INTACT

Sue Hampton

TSL Publications

First published in Great Britain in 2020
By TSL Publications, Rickmansworth

Copyright © 2020 Sue Hampton

ISBN / 978-1-913294-41-0

Cover image:
Jill Hipson

DEDICATION

To Leslie
with love

1

Mags knew what that meant.

"Counselling," she repeated, trying not to make it a question. She knew she sounded stunned, even though she'd sensed it, really – that what he felt was less, and shrinking. "You could have told me after my birthday."

Ridiculous as it seemed, she would be sixty. Could a woman reasonably be called Mags after that? The name had stuck way back in the past, when she was the one starting university like their twins. When she was trialling a new way to be wild again. These days she should probably revert to Maggie, or even Margaret, like an old churchgoer.

She watched her husband pulling odd socks onto his feet. The winter sun through the window lit his hair. Sandy with grey streaks, it was still something of an eruption. Mags knew the feel of it, almost animal in its body – except for the delicate hair sheltered under the rest at the back of his neck. That could belong to a baby.

Now there might be too much of it because he was struggling irritably with the jumper over his head. Another time Mags might have laughed, or smiled like a mother with a boy making a meal of things and emerging tousled.

Making a small grunt, he stood facing her. His shoulders rose and fell. The clock said almost eight; she should be up and dressed and pouring coffee. Would the day have run differently? Not, she supposed, if this disaffection of his had been percolating too. Ah, that was the wit he'd be missing.

"It's grown," she said. "Not just your hair." She always protested when he said it needed a cut. "The age gap, I mean. Is that it?"

He shook his head. "Not really."

She looked behind him to the blue-whiteness of the first painting he'd given her, one she'd never liked as much as she'd wanted to, even though as a gift it had been beautiful, and personal too because she loved snow. He'd surprised her with it before he needed her naked in front of his easel, and its emptiness had felt disturbing at a time when what they did most was laugh, in and out of bed. Perhaps he should have titled it *Foreboding*.

"Not really," she echoed, the emptiness unfamiliar. It was different every time, the breaking up, and painfully the same.

"If you won't go to counselling then I guess it's over. I could stay with Ben."

"So an ultimatum?" He didn't answer. Ben was his favourite brother. "You told him before me."

"You talk to your friends."

"Lovingly," she said, her voice so low it might have been muffled under the duvet. She'd like to slide further beneath that now, seal herself off where nothing could reach.

"What?"

"I only talk about you lovingly."

"Don't make me feel guilty for how I feel, Mags. I'm sorry if you're happy."

His tone suggested she was mistaken about that. "I was, yes."

She couldn't evaluate it now, the precise level, but happy enough, more than enough. She saw he was waiting, expecting an admission of some kind. The silence inside wasn't new, just disabling: a feeling too big to express. She used to have more words.

"Maybe we're just two people who can't sustain it long-term. Maybe most people are."

It was his way of reminding her that she of all people should know this by now.

"Oh yes, no sweat," she said. "I'll just dust myself off and start again. I've never done computer dating but there's a first time for everything. *Woman, sixty, four kids with three*

different men, would like to make something last this time.
They'll be falling over themselves."

"They're hardly kids." He moved to the door. "Even mine."

"Ours," she said, flatly. "You're assuming they'll just shrug
it all off." Like him.

"The twins have each other; we're peripheral really. And
eighteen is the new thirty, you know that."

"Ah, of course! They'll say *Whatever*. Will it be a WhatsApp,
or a DM on Facebook? It would condense to a tweet, I guess."

"Mags, they'll survive. So will you."

He was as skinny as ever; she knew that backside in the
loose jeans, loved it like the nose that fitted against her
cheek and the texture of his skin that was always warm. He
was dressed and hesitant, as if waiting against his will. A
horn outside reminded her that London was thick with life
on the move.

He'd edged away; now he was facing the door.

"What happened to counselling," she asked, "by the way? Is
it a euphemism now, like *trickle-down economics* for *rampant inequality*?"

Rampant: it was what he'd called her in bed. She couldn't
be sure he remembered.

"Mags, leave it."

She glanced out of the window. It was a beautiful day. "I
think you'll be the one leaving."

"Look, I have work to do. Let's talk tonight."

"Or tomorrow, at my birthday meal?"

She didn't want to be petulant, self-pitying either. If she'd
allowed the truth in, she could have prepared a speech,
drafted and edited like Dan with his poems. Dan who had
cheated on her. And that would be it, she realised: history
repeating itself at her expense.

Turning, she saw Rudi had gone. But that was always the
plot twist with men – hers anyway. This time it would be
Charlotte, the PhD student with all that red hair. He'd
painted her gleaming cross-legged on a bedroom floor with a
hairdryer in one hand. Oh but only because his usual subject
for nudes – all eleven of them through the years – had told

him she was too old now, that mirrors were scathing, and shop windows traumatic on a bedraggled day. Not because, he'd insisted, he didn't love every inch of her.

The light was bright for November and the walls needed painting. When she left Dan she'd cried partly for the mural she'd worked on every time Genevieve had slept in the fancy cot his mother had bought them. A few years later, when she needed to double up on baby gear, Genevieve used to ask, "Do you love me even more than Simon and Kara?" Not the standard accusation that she loved her less; that wasn't Genevieve's style. She'd been good with the twins, especially when they were as alike as a pair of Teletubbies.

Perhaps it had been different for Cameron, the one who'd carried so much hurt when she was young and trying not to disassemble. He hadn't bothered with jealousy, acting the big brother or anything much. And now that he was on the other side of the Earth, he didn't bother with his mother back in England, either. How, still alone at thirty-eight, could he be so secretly scattered? Perhaps because she had set such a shambolic example when it came to patched-up and reconstituted family.

Time to be busy if she could imagine how and why. Like everyone else in this loud, enlightened city. She remembered it was before death that her mother reran her narrative. *"Life,"* she could have told Dan, in those days when he was willing to comfort her, *"is a harder kind of dying."* A killer last line but not the kind Dan needed from her. He never let her invade his poems, even the early ones about her. She'd been Dan's muse long, long before she was Rudi's model. And this – now, lying here with the day not so much invaded as severed – was where it always led. To a bed a man had left, or used without her.

She checked and found it was nearly a quarter past. She'd rather be on a check-out today. Less space in the head, more people. She shouldn't have let him close that door just because it was too shabby for his own swelling status. A computer screen was no mortal use; she'd rather leave it dead and kick some leaves around.

8

"I doubt we're hardwired to love for long." Hadn't Rudi said that, or something along those lines, soon after they met? He'd as good as warned her that when the heat went, he followed – emotionally, then in shoes. A small, well-hidden part of her had always feared that without the sparks flying around the sheets she was just a rather tiring oddball who made stories out of people's lives when she had no idea what was going on inside her own, and laughed at things that only kids found funny.

Perhaps she would skip breakfast and let the emptiness nag from inside. She pulled on yesterday's clothes, remembering his comment about colour clashes and pattern collision.

"There's so much I could teach you if you really wanted to learn." That was when she'd said he had no faith in her as an artist. He'd counted on the endless depths of hers in him, oblivious when it dribbled away. But maybe not. Maybe like her he was mourning the old abandoned Mags who loved his work so much she couldn't stop verbalising it unless he took her to bed.

It was caring so much that made her bandy words around like a sword meant to snag his skin: *integrity, principles, ideals.* But all the time she'd kept on loving him anyway, like a mother loves a son she can't really approve.

Walking to the supermarket where she no longer worked, Mags remembered June 1999, when Prince was still partying but the Millennium Dome wasn't quite finished. Blair was PM but not hated yet, and Screaming Lord Sutch had just hanged himself – sad news that had broken that day and seemed to deserve a mention.

"Why do you care?" Rudi asked, drinking red wine at his opening.

The exhibition was about damage and she'd gone because it was close enough to walk there in her lunch break, but also because in the poster he looked gorgeous. Wearing a linen shirt, a rock star silky black jacket with jeans and a man-necklace, he had hair she envied and green eyes that felt intent. His question wasn't combative but curious and came with a slight asymmetrical smile.

"Oh, a reminder that I'm not a girl anymore and the Beatles are down to two," she said. "I made the connection because he must have been damaged too, and we all thought he was just bananas. Wonderfully mad, like a boy chasing around making elephant noises."

"Remind me," he said, smiling again. "Elephant noises?"

"Cows then," she decided. "Only kids these days probably don't know what a moo sounds like. It's not even a sexist joke anymore." She looked at the wine in her glass, which had lowered its level rather quickly for lunchtime on a work day. "Sorry, I'm talking what the Americans call baloney, which is more fun than crap."

"I'd say you're just wonderfully mad," he said. "Or just bananas."

Mags grinned. "That's the nicest thing anyone's said for a while." Since, in fact, Dan stopped pretending the romance was alive for reasons that turned out to be a cover, to avoid the unpleasantness. He'd been gone seven months. And she shouldn't assume, she told herself, that this was sex talking just because she could do with some. A man like Rudi Shaw wouldn't go short.

"So if I said your work ..." She paused, to get it right the way Dan had with his poems. Not so much Jake, she thought, her first creator – those songs of his all came fast as greyhounds out of their boxes, and like the dogs were hard to tell apart. "Is savage and spare, and probably haunting? You'd discount it as the ravings of a madwoman?" She was pleased with that. And she savoured the words, because she'd fielded fewer lately, with Dan gone, Genevieve heavily pre-teen and Cameron backpacking.

"Well," he said, "I'd feel I needed more evidence – and compliments – over dinner."

"I have a twelve-year-old daughter," she blurted. "Babysitters for those are in short supply for some reason."

"Then lunch tomorrow, if your work allows? There's an Italian that serves fast and they do a Malbec that kicks this into touch."

Mags realised she was pulling some kind of face. She knew the place he meant and wouldn't want to pay their prices, even for the breadsticks alone.

"The thing is I earn peanuts. I've never had Malbec whatever it is when it's at home; the £3.99 offers do me at weekends." She'd started so she might as well finish, better now than later. "I'm a cashier at a checkout eighteen hours a week. And my ex is a poet, so child maintenance cheques aren't like bonanzas and I need a little top-up from the welfare state."

"Good for the welfare state." He reached for the wine bottle on the small, glass-topped table. "A bigger top-up. Your shift might fly by."

"Or I might forget how to operate the till." She didn't stop him pouring.

"But you're into the arts."

"Oh yeah, I have a degree in the *Fine* kind."

"And you paint?"

"Not a lot."

"But you would if you could."

"In a different life."

Someone younger and more doll-like than Mags tottered over on heels and put a hand on his arm, telling him with scarlet lips that there was someone he must meet. A man in a suit with a ponytail raised a hand. Rudi looked past her to smile; Mags edged away before he did.

She could go around again; a second look always revealed so much more. Telling herself that this – with the wine in her hand, and the nibbles she'd already disposed of – was all a treat in itself, she tried to delete the girl who made her suspect that if Rudi Shaw liked her, it would only be as a diverting oddball, a bit of a break from the arses. She should focus on the work. Around her the paintings on white walls were far from decorative but stunning in their own bleak way.

11

She stopped at the one he called *The Abused*, surprised that she hadn't noticed the title before. *"You should have talked to me first,"* she might have said. *"I could have broadened your definition of that word."* Then she would have added that she wasn't a victim; she'd left that status behind. The colours in the centre of the abstract were so muted she imagined him paying women to cry over them so the brush-strokes bled. It made her think of the way eyes looked when they brimmed.

There was a hand on her shoulder. With the other one he passed her a card.

"If I don't hear otherwise I'll see you at one tomorrow. No cash necessary – I'm an unreconstructed male."

She'd feared as much but gave him credit for awareness. Without waiting for any response, he smiled and rejoined his colleagues. Mags looked back at the painting that pleased and hurt her most, then put down her glass, not quite empty, and left.

The street seemed deafening now, and grimy too. A waste-land, she thought – for all the new architecture making a minimalist show of itself. Passing the supermarket where she used to exist, Mags was feeling the cold in spite of the blue above. The shop front was all premature Christmas red and tinsel excess. Marriages ended every day, thousands of them, and people pulled on their coats and shoes and caught trains or buses or turned the car radio on. They arrived at work and covered up with overalls or helmets, or touched up their lipstick and checked their tights for ladders. Time ticked by at the standard pace and soon there was lunch to eat. It was all right for Rudi. He could lick his dinner from a body with no creases.

But she'd loved him. Loving was never the problem.

She pictured him alone at work in his studio where he liked order at all times. She had questioned it not so long ago, as if neatness in an artist was a character flaw, a symbol of the selling out she never actually claimed he'd done, not directly. Once he told her what she wanted from him was a kind of

12

Vincent madness – but that two nutcases in one house might be one too many.

He'd be arriving now, hurrying up the steps that kept him fit like sex used to do. Could he paint through this – through freefall and grief, disjunction? In a back room, stacked behind two experiments she encouraged but he called mistakes, was the portrait that provoked, "My thighs can't really be that big." He'd teased her frown away with strokes of the flesh in question. "You wanted uncompromising," he said later. "You're big on truth." He'd caught her spirit and humour but a kind of awkward defiance too as she stood in the bathroom doorway, her hair neither wet nor dry.

"Mags," she muttered, Thom Yorke singing in her head, "you do it to yourself."

2

Mags spent the day walking, window shopping Scrooge-style and drinking coffee. Feeling unready for communication, she reflected that motherhood and repeated readjustments had made her careless with friends. She supposed news like hers would break but how exactly did she share it, in words? Where would they come from and wouldn't they tangle and glut like spaghetti, and slither hopelessly out of control? In her supermarket days she'd been Mags the shoulder to lean on when she wasn't Mags the loon, but she didn't fuel gossip. Some of the girls only found out she was with an artist after she'd married him, and as for her own back catalogue, she'd left them literally clueless. "No guilt I hope?" Rudi had asked and she'd shown him a fist with a grin. As if, she meant. But other people could lay shame like a shroud. They'd tried it with Genevieve, as if it was a mother's fault when a girl's mind lost its way.

She was on her way home that evening when her phone rang. Seeing his name she considered cutting him off before he could begin.

"How has your day been, honey?" she asked in her best American accent, and imagined smoothing a pretty little apron and patting pristine hair. Then she pointed out that she hadn't even looked at his emails or been home to answer any business calls. "Professionally I consider myself fired. How are Charlotte's office skills?"

"Listen, Mags, I've left you a note but if you want to argue anything in it, you can call me. There's no rush and we don't need to do sniper fire."

She knew she had to do better this time, way better than the Mags who had run from Jake. But with Dan political game playing had proved about as good a fit as the Bunny Girl costume would be now, the one she'd bought as a post-modern gesture in '85. The one Dan had peeled away both before and after the party.

"You can be yourself," Rudi had promised. "That's who I want." Maybe even artists who thought they could see right through to the soul were really blinded by the textures and curves. She shouldn't have trusted him to look at those like Rembrandt. My God, the light inside that old woman with the gnarled hands! Had Rudi ever really seen it?

"Mags?"

"That's me."

"I've made a few birthday suggestions but I understand, whatever ..."

"Very thoughtful."

"Just let me know."

Rudi could be effortlessly reasonable. It always thickened the fibres of his voice to deep-pile softness.

"Sure."

Mags cut him off. He could stop painting and present on TV instead; she could just imagine him talking earnestly to camera about the genius of Degas and his skin tones, as if Mary Cassatt never existed. "You do enjoy your obsessions." He'd said that with a smile, as if it was a trait he found winning, like her naked body pressed against him – in the days when Italian restaurants with Malbec were set aside for lunchtime sex. Remembering, Mags wondered why it was only in retrospect that she felt patronised. Presumably because at the time her overriding obsession was him. And his was only ever the art, or rather the reputation it gave him. But could he capture Cassatt's tenderness? Did he even rate it?

Ah, thought Mags, *so hate begins.* She told herself she didn't want it, couldn't live with it, not with so much ugliness twisting Fascist faces, not with the twins telling her it was a scary time to be young.

No need to stop loving. Better to step it up. She increased her pace and wondered about an Indian takeaway for one. Also what the twins were going to say or feel. Kara was still Daddy's girl: "He doesn't … like … undermine me." "Do you mean I do?" "See, you don't even know!" With Simon the reflex response to most information had been, until recently, that *it is what it is* – which was an equally evasive variation on *whatever* masquerading as a philosophical, neo-Buddhist acceptance of everyone and everything. Mags had told Rudi she was waiting for world events to shake him out of that kind of peace because frankly no one was entitled to it anymore.

The sky had faded and rain was falling, but not enough to justify a rummage for an umbrella with dodgy spokes. Grimacing, she saw that someone had walked a dog without bothering with a plastic bag for a glove. The result had been trodden through and smeared ahead of her. Mags remembered a conversation with Rudi about Duchamp's urinal leading to *fag end art* as she liked to label it.

"If a spider's web can be art," he'd pursued, "why can't a turd?" They'd come across one, smooth and steaming.

"Because," she'd told him, "there's no awe, no tenderness, no spiritual encounter. Because no one wants to linger. No one gets their phones out. They just gag."

So he'd pulled out his phone and crouched closer as if to inhale.

"That's just being a boy," she said, pulling him away, "not an artist." It was ongoing, the gender spat. Wasn't there an age limit on that? But when she started those lunchtime dates with Rudi she was forty-two and her heart never actually stopped under the strain.

If anyone asked her whether he'd been faithful over eighteen years, she might have to say it was what it was, whatever, for all the difference it made.

The front door wasn't locked. Stepping inside, she ignored some unsolicited post and picked up a note in his beautiful handwriting, styled with a turquoise sharpie.

Mags, you are a highly individual, complex woman and your heart's too big to frame. But like the world we have both changed. I know you're hurting but I hope that when the drama feels less intense we can stay close. There's more to love than two names on an electricity bill. Or even monthly sex. I will of course continue to fund the twins' education (and lifestyle!) and am more than happy to buy you out and help you find a suitable flat. Regardless of income, let's not argue about money. I can pay your rent indefinitely if need be but maybe this will provide the impetus you need to make more of yourself now the twins are adults and you can do what you want for the next five or ten years. If you want to keep or sell any of the paintings I gave you, just say. I don't need a divorce unless you do, just space to breathe.

I'm more than happy to take you, Simon and Kara out for dinner on Saturday night if they're still coming back for your birthday. It might be a civilised way to tell them what's happening.

R x

"It's my party and I'll bleed if I want to." In her head she sang it, danced ...

She reread the phrases he might as well have italicised or highlighted in bold. Monthly! Civilised. Close. He didn't need a divorce unless she did. Just room to breathe?

Mags put the kettle on and sat in front of the note, examining all the crossings out and guessing at what they were going to be. For all the flamboyant flourishes, he said he didn't trust words.

Frustrating? Wasn't that a direct result of the difference between minds? She had no problem forgiving people for their habit of not thinking, reacting or behaving exactly like her. Especially Simon with his refusal to react at all until the world forced his hand. And she totally refuted the suggestion that she'd changed like that world – which had swung brainlessly and heartlessly to the far right and started picking targets to spit on.

Was she going to reply to this?

The kettle boiled. She immersed a teabag and poked it too hard with a spoon, tutting at a black cluster of leaves that broke out and dispersed.

"All right," she said out loud. "Survival strategies."

Checking the time, she called Kara, wondering whether to leave a message asking her to call back. But instead of a voice mail, she heard a daughter who sounded tired.

"Bad time, love?"

"Not specially. You OK?"

"Well, not especially I guess. Your dad wants out."

"Out? What's happened?"

"Nothing particular as far as I'm aware. But it appears we're splitting up."

"God, Mum, is this like your modus operandi?"

"I'm sorry?"

"Relationship meltdowns. As in four kids with three fathers ..."

"I'm not planning any more! And as this isn't my idea, I don't think I'm operating at all."

"Look, can't you go for counselling or something? I'm in line for a First and this is going to mess with my head."

"Kara, you don't let it. It doesn't have to. It's your life and you can take control of it."

"Like you do?"

"I do and I will." Mags could tell Kara was unconvinced. "Your dad wonders whether you two will still be coming home for my birthday meal on Saturday night. I understand if that's a no."

"I'll talk to Simon. He's in love, did he tell you? I told him not to waste his time. What's the point?"

Mags waited but couldn't hold back. "Love is the point, Kara. It isn't always eternal but it's all there is and it doesn't have to actually die. I want to keep on loving your father if he doesn't make that utterly impossible, and I'm certainly going to love you and Simon until they pull my plug, whether you like it or not, so don't go all cynical and angry on me because I've never committed thinking it might end like this."

Kara was quiet at the end of the line. Mags wrinkled her face at the anaemic dance music she could hear beating stupidly on.

"Well it always does. No wonder Genevieve is such a mess. And as for Cameron, I mean who *is* he?"

At what point, wondered Mags, did teenagers shrug off the self-cocoon, acknowledge how the world might look to the butterflies out there, and concede the possibility that some of them were working overtime on their wingbeats so they didn't nosedive into mud and get crushed by the nearest boot?

"I'll call Simon myself," she said, "and he can tell me all about it."

"Mum … I'm sorry Dad's such a wanker."

Mags let loose a laugh, and imagined Kara holding the phone from her ear.

"God, Mum, nothing's funny." But the voice was softer now. Was that a little peep-hole in the cocoon?

"I know. But things with you …?"

"I've got to go now, Mum. Don't … like … fall apart."

"I've no intention!" She wasn't sure how well the strength she meant to show was travelling. The conversation ended with, "Love you," echoed back rather faintly.

Mags drank her tea and dipped a biscuit in it. She'd call Simon later, if he didn't call her first.

Their twins had always been wanted, right from the test result.

"But Rudi, you're glad?"

She nodded, smiled. Two pea-sized hearts audibly beating. It felt overwhelming but right at last. Maybe this time she could be a serene Renaissance Madonna right through birth and beyond, even with everything doubled. As Rudi stroked her hair, relief swelled and warmth rose through her, because sometimes in those first eighteen months being a stepfather had seemed more than he'd voted for.

Up in her bedroom Genevieve was already telling her friends. She'd recently decided that babies were the cutest thing and only a few weeks earlier alarmed Mags with the declaration that she was going to have one when she was sixteen, leave school and get her own flat. So just for once, Mags thought she might have managed a pregnancy that was perfect timing and could give a new meaning to home education.

From the kitchen she heard Genevieve lollop downstairs like a Labrador. Mags stood with Rudi's arms reaching across her chest from behind and his mouth pressed to her neck. He looked up and probably gave her daughter the same kind of hopeful smile. Was thirteen really too old to be jealous?

"I can be their fun mum," Genevieve told her. "You'll be more like a granny." Then she winked. "Joke, Ma! Shall we have some champagne to celebrate, Rudi? I can have Mum's share."

"Certainly," said Rudi. "Let's go!"

She muttered in his ear as he waited for Genevieve to touch up her lip gloss: "Laissez-faire père."

"Your soft touch husband," he murmured, and stroked her belly, his lips meeting hers.

"Not in front of an impressionable teen," Genevieve told them. "Come on. Can we have Bollinger?"

Mags didn't believe in splashing cash or rearing a brat, but the pair of them seemed so much happier than she'd foreseen. She suspected that as a first-time father, Rudi might be unaware of the ways her long body would remodel itself. Maybe he could explore and discover simultaneously in a series of swelling nudes, a variation on time lapse photography. Oh God! Was that the plan?

Emailing Genevieve in Brighton before Kara could contact her (she hoped), Mags wasn't sure she could predict the response. She assumed the two step-sisters who communicated on various platforms, most of which she didn't understand, weren't remotely the same as the daughters on the end of her phone. Their mouths would certainly be fouler; they'd roll their eyes audibly over her. But how close were they, really? And was Genevieve really that much more of a mess than the average thirty-year-old who hadn't quite worked out who she wanted to be?

She kept her email short and had hardly had time to make herself another mug of tea when the reply landed.

Honestly Mum I'd recommend staying single. Rudi didn't really commit to either of us and the twins come a long way second to his career. I'll never surrender myself to a man the way you did to him. I mean, who are you? Do you even know? Apart from a goofy patch-up Mum that is.

You're sixty tomorrow. Why not find out?

Love you. XX

Mags realised she felt numb now. She preferred wacky to goofy but patching up had been the only option, and sometimes it had held. She heard the old *Who* song in her head and supplied a few answers in her head.

Home-maker (serial). Wannabe genius. A dreamer. No, make that a hoper.

She unplugged and went to bed.

3

The tree house was for her. He'd carved M on the small door.

"Grampy, you little belter!"

Maggie clung to his thin legs but not for long. Racing towards the tree, she paid no attention to Daddy's complaining that she must "Show respect please!" but she did hear Grandma laugh.

"I hope it's not too high!" called Grampy after her.

"She loves a challenge," Mummy said.

Maggie saw that Grampy had hammered in some metal grips or footholds. Breathing hard, she pulled her way up. It was her favourite tree because it had its own life that nobody could guess so it was full of secret stories. It reached so high that the leaves at the top could probably tickle the clouds.

The door had a knob like Grandma's kitchen cupboards and she tugged it with one hand as soon as it was level with her head. Then she grunted her way up to the final step and crawled in, hands first. The house didn't tilt or wobble, even when she jumped and Daddy cried, "Sensibly now!"

There were thick shutters at the big window, like the drawings in story books with cottages in woods. She opened them wide and leaned out, smiling down on the grown-ups. Then she waved like the Queen.

"I'm mad about it!" she called down.

"No comment," said Daddy, but Mummy and Grandma laughed and Grampy said, "Excellent!"

Grampy had even built her a table and chair, and a little bookcase. Everything was wooden but he'd smoothed it. Maggie took a deep breath because she loved the smell. Lying down on the small blanket he'd left up there for her, she rested her head on a cushion and gazed at the roof with its peekaboo square patterned by shifting leaves above. It would be funny if one day a squirrel came and sat there because she'd have a close-up view of its bottom. Daddy didn't like her talking about bottoms and some words made him crosser than others. Grampy didn't mind those things. He was the one who called her a little belter anyway and he really, really loved her so it couldn't be rude.

Maggie didn't want to be a bossy teacher like Daddy when she grew up. Mummy was kinder and when she took drawings down from the pin board to make room for new ones, she

put them safely away in a big folder and called them treas-
ures. She never threw them away even when the arms came
out of the heads. But once when there was a spill Daddy put
a painting in the bin before it was even finished. Mummy
didn't turn witchy when paint went places it wasn't meant to
be. She just said they must clear it up before Daddy saw.

Maybe, Maggie thought, she would paint a mural inside,
where Daddy was too big to squeeze in and complain about
mess. Besides, this house was hers. Daddy didn't like her
clowning but the birds might. She could sing back to them
and if she spent enough time up there she might learn their
language like Dr Dolittle. If only Gramps and Grandma lived
nearer, she could have lessons every day.

"Grampy!" she yelled, and leaned out of the front door. "It's
like the song." She began to sing it, loudly because they were
a long way down. "Do-diddle-iddle-iddle-do. You built a world
of my own that no one else can share."

The tune didn't come out quite right. Daddy liked the
Seekers more than the Beatles but not as much as violins
that sounded really sad. He didn't clap like Grampy though
so it must be showing off again.

"That's enough to scare a crow!" objected Daddy. He called
her a scarecrow some Sundays when she wasn't smart
enough for church.

Grandma said she'd put the kettle on. "Do you want me to
throw Teddy up?"

"It's all right thanks, Grandma. I'll be making some special
friends any second."

The tree fairies were probably shy and their green wings
made them hard to find but the tree trolls would soon be
squeezing through the floorboards with their rubbery scowls,
wanting to pull her ears. And Gramps told her a story once
of a little elf called Tripelski who could turn mean people into
slugs, and magic up rainbow ice cream for children who'd
been scared. She hoped he'd visit if she called his name until
the wind caught it and found him.

"Tripelski," she whispered. "It's me."

Mags woke on her big birthday remembering the tree house her grandfather built her, when she was still a solo child. That was before Georgie came and she loved him more than Teddy or Tripelski. Georgie, who called her Mags way before anyone else knew that was her rightful name. After he *went back* like something from a shop that didn't work, there was a kitten she refused to love instead – until it was squashed on the road and for a few soggy days, she didn't care about anything anymore. When she held a funeral for Kitkat, she was mourning Georgie too because he could be dead for all Daddy cared.

I'm astonished, her father wrote decades later, weeks after her own impetuous, simmering letter, *that you even remember the boy's name. It was a brief trial that failed in ways you couldn't have understood. No, we have no way of tracing him and I can't imagine why you would want to try. Doubtless we will all have been forgotten long ago.*

Those were days of minimal communication with Daddy, who couldn't be any more civil to Dan than Jake. The rage she felt when she scored his Victorian handwriting through with red! For a while, that fury had overwhelmed the rest, like the Dark Lord in a movie. Boy heroes had fight in them; Georgie didn't know how.

She should have focused on loving – and finding – Georgie, not hating Mr Mean, as she called him in those tree house days. And she should have known that after Daddy died it would be a bit like the kitten all over again: a love surge, a grieving for what could have been.

"You're telling me," Rudi said, on the way home from a Sunday afternoon visit when the twins were small and her father obviously found everything exhausting, "that they didn't keep this child they adopted because he was gay?"

"It wasn't Mum. I could tell she'd been sobbing. Georgie wasn't *a real boy*. That's what Daddy said when I asked him why. Gay, trans or just soft-hearted, how do I know? Maybe Georgie didn't."

When he arrived he looked like a street urchin in a Charles Dickens hardback and seemed scared. She didn't know exactly what fostering was but she wanted a brother and he was shy and wild, like a bird could be: hard to catch but easily broken.

Mags hated the way adults kept the truth from children, and stole chapters of their own stories from them – a bit like throwing away paintings that could never be finished, or found. She'd told Rudi she needed to trace Georgie, but even if he wasn't dead, he wouldn't be the sort to play on Facebook and Daddy was probably right: he wouldn't remember her now.

"I doubt it," Rudi had said, because in those days he still thought her memorable for reasons she enjoyed. But at that point a quiet online search had yielded nothing.

Now Mags looked to the other side of the bed and realised she could still smell him. And maybe, if she tried hard enough, Georgie too.

"He's just nervous because we're strangers and it's all new," said Mummy, who was wearing a crisp new dress that swelled, and fell in folds from the waist. It made her look like a Ladybird mother.

"Georgie," said Maggie, "it's all right. You'll get used to us, like cabbage."

She didn't like cabbage yet but she didn't retch anymore unless she tried. Georgie had sore skin breaking up on his cheeks. He wasn't pretty and his hair didn't lie smooth. His legs were skinny and beneath his long shorts there were enough scars and scrapes for a pirate. His shoes looked much too big and heavy and his eyes were too dark and deep for his face.

"What's cabbage?" he asked. "Mags?" Sometimes he used her name instead of 'help'.

"Something you have to eat if you want ice cream," said Maggie, with a sideways glare at Daddy, who looked stiff except when he was suddenly jolly. That switch was so jerky it almost made Georgie jump.

"There's no cabbage today, Margaret, so don't give Georgie ideas. Let's skedaddle into the garden and play some footy, shall we? You like football, don't you, Georgie?"

Georgie looked at him as if he'd spoken in Russian. He didn't move from the kitchen chair where he sat very still even though Maggie was pretending she was on a swing.

"Of course you do," said Dad. "It's a good ball. I bought it yesterday because you were coming."

Maggie frowned because she'd asked him oodles of times for proper oil paints and he didn't seem to care how much she needed them. Daddy was standing now. Georgie looked out to the garden and back to Mags. She held out her hand and he stared at it for a few moments before he took it and let her lead him out to the garden. The school gardener kept everything neat but the magnolia kept splashing patterns over the plain green and Mags loved it.

Daddy started showing off with the tips of his shoes, scooping up the ball and crying out, "Woooo" and "Oh-oh" as he struggled to keep it under control and off the ground like a pro. When it escaped in her direction, Maggie stopped it under her foot and then passed it very gently to Georgie. But he didn't kick it, even when Daddy said, "Whack it, son. Come on."

Then Georgie looked at the flower border and Maggie saw his face loosen.

"I'll show you," she said, and took him across and around the lawn to name the trees for him. He repeated them and she didn't laugh when he got the words a bit wrong. She just said them again, properly but kindly like her teacher would. Then Georgie ran off, crouched down on his haunches and picked up a magnolia petal, big and pink, from the grass beneath the tree. He stroked it between his thumb and forefinger and his eyes brightened.

"It's tough," he said.

"Yes," said Maggie, and started collecting up the petals and filling her pockets. "It's stroft. That's soft but secretly strong. I just made it up. Let's make a petal painting."

Georgie didn't argue. Realising she couldn't hear any kind of rhythm from the football, Maggie looked round. Her father had lit his pipe and folded crisply into a garden chair, watching them from behind his sunglasses and a copy of *The Times*.

Mags tied on her dressing gown and then, in front of the bathroom mirror, rummaged through and shook her hair. She didn't see why, in a global and digital age, she couldn't trace Georgie Barkle. Was that really his name? Georgie Barkle who'd lost his sparkle: that was her private rhyme. He'd lost it somewhere along the line of his five or six years, but found it again with her and the magnolia, the lavender, watercolours and wool.

His middle name was Isaac. She remembered that, because the story about Abraham being ready to kill his own son if God asked him was so horrible and she'd told her father so, even when he insisted that it was only about trusting God. "How can you trust a God who asks people to do THAT?" she countered, and he told her he didn't like her attitude.

Downstairs, she made tea and logged on to her PC. Nothing on Facebook or Twitter. Mags wondered whether Georgie might be Georgia now. Then she felt guilty, as if she was making the same assumptions her father had, just because Georgie was sensitive and delicate and hated sport, speed and elbows, and gangs of boys making a racket. Men could be gentle souls too, for goodness' sake – although if he really had been trapped, as they said, in the wrong kind of body, she hoped he'd freed himself long ago. Whatever and whoever, she hoped he was *stroft* himself.

She tried a few variations on the name but it seemed technology couldn't deliver.

"Ah well," she said aloud, "if we're meant to reconnect after fifty years, we will. And I think we're going to. I insist on it."

Is this your way of bringing on a sub the day after another husband leaves? Well, not exactly, she thought in her defence. There were computer dating sites for that. There might be gigolos inspired by Richard Gere – and who wouldn't be? Rudi would never admit to such a thing himself but there was something about him, something of a strut that said he wasn't for taming. Something that wasn't really husband material – but perhaps that was what she looked for; at least, it was what she always found. *And why, Mags, would that be, do you think?*

Maybe she should see a counsellor after all. She should do something, because reliving the past through the steam from her tea, and smelling an absent man in her bed, didn't really count as anything. Then she had an idea, returned to Facebook and searched again.

Georgie Stroft. As Kara would say and Mags hoped she herself never would, not out loud: OMG.

Georgie wasn't feeling up to much. He could tell, looking down on the street, that the wind was the scowling, snarling kind, nipping at flesh and burning eyes. But the men in suits heading for the station had their armour on. It didn't only protect their ankles like skirts never could; it fitted them for the marching ranks where they could be anonymous but respected anyway. Georgie stroked the loose fabric draping his thighs.

Draining his mug of coffee, he returned to the laptop on the kitchen table. No new emails since he'd left his Inbox to dress. Facebook, then. It had been a while. Surprised to see a Friendship request, Georgie stood a moment, leaning over the screen, before he sat down.

Mags Shaw. Georgie had only known one Mags and she was a child, just a couple of years older than him. He didn't remember her surname then, because it was the same as the man's, the one who didn't like or want him. The Mags he knew climbed trees. There was a house in her granddad's sycamore and it was the coolest thing he had ever seen long before the word was the thing to be. That Mags wouldn't change her name for a man.

Mags Shaw's was an emotional profile, not a selfie, and in it was something he knew. He was scrolling down the page now, and there she was with her arm around a beautiful man who thought he was someone. The black and white gallery around her was chic, but she wasn't. Her clothes were layered and rather random; her hair was almost as purple as red, and piled up in that careless, arty way of women who were academics or campaigners on marches. But then lower down her wall he found another picture where she'd plaited it, not very neatly, and let it be grey. Envious, Georgie could imagine the weight of it. Was it the turned-up nose he recognised, above full lips? Could he really have said what colour her eyes had been before he found the brown ones smiling? A tall, thin child, she was a straight-down woman, loose and free beside the husband who rated himself.

Georgie was looking at the bio now. Married to Rudi Shaw, who had a website and a reputation, and wouldn't be pleased Georgie didn't know what it was. Clicking on the link he understood why. He preferred leaves when there was air to stir them, they might drift away and they'd certainly die – as opposed to thick, brush-stroked simulations that had never even lived but cost the earth. He had an idea that art wasn't really life and that made it shallow, but he knew people like Rudi would despise him for that. Georgie returned to Mags, who loved him. "Be stroft, Georgie," she said, when they took him away and she was crying. Or was that just in his head?

Mags remembered too. Otherwise how would she have known who he was? Georgie Stroft. She had given him his identity but he hadn't expected her to hold on to it and he felt suddenly moved, astonished, grateful.

He could message her now. *I am happy to be found. You are my best childhood memory. x*

He waited but she probably wasn't the sort of woman to live online. At least, he hoped not. Such a fearless girl; he must have spent their time playing together with his eyes wide, awestruck. Her spirit was double his, brighter, tougher. But she would have changed, to state what they called the bleeding obvious. She had probably gone out now, into that wind that was enough to keep him indoors, but to do what? Not to climb a tree. And that seemed terribly sad, so sad that he found himself crying.

Mags was clearing some of Rudi's things into a suitcase when she heard the door open downstairs. She stood, still and silent, listening. Then she smelled the lilies.

"Mags?" she heard. Not a trace in his voice of the last few days.

Now he was on the stairs. The smell thickened. She emerged onto the landing and stared at the physical reality of her husband, hair washed and blow-dried, beads and feathers tied at his neck, his linen shirt undone to show fair hair she knew in the dark. In his arms the lilies erupted, their scent enough to block anything she might have said or done.

"Happy birthday," he said, and smiled, presenting them.

She kept her hands by her side. "Thanks. But I'd rather keep loving lilies if it's all the same to you."

"It isn't necessary ..." he began.

"To taunt me?"

"That isn't the intention, Mags. Come on, you love lilies more than you loved me anyway!"

"Is that a joke?"

"You're the joker. Find the humour, Mags. You usually can."

She laughed. It started off like a stage direction in a script but it rocked around like a rowing boat in a squall. His look was disapproving, impatient. With the lilies in one hand he reached for her arm with the other, closing his fingers around it to steady her. To stop her.

She broke away and ran downstairs, telling herself she wasn't fifteen. She took a bottle of red wine from the rack in the kitchen and unscrewed the top.

"Thanks," he said. "But I'll just arrange these for you and head off."

She placed one wine glass on the table and filled it. "They're art already, Rudi. They don't need you." Her voice was calm, low-volume, a surprise. "Me and the lilies, we can do without your touch."

He was rummaging for a vase. "The twins are on the way."

Ah! She'd had her phone off. She took a sip of the wine, but the lilies he'd left lying in front of her on the table overwhelmed everything.

"Don't forget how capable you are, how brave," he said, "how fucking extraordinary."

She played the bashful damsel at the joust, over-praised. "Pray, Sir Knight," she breathed, hand spread above her chest. "You flatter me."

"We'll be friends in the end, Mags. I know we will. I won't have it any other way."

She wanted to say, sardonically, that it was decided then. Or that she might have it any and every other way. She wanted too to be serene, a Statue of Liberty kind of abandoned wife, towering over the tawdriness of him, the crass predictability. He used to say he loved her passion.

Now he was running water to fill a vase her mother had given them. The wine stung. Or was it the lilies?

"I'm sorry. I never meant it to be forever. We're neither of us good at that."

That was something he might have mentioned eighteen years ago, when he said she was a faerie queen and he was her helplessly adoring servant boy.

"Yeah, let's get real," she said quietly. "This love's had its shelf life. Bin it and get the new line in."

Her gesture was bigger than she meant and swept her wine glass off the table and into pieces. Wine splashed the wooden surface and tinged the curving petals of the nearest lilies. She grabbed them by the wrapping and took them to the sink, while Rudi swore quietly and leant past her for a cloth. Inhaling the perfume, she stood facing the window and heard the crunch and clink of glass and the scrape of the brush into the dustpan. It was hard not to turn and look because the clearing up took a while and he was cross; she felt it in his breathing.

"I'll leave you to your lilies," he said, at last.

"Good," she said. "They're taking me high and I ain't comin' down."

"It'll be all right, Mags," she heard.

"Yeah, yeah!" she drawled, and waved a hand. It was only when the door closed that she realised she hadn't asked him for his key.

The lilies he'd left behind were excessive enough for any Private View, and without care he'd displayed them to heady perfection. She stared at them and pictured the mother who taught her to breathe them in and then swoon like Marianne Dashwood – but straighten right up at the sound of Daddy's footsteps. In her mind she drew them, stroking the lines, suggesting the texture. In a small room and summer heat, she wondered, with door and windows closed, how long it would take to die in a kind of sexual ecstasy? Lifting the vase, she took it to the worktop so the light could frame them.

It had been so long since she'd climbed a tree. Hurrying back to her laptop, she nudged its screen back and checked Facebook, just in case, telling herself not to be foolish.

And there he was, Georgie: her saddest childhood memory. Her reflex was to exit, as if she'd discovered a secret too big to share or keep.

"My daddy was a bully," she murmured. "I'm sorry, Georgie."

It was a lie and true too, because Daddy was all things to all people and Georgie could only be himself. Mags remembered her father the bon vivant, with a different glass for each *tipple*, his hair smoothed to a gleam and his laugh carrying upstairs where she was meant to be sleeping. But when he gripped the lectern on the stage in the school hall, with a voice that could surge and hold the silence, he was the Bishop, guardian of his boys' morality and solemnly proud of his own. And sometimes he was the brooding darkness behind his newspaper, snapping at anyone who passed by. Worse was the Father Who Knew Best with his patient, sing-song endurance – until he yelled that she'd pushed too far. But she had to push, because her mother didn't. It didn't mean she hated him, not then. She'd spent most of her childhood wishing he could make her love him properly. Or believe he loved her more than now and then, which might be much the same thing.

31

Mags wondered whether Georgie had forgiven her father for rejecting him. Probably he wasn't the first or last to do that. She told herself to forget the past because her present had Georgie back in it. Maybe she could say the same for the future.

Hey Georgie. It's so great to see your face, playmate. Wish I had a tree house to invite you up to. What ARE you up to? Whatever it is, you don't have to tell me. I'm just glad to know you're out there and remember me. X

Georgie looked fine in his ruffle-necked top and lacy cardigan over a draping skirt. No vampish Rocky Horror style, no bling, satin or make-up. It looked as if he was in it for the bright colours and soft folds and a lot more besides, reasons she couldn't really guess and he might not choose to explain. His face was oddly the same as she'd known it, apart from a few soft folds of its own. His hair was less vivid now, but fell smooth and free; time had tamed the quirks that provoked her father. The nose was still what they called snub and the freckles were everywhere. Looking out at the world, his gaze was steady and closed. It made Mags glad she'd seen his smile. Not that it had lasted long before Daddy peeled it off like a hero unmasking a villain.

"You're all grown up, Georgie Boy."

Mags shuddered at the sneer she imagined on her father's face, and shut down her laptop. A pile of cards fell through the letterbox but they could wait. She knew exactly who'd addressed each envelope but that made her regret the handwriting she never saw any more because she let go too easily.

If the twins were on the way she'd better get sorted. She remembered Kara's name for their unit of two: *Kimon* coming! They were a classic split cell for a while, until the sexual divide that didn't faze Rudi because he didn't see it.

"They'll be eleven, Mags. They can't stay in yellow babygrows for ever."

"But all she wants for the birthday is shoes she can't walk in." Daddy would call them prostitute shoes but she wouldn't resort to him as back-up. "Apart from nail varnish and lipstick. Apparently you can buy false eyelashes named after each of *Girls Aloud* and she wants them all."

Rudi was on his laptop answering emails and Mags wasn't sure he was taking this seriously when it felt like a crisis she couldn't avert, not without upping sticks to a tree-roofed part of South America not yet known to technology and commerce.

"Rudi? I don't want media stereotypes for children."

He grinned, which meant she was exaggerating again, making an issue out of normality. "Is it better or worse in your eyes that Simon wants a computer game and football boots? Would you rather he asked for a tutu?"

Mags pictured Georgie Barkle, the boy she tried to save from Mr Mean. She narrowed her eyes and told Rudi not to be homophobic, which made him laugh out loud. "And yes, I might!"

"You know he's the softer of the two and that's fine." Rudi drained his coffee. "And Kara's pretty feisty for this girlie you're trying to paint here. Kids go through phases. Ride it."

She knew he wasn't wrong but then neither was she. Rudi reminded her of the time Simon rearranged the flowers she'd just dropped into a vase, and she didn't know whether she felt proud or shamed.

Then Kara burst in, peeling off rubber gloves and picking straw off her sweater.

"Finished already?" asked Rudi.

"Well I've had enough anyway. Trust me to ... like ... land the hamster with Irritable Bowel Syndrome! Si's whispering sweet nothings to the pair of them while he shovels rancid sawdust and mountains of turds. He's so weird. It like ... makes him happy."

"It's a responsibility, love ..." began Mags.

"Si's taken mine and he's welcome so like ... win-win, right? Gotta shower. I'm going round to Bev's to watch this cool action movie called *Taken*."

Rudi said he'd walk her round and collect her later. When she'd gone upstairs he smiled at Mags as if he'd won a point.

"I'll help Simon," Mags told him, and pulled on the rubber gloves.

Maybe Rudi was right. Now they were closer again, Kara was studying hard and Simon was in love with a girl who was bound to be sweet. Mags examined the contents of her fridge, and wondered what Georgie kept in his.

4

Mags returned from a brisk, windy walk to the park and began to make a cake. Listening to a programme on the radio about Gauguin brought her to a sticky standstill as she cried, "Miss Tralee! I hope you're listening." Miss Tralee from Hedderford Junior School called herself Gauguin's greatest fan. It struck Mags that since she'd outgrown her first uniform, adults from her child's world had been busy dying. Even Miss Tralee, who was so pretty and young. The other girls were always telling her, often in little notes and cards, that she was the best teacher in the whole world, because they loved her shoes with heels and her bobby-dazzler blonde hair with flicks. Mags liked her best when she wore a man's shirt that was much too big for her and stiff in places with Jackson Pollock paint. Not that Mags knew who Jackson Pollock was when she was ten. She only knew she loved the colours that came from the tubes: shiny wet and more alive than anything else in the dusty old school building.

"You love it, don't you?" Miss Tralee asked, stopping on her route around the desks to watch her paint.

"With a passion," said Mags, feeling grown-up and special.

Someone behind them sniggered, but Miss Tralee nodded, smiled and then winked.

"That's the foundation stone," Miss Tralee told her, and Mags knew that meant she was an artist too. Then Miss

Tralee showed her how to make her strokes feathery for a change, so that the clouds could float instead of sinking straight to earth. "Try not to get coated this week, Maggie," she whispered before she moved on, "or I'll be sending another abject apology home."

Mags remembered, years later, winning the Art Prize at High School and knowing it was Miss Tralee she should be thanking if she could find her. Miss Tralee would celebrate a lot more wholeheartedly than her father, who considered Art time off from proper subjects and as such, a weakness. It was Grampy who bought her an easel and oils, but she knew the idea had been her mother's – one that would have been overruled at home.

Mags looked at the kitchen clock. Checking her phone, she realised she'd missed a few messages and the two of them would be here any moment. And now that it was time to fold in the flour, she found she didn't have enough. How ridiculous! Would grated potato do roughly the same job, with more personality?

She heard the doorbell. The twins both had keys but presumably their arms were full of birthday gifts. Opening the front door, she found Simon with a black bin liner full of washing – and Kara looking as scrawny and stiff as a model on a catwalk. Wasn't she eating?

"Happy birthday, Mum," said Simon, and she took the washing bag. "If it's still happy at all, you know ... but I suppose it is now we're here!"

"Yes, Mum loves the gift of your rancid underwear," muttered Kara. "Thoughtful, and so endearingly male."

"No worries," she breezed. "I've had my washing halved just lately."

"Dad's a shit."

"Not what you just told him," murmured Kara.

"You've seen him?" checked Mags, reminding herself that she should hope so.

The twins received it as a statement and raced each other for the bathroom. Then Kara turned into the master bedroom just before Mags could call, "Use the en-suite."

Mags made coffee in the percolator and grated the potato at the same time. She was just slamming the cake tin into the oven as the pair of them broke into the kitchen like slightly hungover commandos on a raid. Kara sat down, arms on the table and shoulders lowered towards them. Simon's phone rang and his whole body responded like a ribbon to a stroke of the scissors.

"Hey," he purred and left the room.

"He's like virtually sick with love," said Kara. "It's a wonder he can stand."

"Is she nice? Do you like her?"

"You mean would *you* like her? She's a bit girlie for you actually." Kara smiled sympathetically. "I got you a present. He was too busy shagging." She bit her lip. "Simon, I mean." Grimacing, she drew her head back from the lilies. "They're overpowering. How can you stand them?"

Mags moved the vase from the table to the work top. Cue for another swoon which she overacted a little.

"Anyway, here you go," continued Kara. "I didn't know what … well, I bought them before unexpected developments, obviously."

The card she placed on the table was swollen by theatre vouchers.

"There must be something tragic on somewhere. Maybe you can persuade a friend to go with you?"

"Maybe I can," said Mags, trying to estimate the chances of that friend being Georgie Barkle. She kissed Kara's cheeks. "Thank you, kiddo. Seriously radical."

Kara pulled another face. "Mum, catch up. Radical just means radical now. Like no one uses it, except activists."

"Ah, but it's my favourite word, apart from guts."

"That's because you like to think you have some, Mum." The cheeky smile came a bit too late. "Shall we have some birthday bubbles then? No need to wait for Simon to finish his phone sex."

Mags stood. The lilies must be fuelling her. "I intend to use my guts along with the vouchers, Kara. I intend to be as radical – original meaning – as I can manage. And I don't give a monkey's aunt what other people do or say. But I have the kind of wine Dad wouldn't countenance, if that'll do you."

"OMG," muttered Kara, and picked up her phone. "Mum, don't lose the plot along with Dad, O.K.? Fill it up."

Mags poured the wine and hoped the cake was going to be sensational. For a few minutes she sipped, checked and sipped while on a tiny keyboard Kara's thumbs passed a dexterity test Mags would fail. Waiting, she rose and danced to some music in her head, which happened to be Hawkwind's *Silver Machine*. Facing the lilies rather than Kara, she found herself grinning like a girl who'd just chalked VIRGIN on the back of the Latin teacher's jacket. Except that she never had. That was Linda something and even at the time she'd called it cruel. What had Georgie suffered in his teens?

"Mum!" cried Kara. "You're like scaring me. Simon, help!"

Flushed now, Mags let her arms do their last swirl for the time being and turned, wearing her most demure and conventional expression. After all these years she realised she still hadn't reached that place where she could be wholly and hopelessly Mags instead of Mum. They couldn't handle that, bless them.

"No wonder Dad left," muttered Kara. "But I'm sorry anyway. I just feel …"

Mags sat and assumed mother-counsellor position. "Annoyed?"

"Yes! With both of you. I'm not ready to deal with it, you know? But I love you and it's a crap birthday. Poor mad Mags."

Simon walked in with a grin to find them hugging.

Mags didn't feel ready for anything much herself, but it was wonderful to see the happiness flowing right through him and spilling out like a kind of aura.

"Wash your hands," Kara told him.

"Yes," said Mags, "the cake should be done. There are candles somewhere." It was only while she searched, standing on a kitchen chair, that their mainly non-verbal banter helped her to understand the hygiene issue, gesture and accompanying smirk. She winced into her kitchen cupboard, produced one candle with rather a small, black wick, and tried to remember how adorable they had been with their teddies, Yobbo and Bob, who were family and best friends and lived in a house made from painted packaging. A house Rudi had binned one day when she'd taken them to the park because it interfered with the aesthetics of the lounge. That was probably the day she should have left. Would have, she thought as she tested the cake with a forefinger, apart from the rampant side of things and the fun of making him laugh…

It was his house after all and this time round she could find better accommodation than the dump she'd rented when she ran away from Jake, with five-year-old Cameron sobbing as she coaxed him into the taxi with a teddy pressed to his chest like an evacuee.

She tipped the cake onto the rack while Kara looked up from her phone to berate Simon with, "Not even a card, you useless turd?" and Simon ignored her with the question, "What kind of cake is it? Looks awesome."

"An experiment," she said. "Ingredients classified."

"Not for me," said Kara. Mags felt irrationally disappointed. But Kara reached for the matches and told her, "Sit down then."

The candle took a while to light and they sang very badly but it was enough in any case to draw an embarrassing tear. They'd keep the house, like their dad. It would make no sense for them to keep a third kit at her new flat, wherever it might be. They'd come home, and fit her in between catch-ups with friends. Their beds were here, like everything they'd need.

"Mum …" said Simon, and reached across to her hand but didn't quite touch it.

"Women turn sentimental in their seventh decade," she said. "I'll get pills for it."

"You'll bounce back again," Simon continued.

Mags read his expression change to suspicion as he bit into the cake.

"I'll get a better bra too."

"Mum!" It was Kara this time. "Behave, all right? We love you but we don't want you going totally bonkers just yet."

"Oh, on that subject," said Mags, with half a mouthful of cake because she didn't see why she shouldn't multi-task, "I've hooked up with my childhood sweetheart on Facebook – the boy Grandma and Granddad fostered and then gave back." She waited for dramatic effect. "Georgie. I found him."

"OMG does he know?" asked Kara. "That he's next?"

Simon glared at her.

"Sorry, Mummy," Kara told her sweetly, and attended to her phone.

"So who was this Georgie again?" asked Simon.

Maggie found little Georgie in her bedroom, wearing the dress she'd only put up with once, for a silly party at Daddy's school where she wasn't allowed to play. It could have made her laugh but something wasn't funny. He was spinning in front of the mirror with half a smile on his face so she guessed he liked the lacy trims and the shiny bow tied at the back. Daddy had been cross because she spilt orangeade on the front and Mummy hadn't quite scrubbed it all away.

She stood a moment in the doorway, stopped by surprise. Georgie's forehead creased, with his nose and mouth lifting towards it.

"You look nice," she said. "Like Alice in Wonderland." She didn't think that was what Daddy would say. "Let's keep it in the tree house at Grampy's and you can wear it every other weekend when we ask the tree fairies to secret tea. And dancing."

He nodded. She helped him pull it over his head, which reddened his ears. He dressed in his own clothes and she saw how awkward he looked, as if he couldn't plant his legs once they came out of long, stiff shorts.

"I'm a secret too," he said, his eyes appealing.

"A beautiful secret," she said.

She knew he loved her best in the world the way she loved him. She might marry him one day because he never made her feel small or wrong. Nobody said what had happened to his mummy and daddy even though she'd asked a million times, but he was sad about it. Sad that they died? Sad because they didn't want him? Maggie didn't know which was more horrible. Sometimes she thought Daddy didn't want her much but then sometimes he'd kiss her on the forehead and call her Poppet and she liked him again. Maybe if she was good at something else, not colours that wouldn't stay behind lines. Maybe if she wore the party dress on Sundays ...

But it was Georgie's now. She'd promised, more or less. She could find a hairband for him too – her best red velvet one. She was good at losing things, so that lie would be believed and not the bad, Hell kind.

They looked at each other as they heard footsteps on the stairs. Maggie pointed to her small wooden chair and Georgie sat in it. She grabbed the nearest book, opened it at the last page and said, loudly, "Shall I read it again?"

Behind her she heard Daddy stop. She knew it was him without turning – his tread, his rhythm, his smell.

"The sun's shining, George!" he cried, opening the door. "We need to work on your batting."

"I'll bowl!" said Maggie, hoping he wouldn't notice the dress because then he'd want her to wear it.

"*I'll* bowl," he corrected her and she saw Georgie's eyes shrink with fear.

"Oh but Daddy," Mags said. "You must be much too tired. Have a nice cup of tea."

"An Englishman's never too tired for cricket, eh Georgie?"

"Georgie would rather have another story," she dared.

"George can speak for himself, Margaret. It's not for you to decide what boys prefer. Come on, now, lad. You've got some catching up to do."

Maggie looked hard at Georgie, willing him to tell the truth about what he wanted, but scared too that if he did they would both be in big trouble, because she'd get half the blame. A bad influence, Daddy had told Mummy when they didn't know she could hear. That was what he thought she was.

Georgie's whole body had sagged now. He looked as if he'd like to melt away. His eyes were downward and he didn't speak.

"For crying out loud, boy, a cricket ball won't hurt you."

"They can, Daddy! They can knock you into a coma!"

"Margaret, I've had more than enough of you interfering and knowing better. I'm not going to bowl a fast ball at the boy's head." He turned to Georgie. "Your hair's a terrible mess. Give it a brush and I'll see you in the garden in two shakes of a lamb's tail."

Georgie didn't react. Mags glared at Daddy's back as he walked away. As soon as it was safe she put her arms around Georgie and stroked his hair a little flatter.

"Mags?"

"Take no notice," she whispered. "He doesn't understand."

But why didn't he? He was a grown-up who knew all the world's flags and capitals and dates of the country's kings and queens. He knew how many runs England scored in Test Matches long before she was born.

"The lamb?" asked Georgie faintly. "He wouldn't hurt it?"

She was puzzled until she laughed. Georgie wasn't used to fields, farms and forests. "It's gibberish," she said, "like Jabberwocky but not as much fun. It just means you'd better hurry."

Georgie set off towards the door but didn't get far before he turned back to hug her tightly around the waist. "I can't hit the ball," he murmured into her jumper.

"It doesn't matter," she said. "Daddy only thinks it does."

She would find an excuse to interrupt the training the moment she spotted tears welling. She didn't mind drawing blood if she had to, as a distraction. She had a compass that might work.

Since she was perfectly sure she'd told all her kids about Georgie, Mags didn't feel like beginning the narrative now. The time when they asked, "Tell us funny stories about little Mags," was long ago and felt faraway, further than Georgie and the tree fairies. In this particular tale Daddy might as well be the evil one swishing his cloak while the audience hissed. And she hated to think of her mother as some virgin in white, trailing blood. But didn't she ever yell at him, "HOW COULD YOU?"

"Mum?" barked Kara, phone still in hand. "Calling Mother wherever she is."

5

Abida, said the landline that evening when the twins were at the pub. Usually Abida just knocked at the door, sometimes in her red dressing gown with satin trims.

"Simon told me, Mags. Why didn't you say? What happened? Are you all right? Silly man! He'll see sense, you see."

"But what if sense is what he already saw?"

"Naughty," she said. "What possessed him? Is he playing away?"

Mags said she assumed so and for a moment Abida had no more questions as she tutted and called Rudi a foolish boy. Abida was eighty-one but energetic. Although she preferred to be as emphatic as possible on most occasions, much of the conviction was in her phrasing and hands. Her voice was soft and light.

"I'm going dancing," she told Mags. "Salsa Night. Come with me." It was like the gentlest of instructions, hard to resist.

"I can't, Abida, I'd get all the steps wrong and out of order. But thanks."

"I know you love him to the moon and back. Isn't that what they say on Facebook? I love that, it's so dreamy. I'm sorry, dear Mags. He wants to be a boy I'm guessing."

"You could be right."

"And you had no idea? No inkling?"

Abida spoke with genteel care and relish, and the last noun was bell-like. She especially loved the phrases Mags could teach her, the almost-extinct or never-anything-but-rare ones she'd never heard on TV. Suddenly Mags felt guilt and shame because she'd learned almost nothing in exchange, apart from 'salwar kameez' and she wasn't sure how to spell that. And she'd turned down that wedding invitation because something important of Rudi's came first. Mags hoped she'd been a good friend as well as neighbour but intimacy with other women was something she'd avoided since Dan made a lover of her nearest confidante. Betrayal: a word that couldn't be aired without a flinch, crack or shake, and for her always passive. Hard to imagine how it would feel in the doing.

In any case, there was blurting out nonsense for the hell of it and there was self-exposure. It was a kind of surgical scrutiny and she found herself lacking. No, she'd rather hear one of Abida's childhood stories than try to shape this latest episode in her own – unless she could fabricate like the tabloids, of course, and pass it off with the same success.

Although she hadn't answered Abida's question, or registered what followed, now she cried, "Eek, Abida! Do you think Rudi's enough of a celeb to trend on Twitter?"

"Ah, Mags, dear, you know I don't tweet. But I'm an old hand at dance moves and I'm utterly determined to take you out to strut your stuff."

Mags hoped for the kind of voice tone that signalled a call being wound up, but remained bright and grateful too. "You get your dancing shoes on, Abida. If I ever want to spill my guts I'll pop over and you can find a bucket. You're a sweetie but I have to keep breathing and I find that hard once the guts have sloshed away."

Mags pictured the pained and genuine sympathy on Abida's still-smooth face. Her dark brown eyes would be damp now and her head would be shaking. Abida couldn't bear anyone crying without her joining in.

"Dear Mags, it's so unfair. Remember I'm here, bucket ready."

"I will. Party for two, off you go."

Mags had drunk too much for the time the clock showed. What if the twins wanted picking up later? She pushed the cork back in, splintering it and allowing it to jut out awkwardly.

Betrayal. At least with Dan she knew it for what it was. No evasions and no lies. Rudi didn't have the guts to confess. Or perhaps he was too much in love to paint his new muse in scarlet. If it really was post-grad Charlotte of the tempestuous mane, she was barely a woman and arguably exonerated, but it was hard not to begrudge her everything. The feeling. The lushness of it, like a Gauguin. The colours so deep and the world thick with the scent of lilies. The charge of his skin. The tsunami that obliterated the landscape as it used to be. Passion: what he'd loved in her until, she supposed, she lost it. Outgrew it. Remodelled it, or time did, or sod's law as girls used to say at school, with no idea what it meant.

She should pity Charlotte, or whoever it was he was chasing. He was a man who didn't know how to keep on loving.

And did *she*? How could she know?

What if Jake hadn't slapped her face, pushed her out of the back door into the garden and turned the key in the door? If Dan had given up being Dan? If she'd remained Rudi's model, kept her stomach flat and held back gravity when it tried to drag down her breasts – or not cared, kept it brazen, believed herself still the *strumpet* he liked her to be?

How exactly did she know she was better at loving, with no chance to prove it?

She could say because she never stopped loving any one of them, not totally, never let the ashes scatter but stored the jar somewhere secret. Was it like that for teachers like Miss Tralee, when one class moved on?

She could say she knew because of Georgie, but that might be a lie. She wouldn't know unless they met and the past morphed into the present. It was a passion of a kind. Not about bodies, but souls: young ones, and purer for it. That was when bodies were smaller but souls hadn't yet shrunk. Maybe those blackened and shrivelled like a smoker's lungs,

44

with every inhalation of hate, every outbreath of venom. But what else could have connected the two of them, except a better kind of love?

She should have saved him. But maybe saving was what he needed still. She guessed most people did, one way or another, and sometimes from themselves. Deciding to check whether he'd messaged her, she took a few more sips of wine before she found he had.

Mags, it's you! I can see your small self a few layers down, still visible. I'm overwhelmed and a little shaky, truth be told. I loved you very much but you must know that. I want to say let's meet. You're in London after all. But I'm afraid too. Silences between us would be painful and missed connections worse. They say the past is another country so maybe we should accept that we're both migrants. I ramble now, you see. I'm not sure I'm any more whole than the boy you knew, which is a kind of warning because you look so complete. G x
P.S. I changed Barkle to May.

She read it again, wishing it was on a notecard so she could slip it in the photo albums. But this was the present. She would meet him; how could he suggest otherwise? She would allow no silences and they would connect with natural ease. At their cores they would be unchanged and the rest would peel away. She breathed out because she must do this right.

My husband's just left me and I think I'd be in pieces if I could find them. I'd like to avoid art galleries for now. There's a vegan café … She found him a link and inserted it. *Wed or Thursday? 7:00? X*

O.K. Mags drained her glass. Recklessness. Damage. Dependency. She had four kids already and he might need her still. But she liked to be needed anyway.

Thursday at 7. I know it! I was there a fortnight ago. See you soon. G x

Off to dance with the tree fairies now, he added in another blue bubble. Mags smiled.

"Bring it on," she muttered, and made some strong coffee.

45

After beginning but abandoning a TV drama she'd only half-followed, Mags played Janis Joplin for the first time in many years, and fetched the photo albums that had come her way after her mother's death. She'd already flicked through the three volumes but now she wanted to be sure. Not one photo of Georgie Barkle, even though she remembered posing with a protective arm around him. She supposed her father must have thrown those away after they came to take him back. But she could imagine her mother keeping one secretly, in a covert rebellion, and it disappointed her that apparently she hadn't dared.

No need to blame Mummy, she thought. She hadn't put up enough resistance herself, for all her father's complaints about her behaviour. Time to make up for that in her old age ...

Most of the photos were black and white. Her father had a Box Brownie with a miniature croquet hoop on top and a worn leather case. He didn't let her use it because it was delicate and complicated, but bought her one of those instant print, peel-off jobs when she was about sixteen, as if that kind of cheap trash with its overbaked browns, undercooked contrasts and unnatural sheen was quite good enough for her. Mags would have liked to be a better photographer than her slow, precise father – or than Rudi, framing with something he called instinct although it looked to her like neo-spiritual focus. But both of them, somehow, were masters of technology that made her stupid.

In a black and white square with a border, Grampy was there with her and Grandma, at the foot of the tree where he built her the house – looking too old and thin to shin up there to install it. His face was faintly dappled in a way Daddy would have thought arty, and she was nudging in between the two of them as if she wanted to burrow. "Can't I stay longer?" she used to ask when she spent a weekend or a week with them, in the long attic bedroom that belonged to a story. She used to imagine a secret passage hiding under the slightly bumpy wallpaper, and pretend when they found her in the kitchen that she'd crawled along and slid down it. The

46

real world must have been dark then too, but the darkest thing she knew was Daddy. His temper. His ice.

The phone she didn't really understand heralded a message telling her she could go to bed as the twins would both *stay over*. No mention of where; they had so many friends, And she ... well, in the old days hers got lost with break-ups, house moves, job changes. She'd never been one for letters, and phone calls could feel so invasive. Loving and losing – that was the pattern, and it seemed more real than all these digital connections based on being in the same club on the same loud, hazy night.

She fingered through a few more photographs. Her parents at their wedding: the pair of them turning to each other as if quite alone, in an image that was never framed. Not a Fifties shot at all, it was so intimate that she imagined her father resenting the intrusion. Her mother's girlishness and shine were moving but troubling too. In this moment she was utterly abandoned, and anyone would think him capable, looking at his bespectacled smile, of giving back. But how long could she have kept loving him? Until he gave up Georgie? It was hard to believe she let him touch her after that. Impossible to respect her if she did.

It was a cruel picture. Suddenly she wondered whether the truth was the other way round, and Mummy fell short of his high standards, sharing his bed believing she no longer deserved his love. Another pattern. Either way, it was a picture that couldn't have kept its place on a shelf.

Mags remembered Genevieve telling her relationships were "such total shit." Now the secrecy of the marriage she'd grown up with seemed shocking. Who was her father when he wasn't Daddy, or Sir either – when they were a couple, not a family? It seemed ridiculous and painful that she'd never know.

But she would know Georgie.

"Why did you marry Daddy?" Maggie asked, squinting up through sun.

"What a question!" Mummy smiled it away without an answer, like a joke. She was sitting in the garden with a bowl of peas to be freed from their pods. She wore a pinny over her summer dress but she was always clean.

"Why can't I have a brother or sister? Daddy would like a boy better than he likes me."

"Oh, Margaret!" Her mother's smile was different this time. She never told Maggie not to be so rude. "It's funny you should ask that."

Maggie jumped up from the step and all the peas in her lap fell onto the stone. "Oh bothering bandicoots!" she cried, watching them scatter. She looked at Mummy's tummy but it wasn't a baby curve. "Tell me! I can't *abide* secrets!"

"Daddy said ..." Her mother stopped. "Can you keep one, so that I don't get into trouble?" Maggie nodded repeatedly. "We're going to foster a little boy called George who's had a sad life."

"And make him happy!" cried Maggie. "Why was he sad?"

"That's private, dear, even from Daddy and me. But you'll be kind to him, won't you?"

"You betcha bottom dollar!" Daddy didn't like her talking American but Mummy just shook her head and kept smiling. "He can come up in the tree house if he wants."

Mummy told her to pick up the peas but it was more fun to roll them like marbles and whisper, "Kapow!" when they collided very softly. She was looking out for ants because it was funny when they lined up and carried food away.

Daddy might be happier with a boy to play with the things he liked, with balls and bats. Then he might do what he was always telling her: "Take that frown off your face!"

Maggie noticed that birds were starting to take an interest in the peas. Suddenly she imagined their throats blocked with the hard green balls and them all spluttering and falling down dead with their legs in the air, so she began to squash the little green balls with her feet. Mummy was too busy shelling to tell her off but she said she mustn't bombard George with questions.

"Not even, *Where do unicorns sleep? What's the best way to shrink a giant? Or What do trolls eat for breakfast under bridges?*"

Mummy said she could try those but she wasn't sure George would have any answers. Maggie had plenty; she just hadn't chosen the best yet. But she didn't think boys cared about things like that.

She hoped this one would be different.

6

Mags began the day marked 'Georgie' by rubbing away the pollen stains from the lilies with limited success, and then forwarding all 379 of Rudi's dormant emails to his personal address. She recorded an automaton-like message that said Rudi Shaw could not be reached on that number, giving his mobile and ending with, "Good luck," as if they'd all need it. She failed twice to catch Cameron at a good time and he hadn't managed to call back to "talk properly" like he promised. Genevieve seemed to be settling for email these days, or preferring it. *I'm aiming to take more control*, she'd said in the latest. So Mags had replied, *Control is an illusion, sweetie. Accept that or you'll have no peace. It's a lot less fun than freedom too, so fly! Just make sure your wings aren't made of wax.* Then she'd had to send another more responsible message about living consciously, and joking that her account had been hacked by a headcase.

For the first time in a while, she spent some time sketching – beginning with the lilies and staining them, once she'd located the pastels, with exaggerated dark red that dripped like blood. "Poor," she said aloud, and tore the drawing in half for the recycling bin, wondering whether it would be fair on the lilies to throw them on top of it. "Too conventional," she added. She needed a better idea and in the absence of such a thing it was time she cleaned the house.

Early that evening she remembered her advice to Genevieve as she set off to meet Georgie, reflecting that this was a kind of flying and she must never give up on adventure. The end-of-the-day carriage felt stale. She could smell saturated fat, beer, sweat. As the tube raced into central London she wondered about these other lives sealed up around her. In the midst of so many tablets and phones keeping people separate in spite of the crush, she wanted to collect them all like a teacher, pair their owners up and make them lock eyes until something cracked open between them and lived. She could try that with Cameron if he ever flew back again – just the two of them, with no devices and precious little space in the way. She could picture how shifty it would make him, but if only he would let go of his ideas about people in general and her in particular, and allow himself to be …

What would he be doing at this time of day? She had little idea. But then he probably wouldn't imagine her heading off to meet Georgie Stroft in the top Rudi once said made her look more Woodstock than usual. Mags stroked a few of its textures: the velvet strips, ribbon, lace. In the window she checked her hair and found it equally untamed – just the way it used to affront Daddy, except that now it was fading to matte as well as grey. Maybe she'd try blue soon, a shade Monet used for snow.

The familiar route was glittery in the darkness, a few of the lit-up windows framing decorated trees and lights draped under roofs like fringes on an old-fashioned lamp. It wouldn't be November for a few more days and it didn't feel like winter. How long was it since she had done this alone and single?

Maybe he'd have stored away episodes she'd deleted or never even seen. Small Georgie never talked except in the present, but now they both had an excess of past. Mags decided she must try to order hers, and compress it – which might take some practice.

Georgie sat in an armchair, attempting a straight back and breathing deeply as his hands rested on each side. Tchaikovsky's violin concerto filled the room the way he allowed until his neighbour made it back from work. Georgie only liked drama if it was exquisite. With heavy curtains drawn he felt warm and safe but she was out there, on the way. She'd given her number. He tapped it in and looked at the space below.

Mags hurried to squeeze into the Northern Line carriage just before the doors closed. She was finding a place to hold the yellow rail that wasn't too close to another hand, or any unfamiliar body part, when she heard her name.

Dan was sitting below her, leaning back, one leg high across the other at ninety degrees. Still slim and in jeans, he was wearing a beard, the kind the Leftie young men were cultivating now even though it reminded her of a cartoon sailor. Dan's was dark grey, flecked with silver. Mags noticed the hair bubbling up under his neck was no longer dark but his eyes looked such a vivid blue she wondered whether they'd brightened while other colours faded. She had already managed to say his name as if it was a joke. He said he didn't believe it.

"That makes two of us then."

"Do you want to sit down?"

"Why, do you want to look down my bra?"

Mags felt an instant inner contraction of embarrassment at the old reflex but Dan laughed. The volume of it seemed to rattle the space. "I may look like Captain Birdseye but I've still got my memory."

"Don't they all merge?" she asked. "The women, I mean? Their bits?"

He stood. "That's a thought ..." Grinning, he loomed over her, bending around the curve of the roof. He was the tallest human in the carriage and she remembered how unexpectedly they used to fit.

"I'm sixty, Dan. Younger than Elizabeth Hurley. Well, younger at heart anyway."

51

"Looking good," he said, still looking to the seat he wanted her to fill. Their bodies seemed to have drawn closer and he smelt so familiar. What was it with men's skin? Was every one of them made up with some unique molecular structure that triggered its own scent?

She was pretty sure she hadn't seen him for four years – and there had been seven of them then, at his place: Dan and Melanie, Genevieve and a grungy boyfriend who didn't last into the next year, Rudi and the twins, and herself. Eight, in fact, because his mother had been there too, chewing in between her sentences and going outside to smoke in her coat and hat. Which had put an end to Genevieve's six months nicotine-free, because she felt obliged, she said with booze inside her, to keep Gran company. It was the one and only reconstructed Christmas they managed.

She asked how he was, wondering whether he still emptied his glass every twenty minutes, or only when there was a socially acceptable context for alcohol abuse.

"I'm good."

She attempted to raise a sardonic eyebrow at that.

"All right, all right," he said, more pleased than offended. "Rudi not going too, wherever you're off to?"

"How's Melanie?"

"She's fine. She'll be sorry she missed you." He stopped smiling a moment. "Gen told me he buggered off."

"Then why did you ask?"

The youth in the seat next to him rose as they drew into the next station. Dan looked at it; Mags sat down. She'd wanted, at that gathering Genevieve had more or less demanded, to ask him about his poetry. She would have liked him to deliver something in that deep, fruity but slightly laddish way of his. But those longings were hard, in the circumstances, to explain or understand. A kind of self-harm.

Dan was talking about Genevieve now, not in Rudi's weary, disparaging way but with a kind of distance all the same that she found hard to forgive: "She's obsessing as always but I guess there's progress."

Although Mags wasn't sure what he meant exactly, she didn't want to admit it. Sometimes she thought Genevieve talked to *Pa* more than to her, now that she'd forgiven him at last. Infidelity: such an elegant, musical word. Genevieve had yelled the more Anglo-Saxon translation around with such rage that Mags had hated him for snatching her innocence – which was unrealistic, given the words their eleven-year-old daughter had been using since primary school.

"She's still young," she told him. "I'm told thirty is the new eighteen."

He gave her a look. Her men all said she made things up and presented them as figures, quotes, findings, which seemed to her a natural kind of deducing from evidence.

"She's passionate, that's all," she continued, unable to produce that evidence just now, "and searching."

"Like her mother?"

"You're the one who used to spend hours hunting for a word. But maybe you like things instant now – slams and performance and poetry as Smash?"

Dan grinned. "Without the lumps. And the sugar."

Genevieve said he made zero money and never admitted it. Mags supposed she admired the way he managed, in that case, and didn't give up.

"I'm heading off," he said, "next stop. Call me if your date doesn't show."

Mags narrowed her eyes at him and remembered when that was part of their play. He teased; she only pretended to be cross. He had the wrong way of finding her funny – except that mostly it felt right.

"The vegan place Gen likes, right?"

Mags stared. Watching him move to the doors and turn to raise a hand, she realised he was thicker around the waist than Rudi as well as longer. She wondered whether the beard was a fashion statement or the most easily achievable goal on a bucket list – and remembered spluttering a bit when Genevieve asked her whether she'd made hers yet. As if people still died at sixty, like the Tudors. But Dan didn't look like a man who'd still be costing the NHS in another twenty years. His health was a question she must ask Genevieve without alarming her.

Mags knew she could make assumptions that just ran off like dogs off the leash and were hard to rein in. But then Dan had assumed she was on a date, searching for a new man five minutes after the last had quit – as if she couldn't exist independently without one, like a relationship junkie. It showed how much he knew because this was Georgie, her best boy.

"Old Dan really gets under your skin, doesn't he?" Rudi had remarked after that Christmas. It felt like a flaw he was identifying as one who made a habit of staying fond of his even fonder exes. Once she'd called it his Rod Stewart complex, and claimed that he'd proved her point when he seemed rather flattered and wiggled at an imaginary microphone without the leopard-skin leggings.

Maybe they were all her boys. Still, it was unsettling meeting Dan so unexpectedly, on a night that felt verging on momentous. Mags reflected that she could have handled the brief encounter without the reference to passion.

Anything might have happened to Georgie in more than fifty years. It wasn't as if he'd been robust, or average, or destined like the Eton boys for status or power. Dan would have warned her of the possibilities, Rudi too. As if she was only interested in reconnecting as long as he'd mended! Mags wasn't sure time was as good at that as people glibly assured each other, while nursing hurts of their own that never quite sealed up.

"Love can't really be unconditional," Rudi said, in the kitchen, over supper not so long ago, and she didn't remember why. "People are too selfish for that. We use love as a survival strategy, that's all."

She'd been surprised by the wording. "You mean if it damages us we give up on it," she said, "and those are the conditions?" But she hadn't damaged him, had she? She couldn't imagine how. "What about a selflessly giving kind of love that never holds back even if it gets nothing in return?"

"That's charity, Mags, not sex."

"What's sex got to do with it?" she sang with a Tina Turner strut.

He gave her a look, then a little sigh. Looking back she was sure she must have known. It was a trailer when the film was already made.

But she didn't mean she didn't want it, him. "It's a red herring," she added guiltily. And it was no good trying to seduce him then, not because he would have put up much resistance but because she didn't work like that, once the ache was throbbing. Sex was laughter or moonlight and jasmine, one or the other.

This was her stop now and she wished she'd written down how to find the café because sometimes her muscle memory wasn't as sharp as she expected, and it was dark out there. Georgie might be nervous, always was.

As she stepped down onto the platform she stumbled and lurched like a lush, grimacing at the impact on her ankle. People were everywhere and as the nearest freed himself rather irritably from her tilting arm she felt ridiculous. It wasn't going well so far. She made her way to the exit, trying not to limp. Georgie used to look up to her because she was the strong one, when they were both too young to know that was both relative and luck, and nothing to do with her at all.

7

Walking familiar streets, Georgie remembered things better now that Mags was real again, and out there in close proximity. He pictured the way the black moustache wiggled wormily above the man's mouth when he was cross, but sat happily in the sun when no one was disturbing him, and the radio roared with another England boundary as he lounged in his stripy deckchair, swinging the leg that crossed the other. Indoors, watching Wimbledon or the rugby, he'd be straight and tense, and the moustache only twitched in a way that made Georgie think of rabbits. Its owner was Daddy to Mags but always Mister to him, or Sir to his face. Especially when Mister talked about Father that was God, and Georgie felt as if he might be in trouble for something.

"Why can't Georgie call Daddy Daddy?" Mags once asked the mother, who was always flowery with skirts that spread and would have wrapped around him twice.

"We're getting used to things, sweethearts." Plural! He looked up and she was smiling. "We mustn't rush things. We're still getting to know each other."

"Georgie knows me," Mags said, "inside out and back to front and the whole caboodle when it's at home."

The mother never said *Ah, but we don't know Georgie, do we?* Georgie supposed she must have thought it because he didn't have much to say, not to the grown-ups who weren't his parents yet and didn't ask about the real ones.

In counselling decades later they asked him, "Did you ever feel accepted for who you are?"

"Only by the girl," he said. "By Mags."

Now, feeling the wind scour his face, he knew it was just a trial and he was found guilty of something. Not being a regular boy. Not being nice and clean and pure. He liked to think the mother had defended him, pleaded maybe. But she was afraid too when the moustache wiggled.

His Mags was a child and the woman would have had the edges rubbed off, the quirks. Maybe she'd be all manners overlaid. What if her memories broke in, knocked his into shape or bullied them away? What if there was a false note in her voice, a chord struck by a duster and making him sad like it did when the cleaner came to the big house and gave him a look that meant, *Don't you dare, boy*!

The present couldn't connect with the past after half a century. Rudi Shaw had money, fans and a Wikipedia page; Georgie fitted only into corners. Better to leave the girl she'd been intact and bright than let the woman erase her. With all the goodwill in the world, how could she do anything else? And he didn't want to see disappointment in her face, or concern where the love had been. It was all foolishness and adults had told him early on how dangerous that could be. *I'm sorry,* his text began.

Sitting in the vegan café, Mags smiled at the eccentricity of its art, which looked as if children had created it out of scrap. Maybe it was the equivalent of Dan's back-of-the-envelope poetry: fast, fun and fleeting. Except that most of these pieces had been here last time she'd come for supper, with vegan Genevieve, who'd been crowing about converting her until the manager behind the till said they didn't accept the new five pound notes because of the tallow.

"Oh shit," said Genevieve. "That's cool but they're like all I've got."

Genevieve clearly felt shamed, so Mags paid with larger notes and ordered more wine. That night she'd realised how perfectly her eldest daughter fitted the place, with a short, jagged hairstyle and an additional nose stud to add to the three holes in her left ear. Mags was pretty sure the ties from the woven and beaded bands stacked around her skinny wrist were dangling in sauce, but didn't mention it because bangles and wristbands were a taboo. They used to mean lines scored underneath.

Tonight the place was empty apart from three backpacking Americans interrupting one another's laughter. Mags wondered whether she was the oldest customer of the month, and the only one who still liked fish and chips on a Friday. She looked up at the wire and netting sculpture of a female bust: a variation on a figurehead leading a ship out into unknown water, except that the breasts had Madonna cones with spikes. Around the corner hung a 3D collage of pans, some of them burnt at the base and others splashed with ketchup paint. The primitive dove that dominated the far wall paid homage to Picasso, but with a wreath of tissue flowers wrapped around its neck that turned out to be made of white poppies. PLEASE TAKE ONE FOR PEACE NOT WAR, a penned notice said, so she carefully extracted one like a child removing a brick from an impressive tower, and pushed it through a button hole.

Mags was hungry and looking forward to some guilt-free fast food. Georgie was late now. A few more minutes and she'd be uneasy. What if he'd become a Tory, or arrived only to disappear between courses to snort coke in the unisex loo? Thought white poppies were an affront to decency? Preferred Damian Hurst to Chris Ofili and Ed Sheeran to Benjamin Clementine?

Mags resolved to stop being trivial and posy. Anyone would think she was married to a money-making artist with a weakness for designer shirts. She checked her phone because in spite of her attempts to control the settings, sometimes messages sneaked in at a volume only dogs could hear.

He wasn't coming.

I'm sorry to let you down like this but I struggle sometimes, which may not surprise you. Body/mind – who know which leads and which tags along? I hope you understand and can forgive me. Georgie. X

Mags read it more than once, imagining the words in a voice that could be his, and his face as he looked at the screen. Georgie was struggling, and not just as a synonym for living, the way she did herself. She'd guessed that; Daddy helped guarantee it. Not a word, she noticed, about trying again or keeping in touch. It was horribly sad but she'd wanted to get to know him as he'd become and this was a start. He was trusting her, the way he used to, and that was as much of a risk as she'd taken.

Of course I do, and I'm sorry not to see you but we WILL meet and it will be weird but beautiful. Like whale song. I do listening if you want to call, now or any time. Did that sound too much like a therapist when the kids would have said she needed serious time on the couch herself? Maybe the capitals were bossy, controlling? Sometimes texts were harder than the real world. *Here's the hug you were going to get and I hope you feel it. M xxxx*

She decided to order plenty. The soundtrack above the low Brazilian music suggested that at least two of the Americans were kissing but she had to lean around a corner to see them and wished there was a well-placed mirror to make that unnecessary. Kisses were more delicious than anything.

"You're not waiting for anyone?" checked the girl at the counter below the chalked board.

"Independent female," said Mags, deepening her voice and wondering whether she'd shuffled her shoulders like skinhead girls used to do – in TV sketches at least. "Innit!"

"Good for you!"

The tiny girl was Eastern European and probably had to wear children's underwear. Mags would have liked to know what her life was like while she sat her at her table and fed her up, but instead she said, "It's a goal rather than a status. You?"

"I'm quite fine thanks," said the girl. "Katine. I bring your food fast."

Mags thanked her, aware of her looking up to the next customer – a long way up. Dan loomed behind her and she felt a reflex of outrage.

"I thought I'd keep you company," he said. "I'll have what she's having," he told Katine.

"Please," added Mags, with a smile to make up for the manners that hadn't improved.

While he followed her back to her table, she tried to formulate something suitably discouraging, realising that Kara must have told Genevieve, who had passed the news on to Dan. So he'd known all along that it was Georgie she was planning to meet. Together they'd been speculating about her recklessness and where it would end. She supposed Rudi knew too, but somehow she didn't expect him to walk through the door and make a threesome.

"I can't imagine your ex putting up with art like this," Dan said, grimacing at the walls.

"He doesn't have to. Neither do you. I was just going to stuff my face while I read a good book."

"People are worried about you. Genevieve says you're out of your mind – and let's face it, Mags, she should know."

"She's doing well," objected Mags. "Making progress, you said." Gen was holding down a job now but her father had no faith. "And so am I. No baked beans and wine in bed. No wailing through the night. You won't have any childhood friends to reconnect with but I've realised that this boy was, in a way I wouldn't expect you to understand, the love of my life."

It had seemed true until she heard it. She half-expected Dan to remind her, *"What about Jake?"* but one ex was enough. The food arrived to interrupt any thoughts he might have had. Mags thanked Katine and immediately speared her first sweet potato chip. Dan reached for her wine glass and drank freely.

"Hey!" she cried. "You're not maturing with age, Dan."

"But are you? What happened with Rudi Shaw? Did you lose him up his own arse?"

"I have some advice, Dan. Grow up."

"In fact I'm working in the other direction, from responsibility to freedom. It feels heady sometimes."

"It will do if you keep stealing people's booze."

"You're a good woman, Mags. Why don't you make good decisions?"

"I've made at least one, the best," she retorted. "In 1998, July."

Half-suspecting a clueless shrug, she saw that he knew exactly what she meant.

"It's that long since you left me a broken man?"

"It's that long since I left you free to screw around at will."

He held up a hand in a gesture that meant, she presumed, guilty as charged. His food arrived too, and she told him to eat up.

"We're talking about Celtic-Roman times, more or less," she pointed out. "Bring me up to date with the literary world, Mel, mistresses …"

"Mel likes you."

To be more accurate, Mags thought Mel didn't feel remotely threatened by her, which wasn't quite as heartening. Mel was such a straight, scholarly young woman by twenty-first century standards that she must think her poet's ex-wife a fruit cake, a bohemian, old. She remembered Genevieve reporting that she went to a Baptist church these days – which considering she would have called Dan a fervent atheist made her wonder whether she'd ever known him at all.

"She thinks she can free me from Satan's power," he announced with a grin. "I'm not a bad man, am I, Mags?" Her mouth was conveniently full. "You brought out the best in me. The only decent work I've ever produced."

Mags shrugged. "Are you telling me it's over with Mel?"

"I promised her I'd change."

Mags hoped Mel didn't buy that for a minute but then presumably transformations – miracles – must be, for the faithful, built in. If she was Mel's mother she'd tell her some sinners had to be cut loose to wallow in it.

"I didn't know you did promises, Dan," she muttered.

"You're not allowing," he said, "for the possibility of change – over two decades? Haven't you at least modified ...?"

"My eccentricities? I hope not! What would I have left?"

He said being a celebrity's wife must have remodelled her and she told him not to be silly and jealous. When he amended that to, "Rich, then," she opened her hands and looked down at her charity shop clothes as if to let them contradict him. She pointed out that the pursuit of status was a costly business. Dan nodded and sighed.

"I've won a few half-arsed competitions."

"Genevieve said. Congratulations." Suddenly he seemed like a rather grizzled and grubby boy. "Dan, we can't let these things define our work ..."

"You're painting?"

This thought seemed to please as well as astonish him, which was touching, but she didn't choose to answer. Instead she told him that creativity was far too elemental to be reduced to a price tag. Nodding, he asked for another sip of wine and she promised to throw it over his head if he grabbed her glass again – then passed it to him.

"I've always been a pushover as a mother but you need to stop."

"What, all of it?"

"Only the things you like best." She nodded towards the wine but hoped he'd see beyond it.

"I like talking to *you*."

Mags told him that was because he could steal her booze but he shook his head and swore he wouldn't touch another drop. Somehow they found themselves retrieving anecdotes like old school-friends. He recalled with relish the time in their first terraced two-up, three-down, when he locked himself out – while Genevieve was napping and Mags was at work – fetched the ladder from the shed and climbed up to the bathroom – leaning in, one leg first, before he surprised their neighbour on the toilet. Mags said he must have been smoking a joint in the back garden; marijuana made him seamless as well as clueless, a kind of elastic joker with an enormous smile. Without it he could be impatient.

"You didn't need wacky baccy to be a fruit cake," he told her.

"Oh no, I can do that unassisted."

His proof was an account of her sneaking the rubbish out to the dustbin "stone cold starkers." Mags said it wasn't exactly a routine but she couldn't deny it had happened – in the dark, a quick streak only.

"I danced around the washing line, the whirly one," she admitted, "one summer night when it was raining."

"I haven't forgotten. I watched you from upstairs and when you came in ..."

"Yes. Have a chip."

He looked at his phone as he chewed it and she saw Mel's name. He flicked and scrolled impassively before standing.

"I'm going to head off. It's been fun." He leaned down and kissed her cheek, just one. It felt warm and damp with wine and oil.

"You can report that I'm intact. In possession of as many marbles anyone could be bothered to control."

He grinned and she knew he approved her still – or rather, she amused him, in small doses. And this unexpected charge he'd given her evening was quite enough. She needed time now to recover the difference between the evening she'd longed for and the one he'd dropped in her lap. Mags was careful not to watch him leave, or be caught with her face turned to the window. But maybe, for the first time in years, she could approach his poetry with the same discipline, as something entertaining to read on the train.

After a visit to the loo she found a text.

I am a fool. ☹

Bless you, she wanted to tell him. But she mustn't pity him; that wasn't the way they did things. Georgie Stroft was her equal, anyone's. It was what she'd tried to teach him.

That's our connection! She replied, added a kiss and sent it before realising the recipient was Dan.

From Georgie, silence.

8

On her train journey home Mags devised a plan scribbled on the back of a till receipt. *Volunteer at Food Bank. Paint that mural. Exercise. Meditate.* Even the newest of these intentions was years old and the third lifelong. Mags liked silence because of the potential but in practice she always felt a sense of failure and waste, as if she had a mind that jumbled on regardless of deep breathing, hands in lap, candles or sun, and turned everything into a random mosaic of memories and connections that logic couldn't sort or even hold. As for the mural, there was no one to stop her now.

"I was thinking," she told Rudi one morning when the twins were kicking inside an outsized bump, "of doing a mural for the nursery. I might start today."

"You can hardly balance without toppling, honey. That's not good on ladders."

She pushed her fist under his chin; the endearment was banned, along with *babe*. "I'll start at ground level, Marmalade. And I'm dressed for it!"

She was in maternity dungarees and happened to think she rocked them, as long as what spilt out at the top was multicoloured and soft. Maybe Genevieve, who'd painted her nails in five different colours, would join in, but preferably not with her current speciality: skulls.

He put an arm around her waist and listened to her belly while she did up the buttons of his shirt.

"Kiddos are unanimous. Mummy Mags needs to take it easy and not give herself a second massive challenge," Rudi reported.

"No but it'd be cool, Daddy Spoilsport. I thought a whole crowd of aliens half-hidden on a rainbow planet."

He shook his head. "Veto."

"All right, Planet Veto. Where the one-legged vetoids hang from the sky. I'll get the paint later, unless I can use leftovers from the studio?"

"No."

Rudi was dressed and the conversation was over. She went into early labour two exhausting days later with the Babies' Room an undisturbed sun yellow.

In her imagination Mags recreated her own childhood on the bedroom wall he no longer needed to look at. She could return the Rudi Shaw originals before he took them himself. And in the unlikely event of any man ever joining her there, he'd have to understand what it meant to her. As for the aliens, she could paint those for money on nursery walls! She might as well exploit the surname before she shed it. She had a photo somewhere of the mural she left with Dan, and could explain to non-poets unfamiliar with recreational drugs the details he'd requested. Meaning to search food banks before bed, Mags turned off her phone and closed her eyes on her fellow-passengers.

When she arrived home, she was surprised to see a light upstairs. Not Rudi, taking back every word – or only the paintings? It was almost ten, too early surely for burglars. Most likely she had just forgotten one switch. But she rang the landline anyway, expecting her own sniffy message about Rudi no longer being available on that number.

"Mum's not here. This is Cameron. She should be home soon."

"Cam!" she yelled down the phone, and ran towards the house. The door opened and she squeezed him hard, all of him – surely more than there had been last time she saw him on Skype ...

He felt so solid, no give. A muscle man now, so less beer and more tennis in his life these days. Smelling an unfamiliar scent from his expensive jumper, she remembered she had no idea what those days of his were like.

"You're so clean!" she cried, and then laughed at herself. "And handsome! What are you doing here?"

"I'm here for Dad," he said, and Mags saw under the hall light a trace of sweat in the crease under his chin. "You haven't heard?"

"He's dead, isn't he?" Once that had seemed the best solution.

He nodded. "You don't have to pretend to be sorry."

"Cam, I am – for you. I was lying low. Let me make you some food."

He said he'd eaten on the plane. She put the kettle on anyway and insisted she was sure he'd like toast. "I could have got excited if I'd known!" She thought she'd better add, "About you coming, not Jake ..."

"Where were you?"

She didn't answer that. What difference did it make? He hadn't actually refused the toast so she flurried about and hoped the jam she hadn't touched since Rudi left was still safe for consumption, given his habit of licking the knife and then returning it to the jar.

"You must be tired," she said, as he sat straight at the kitchen table and didn't speak or move. Such Australian shoulders, not British at all.

"You don't want to know about Dad?"

"Well of course … but he's dead and you're here, and I'm all over the place with joy!"

Was that what it was? Something other, less complete and much less easy, but what alternative word was there? It had been three years at least and he was well known for lying pretty low himself, on a semi-permanent basis. His hair was crinklier, and gleamed. How could any child of hers be so neat and firm and utterly conventional-looking? He could be a Tory back from some golf club! But it was reassuring in its way. Leaning over him from behind, she crossed her arms around his neck, but only for a moment before he pointed out the smell from the toaster.

"It changes the setting behind my back!"

"I tried to call you."

"I was off duty – as Rudi's PA or whatever I was. I needed space. I didn't expect Jake to use it to die."

She scraped the black from the corners and laid the two slices on a plate in front of him.

"No thanks. Sit down, Mum. I need to tell you. I know you can't forgive him but he's my dad anyway and it's too late now."

She sat. Poor Cam had needed Jake all his life, but a new improved model, not the crappy original. "Too late …?"

"For anything. To get to like him, or understand him anyway. It was a brain haemorrhage on the street."

"So no pain?" Mags was imagining it now: the traffic fumes and noise, and legs buckling. But no face, not an up to date image. She hadn't seen Jake since Cameron's twenty-first and she hadn't known then whether she could do it – present herself whole and stay that way. Jake: the first boy who made love to her after he sang her a song he wrote because he couldn't sleep for wanting her. That was roughly five years before he knocked her against the wall and split her lip with the side of his hand, the right one with the long nails for plucking strings. Before his parents' swimming pool ...

Cameron wasn't responding. She'd always known there might be anger in the mix, perhaps unidentified and without a precise target but niggling all these years under his skin. But he became a boy who wouldn't talk and the habit stuck.

"Can you work out how you feel, love?" she tried, gently, with one hand reaching close to his but not quite meeting his fingertips.

There was a long pause in which she almost added that of course he couldn't, what with the shock, but then he withdrew his hand and said, "I'm tired, Mum."

"Of course you are. I'll make up the spare bed."

She hurried upstairs straight away, sorry to leave him and wondering whether he might join her and help the way he used to like to do, a few lifetimes back. He was Mummy's best helper; Jake thought she made him soft but she didn't want him breathing in Jake's smoke or echoing his language. She used to apologise to Cam on his behalf, with, "Daddy doesn't mean it. He's just tired," or, "It's all right, baby, don't let him make you cry."

In her head she told Georgie Stroft she should have said sorry a dozen times to all her children, for complicating their lives and giving them reasons to be sad, or feel damaged, because loving them didn't seem to be enough. *"Has Jake ever said sorry?"* she imagined Georgie asking. As if!

She couldn't hear any movement downstairs. Had Cameron fallen asleep? She imagined him looking around the kitchen and lounge for clues, but when she hurried back he was still sitting just as she'd left him.

"All ready," she reported.

Now Cameron stood and stretched his shoulders. His smooth, tanned face reshaped briefly with a yawn, only to compose again, impassively at rest.

"Oh Cam!" she cried. "You could be on knitting patterns."

"OK, if you say so. Goodnight then, Mum. We'll talk in the morning."

"Of course!" she agreed, uncertain what that meant. Talk? Would he be telling her all about work, in which case she'd need plenty of strong coffee? Or selling the way of life he'd chosen even though she'd rather stick cocktail sticks in her nipples? Or was it more of an interview he had in mind, a kind of psychotherapy for one or both of them?

He'd gone before she'd managed another embrace so she called after him, "It's wonderful to have you home!" as if forgetting that he'd been an independent adult well before she'd moved in with Rudi. He had no home to come back to.

"Well," she said to herself, and breathed deeply.

"Mum," he added, leaning around the kitchen door again, "would you mind binning the lilies? You know I ..."

"With pleasure!"

Upstairs he made so little noise he might have been a glis-glis pattering about with a fluffy tail brushing corners. Mags liked that idea.

Jake was a hod carrier on a building site near her school. She noticed him the first time she heard the tanned, bare-chested gang of them with their, "Mornin' darlin'"s from above, with a whistle or two.

"Nice tits," one of them called. "Shame about the face."

Someone objected, "Leave her alone. She's all right, aren't you, love?" but she had no intention of bestowing a grateful backward smile. Her breasts felt womanly and full as she walked on, trying neither to hurry or swivel, or to alter her rhythm or frame – as if she wasn't smarting and the rawness of her skin and eyes was a coincidence, and telling herself they had no power as well as no right.

But once she had crossed the road and almost walked out of sight, she risked a glance and he was the one she saw: his coffee-coloured back and his blond hair hanging loose and wispy from his helmet. He was shorter than the others and younger than most, and there was nothing raw about him. He was all looseness and ease.

He was the one who'd defended her, she was sure of it. Not that she needed defending from any man. And that included

Mr Mean, who was being ridiculous and rigid about every-thing, as if a Fine Art course was equivalent to lap dancing. The blond head turned just a second before she looked away. Maggi (with a circle on top of the i) ran one hand through her curls and shook them back from her eyes. As she headed for the school gates she tried to guess his name.

A few days later she was in the pub across the road at lunchtime, after her last A Level exam, with her friends Judy and Hilary who had finished too, and the three of them knotted their school ties around their foreheads and unbut-toned their blouses as low as their bras allowed. Judy and Hilary were smoking and reassured the publican that they'd all been eighteen for months when they ordered two lagers and a shandy. Maggi was the one who started singing, "School's Out!" with as much gritty, snaky relish as Alice Cooper and a confidence the others couldn't match. But she didn't finish the chorus as they took the glasses back to their table, because the hod carrier walked in with a battered old tray and a long order.

"You still all right for Saturday night then?" she heard the landlord ask him.

"Unless I get a better offer!"

"I can't go higher than eight quid. Unless you're bringing Elton John with you."

Maggi could see the others were listening too. Personally she would have said he looked more like a footballer than a musician.

"Let's sit outside," she told the others, even though there was a cool breeze licking through the sunlight.

It seemed a long wait for him to emerge again, and she hushed the others when they tried to talk about him, Judy a bit sniffy but Hilary with an impression of a wide-eyed frog. They were virgins all three of them, although in Hilary's case that was something of a technicality judging from the way she weighted the word *heavy* before *petting*. Maggi had endured a few beery, smoky kisses and been touched on the breast a few times by blokes who didn't appreciate being told to piss off so she supposed that was as light as it got, without a habit and a rosary.

"Watcha," he said, making a show of steadying his overloaded trayful as stray beer ran down the side of a tankard or two.

It was Maggi he looked at before he carried the drinks away; she looked back and warned, "Watch out, more like."

"All under control, sweetheart." He winked and walked on. His shirt was open and flapped in the wind. He couldn't know she watched his bottom but she guessed he might count on it.

A barman called after him, "See you later Jake. Bring the glasses back!"

"Five thirty sharp mate."

That was for her! She was sure of it. It was a kind of date, and she would be there.

He claimed he'd written a song that afternoon, in his head while he worked. A song for her, called *Leaving School*. 1975 was an impossibly good year, thought Mags, wiping the worktops. They met at five thirty and he bought her a shandy with an amused smile. He told her he aimed to be a professional musician but the band he'd formed had just split and he needed to work on more songs for an album. When he left fifteen minutes later he had her phone number and made a show of kissing her hand.

She lost her virginity early that July, after the first private performance of *Leaving School* on a Spanish guitar, in the newly built Barratt house his parents had bought but abandoned for a four-week cruise. There she progressed from shandy to his father's scotch, vodka and gin. At first it wasn't co-habitation, just evenings and nights and then sleeping the days away alone in her narrow childhood bed. She told her mother she was safe and sound and sensationally happy, which earned her a few tearful embraces and repeated assurances that they would always be there for her. But defying her father with a smidgeon of truth led to such volcanic rants that she packed a small suitcase. She spent the remainder of the month painting a flower meadow on one new magnolia wall, cleaning diligently and enjoying for the first time the billowing of her own washing on the line that whirled at the centre of the square landscaped garden.

Now Jake was dead and she'd cured herself of loving him – or rather, that had been his solo achievement, even before what happened in the pool. Not with the first strike or even the second but with their memories, the traces she carried with her long after she'd taken Cameron away and made sure he couldn't find them if he tried. She made a resolution never in future to love so wholly, so theatrically and irrationally, because then nothing would ever hurt that much again.

One hot Sunday they lay naked in the tasteless bed with its orb-like decorations and mock-antique head, and Jake told her it had never been like this with any other *bird*.

"I don't chirp," she told him.

"No, you roar and wail and rock the ship out of the water!"

He always sounded proud of her and she loved it. "Do you mean that?" she asked, soft now, but pressing too.

"Ask the bleedin' neighbours. It's a wonder the fuzz don't knock on the door."

He lit a cigarette and opened a window. It must be almost lunchtime because she could smell the predictable roasts in the new ovens on all sides.

"No, Jake, do you mean what you said about other girls?"

He turned and smiled, mostly with his blue eyes because his full mouth was sucking in smoke. "Of course I do. How could there be two like you?"

"That's all right then," she said, when she might have asked, *"So you love me?"* Not how many girls he'd had, because she didn't need to know that; her father seemed convinced the total was more than Mick Jagger and George Best combined but Jake was only eighteen months older than her and more of a bragger than a doer. Most of all he was a sleeper. If she didn't use sex to wake him, Sundays would start at around the time her parents had their tea, fruit cake and sandwiches with the crusts sliced away for perfect triangles. When she asked him how many songs he had for the album now he said, "A few," or "not enough," but whenever she suggested working on a new one he said he had to be in the right mood and he couldn't think straight when she was there to tempt him.

"Let's go for a walk," she said. "Get some air. A picnic!"

"We can picnic in bed."

"Ah but the teddies prefer the woods, don't you, Ned?" Sitting up, she reached for the one possession she'd taken with her on top of clothes and make-up, *Sons and Lovers* and *Jonathan Livingston Seagull*. Ned was thinner than he used to be, and scrubbier, but she loved his lopsided smile and sad eyes.

"Ned says you're a wastrel and he'll have banana sandwiches please."

"If it's a nice big banana you want there's one right here."

Laughing, she covered Ned's ears and opened her eyes wide with shock. Then holding Ned by one leg, she used him to beat Jake around the head until she let herself be pulled back under the cover.

Mags no longer had a single photo of Jake the way he used to be. Now that he was dead she might have liked to look at him with just enough forgiveness to let it all rest with him. She tiptoed upstairs in case Cameron was already asleep.

9

It was a gift she had: sleeping as if nothing ever happened. Waking next morning, Mags remembered that several things had.

"Such is life," she muttered to the mirror, where her hair looked as if she'd spent the night standing on a cliff edge battered by a south-westerly.

She heard Cameron in the bathroom and shuffled out in her pyjamas to call through the door that the shower water switched in a blink from cold to scalding so best not to trust it an inch.

Would he want cooked breakfast? She could manage beans on toast. What on earth would they do all day? It wasn't as if, like the twins, he had school-friends still around. She could find him a gym, she supposed. He didn't look as if he let a day pass without toning up. How on earth he had achieved his rippling bulk and glistening health with a toxic father and a sport-phobic mother, she couldn't imagine. Jake's body was beautiful in '75, in a carelessly self-destructive, open-air way, but casually compact. This son could have picked him up in one hand and tossed him like a pancake. But was he as gentle as his father was a brute? She would probably never know anything real about him.

Cameron wanted a puppy.

"Not in a flat, darling."

"Why are we in a flat?"

"You know we couldn't stay where we were."

"Grandma said we could live with them. She wants us to."

Mags poured his cream of tomato soup and saved herself a third of the can. It was his favourite. The kitchen was just a space demarcated by chipping lino at the end of a living room that smelt musty, but it made no difference. She didn't want Cam intimidated by her own father, who'd become darker and sourer with early retirement. But for the carefully ironed Marks and Spencer clothes, he looked at fifty-seven like a beaten old man in a Cezanne café.

"Ah but Mum's a grown-up, Cam. We can manage on our own. We'll find somewhere nicer as soon as we can."

"And have a dog?"

"I'll have to get a job, sweetheart, and you'll be starting school."

He put down his spoon with a small splash that caught his protruding chin. "I don't want to."

She leaned over and stroked his hair back from his forehead, so terribly soft it tore her gently to feel it against the warmth of his skin.

"Don't go away," he said, his voice stretching into a sob.

She picked him up even though he was too chunky for that now, a whole jointed being, not a blob of a baby.

"I want Daddy," he murmured into her shoulder.

"Well so did I," she told him, "but sometimes the things we want are bad for us, OK? We'll be just fine, the two of us. We've got each other."

He wasn't the kind of child to be fooled by fist-swinging positivity, American style. He gave her a long look, eyes squeezing in and clouded.

"Daddy isn't nasty *all* the time."

She could have said daddies never were and that was what gave them the power to slay you when you were off-guard loving them. But there must be kind men out there who didn't need to slam women and children with their volume and their long, strong arms, or half-drown them in chlorine-blue water. Georgie would have grown into one of them.

"And you and me, we try not to be nasty, full stop, not even on a grizzly Monday or a sweaty Sunday." She kissed his forehead. "Not even when we've got no chipolatas in the fridge." He hadn't been happy about that yesterday. "And no good coffee for Mummy. Because we've got love and that's enough."

He nodded but she wasn't sure he was convinced. Surely he knew his status had been promoted to everything, the whole caboodle?

"I'm sorry about the chipolatas, Cam. Let's make some Welsh rabbit, eh?"

"Rare bit!" he protested.

Not so rare on her income, she thought. He'd survive, wouldn't he? Had Georgie Barkle?

Her smooth, scented son was quicker with the shower, comb and gel, moisturiser (and whatever else it took) than she might have expected. She'd been looking for a tablecloth that wasn't stained; the dining room had the kind of clean minimalism she thought he'd like with its white walls and muted modern furnishings, even though she hadn't stepped into it since Rudi left. But Cameron said there was nothing wrong with the kitchen table.

"Is there fresh fruit?" he asked.

She checked the fridge knowing full well that the blueberries had turned the day before. He wasn't prepared to try the vegetarian sausages and didn't want to know why she'd drawn a line under eggs.

"Any sugar-free cereal?"

Apparently not, when he checked the ingredients, so she made him porridge which was a bit of a push-me-pull-you debate because he said he did know how but she insisted – only to lose control of the oats. "Aagh. This would keep the wallpaper on, no messing."

"I usually have fruit in it."

The coffee was strong but she told him it would wake him up without the effort of a morning run.

"Mum," he said, "I'm going to see Sharon. Dad's wife. And Granny."

"She's still alive?"

"Sharon's only thirty-eight or nine."

"Yes, I meant ... Give my regards to Maureen." Maureen who never liked her but then shocked her, made her cry ...

"But before I head off to Basingstoke I want to ... Can I ask you some questions, about Dad?"

"Oh darling, of course you can. But I can't vouch for my memory. And I'm not really a neutral observer so you'll have to understand I have an angle."

"No kidding. I'll ask Sharon and Granny too."

Mags remembered she had some hazelnuts and various seeds clipped with clothes pegs. She produced them and returned to the cupboard in search of something else she might have forgotten but Cameron asked her to stop fussing and sit down.

"I know you met when you left school. You moved in with him while Granny and Grandpa were away and then you went off to uni."

The words of the song ran through her head, tune attached and visuals too. *She's leaving school, life's lessons have just started. She's the kind of chick who leaves fellas broken-hearted. First time I saw her with her school tie round her head, I pictured her school uniform on the floor around my bed.* Which for the time was more explicit than lighting her fire.

"He asked me not to. Said if I did we'd finish, fizzle out."

"But you went. You did Fine Art. Did you both see other people in those three years?"

"I promised I'd be faithful. I came back for weekends in the show house. He didn't want to visit me at De Montfort. Too middle-class for him."

"Can you minimise the slant?"

"I am, Cam."

"You were faithful?"

She almost confessed the one time she got drunk as a skunk and woke up in an engineer's bed. The engineer complained she'd crashed senseless. "Yes," she said. "Your dad said he couldn't guarantee to live like a monk in my absence but he'd try. I told him not to bother."

"But you made up?"

Oh yes, lots of making up, most of it naked. "He won me round." He'd said he loved her, wanted her, told her that being apart only kept it fresh. She saved coins to call him from the payphone on the hall corridor and try to find his wanking romantic. But she used to look at her happily married tutor, listen to him talk, and wish she could love a man with gentle manners, ideas, morals.

"It was a mistake." *And when she looked at me and smiled, I knew she was innocent but wild.* "You must have made some, darling."

"I haven't made any babies. Neither of you wanted me, because I came along too soon?"

"I was pregnant half-way through my probationary year. It wasn't planned. I forgot the Pill somehow – and yes, I did hate teaching. Jake thought I did it on purpose as a way out. He was mad with me."

She'd been neglecting her coffee but when she drank a little its strength made her wince. She'd never told Cam his father wanted her to go to an abortion clinic. That wasn't necessary, was it, in the name of honesty?

"I came round fast. I wanted to lavish love on you and I told him he'd be a fun dad. Maureen and Don said we could live with them until we found a place. He felt cornered. But he was glad you were a boy. He sang to you, made up a song about bears with growls in it. I think you were a bit scared."

"I don't remember."

She was glad but didn't like to show it. She'd always counted on him being too young for bad memories. Mags told him Jake really was a fun dad, could be. He just hated losing his weekends, his Friday nights with the lads, his sleep.

"He wasn't ready," said Cameron.

So sympathetic. It was touching – and exactly the line she used to take with her mother. Mags shook her head and twitched her nose. She wondered whether he would be ready himself, sometime, but didn't ask.

"If you want to know what he was like when I knew him, he was sweet and funny, and quick and playful. And sexist and rude. Full of anger and contempt even though nobody ever really blocked him. His parents were classic laissez-faire with a ton of financial support thrown in. Maureen even offered to help look after you so I could work, but I wanted to be a hundred percent mother. Not a hopeless teacher. I think you spared me that humiliation."

Cam didn't react. He didn't want to know about that.

"Was my father talented?"

Oh she believed so. "Things came easily. He could play guitar but he didn't practise. That drove Maureen mad. He tried to gravel his voice but it was pretty really, like him."

She remembered teasing him that he was a softie, that the songs were for romantic females, so he wrote one about killing a girl who tried to make a kitten of him when he was a cheetah that knew how to bite and claw. It was the song that opened his first gig with the new band and his voice was so thick with edge that she walked out and told him her breasts were leaking.

"Mum?"

"Sorry. Maybe I remember more than I thought. Yes, he had talent. I don't know exactly why the band imploded but he was always steamed up about something. Not a great team player."

Cameron didn't seem to be finishing his porridge. She offered toast and promised to watch over it.

"And you left him because he ... assaulted you, but you didn't report him to the police."

Assault. That was one word for it. No watery word for that. "I should have. I disappeared off the face of his earth but I don't think he looked very hard."

"But you loved him?"

"And hated him. Same for him I think. First time someone hits you, or shoves you against the wall, or grabs your throat, you think it's the exception. You find mitigating circumstances like booze or you accept the word *provocation.* The second time you tell him you're scared and there can't be a third and he declares penitence and passionate love. Third time you know you can't let your child be the fourth."

She mustn't get emotional; she needed to match his calm but that was easier for the barrister than the accused.

"You don't know I was in any kind of danger. I can't ... Wasn't it just the booze?"

"I wasn't going to risk it." She looked, waited. Then he shifted and firmed, more upright in the chair than ever, bigger.

"I loved my dad. Even when I didn't see him or hear from him I kept on loving him."

Everything he had said so far had the same steady note, the same slow delivery. His face had barely assumed any expression but reception. As interrogations went, it was lower than low-key but she felt something through it that challenged

78

and blamed. Something that might be in her all along, ready to be raked over and shown the light.

"I know, Cam. It's shit."

He wasn't eating or drinking, and though he looked at her, not the porridge or coffee or wood grain or walls, she couldn't tell what he saw.

"You left me alone at night in that flat."

"What?" No. She couldn't have. But her body felt as if it knew better.

"You did late shifts at the supermarket."

"Not nights, Cam. Supermarkets weren't twenty-four hour in those days." Oh God, she had. Something groaned inside, an old ache. "Only a couple of times. There was a Sixth Former, from the big house over the road, who babysat. Except once or twice she let me down."

"I was frightened, Mum."

She was too. "I was back by half ten. Once or twice, I swear to God." She'd come home and cried with guilt at the sight of him. Hadn't he been fast asleep when she got home and she'd lifted him into her bed with her so she could hear him breathe?

"You said your memory wasn't reliable."

"But I'd remember that! I do!" She placed a hand on his, which was lightly closed. "I'm so sorry, love. You were a good sleeper."

"Only when you were there."

"Cameron, what can I say?"

"Look, Mum, I'm telling you my version because I have one. You meant to lavish love but you weren't a perfect parent. It's worth remembering because you make Dad out to be scum ..."

"Not full-time."

"He hasn't hit Sharon."

"You don't know that."

"Maybe you'd prefer it if he had."

"I wouldn't. I'd hate it. I like to think he matured late, grieved the loss of you – us, even. And learned to manage his anger."

79

He pointed out that she hadn't given him a chance to prove it if he had. No, she said, because she didn't want him to know where they were. That was how afraid …

"Then you shacked up with a druggie who couldn't look after a gerbil."

"Not strictly accurate, darling. Dan only did a bit of weed. He was really fond of you. And I married him eventually."

"I didn't want another father."

"No, I don't suppose you did but I thought you'd be friends."

"He was another mistake?"

"Yes, Cam, yes!" She held up both hands. Never had Genevieve managed this, not with her screams, slammed doors, intense silences. Mags wasn't sure she could stand in the face of it and yet she knew … what? That she meant well? That she always loved them all?

"Mum, I don't want to judge you."

"You could try harder?"

"I really don't. But my dad died and I'm not forty yet. I'm not ready."

"I don't suppose you are." Her poor boy. Had he hoped they would reconnect more meaningfully than Skype allowed? This last week she'd been unready herself for just about all of it. "Call me Ethelred." She really couldn't drink this coffee and she hadn't eaten yet. "When are you going?"

"Maybe I'll have a swim first." He looked at the time on his phone. "There's a sports centre a couple of miles away so I'll walk there and back."

What was it they said about hormones boosting wellbeing through exercise? Mags didn't suppose she'd ever test that theory in person. She couldn't tell how well that being of his was, under the surface that barely rippled even when he really didn't want to judge her. She was trying to remember now all the newsy answers she extracted in calls, probably bombarding him in the hope that one question in five would generate a revelation, an insight, or even just a scene, a location, a storyline.

"If that's what you fancy. You'll be hungry after that lot. I can make a cake!"

"I don't do cake, Mum. Thanks. I'll sort myself out when I get back. Porridge was a bit heavy on the stomach, sorry."

Was that it? By late morning he'd be gone. She asked him how and when he heard about Jake, but he'd already stood and didn't sit again. Apparently Sharon had sent a message on WhatsApp. He'd been asleep but for some reason had heard his phone murmur.

"Sharon's cool. She wanted to build a bridge I guess. Did you know when they first got together she had three miscarriages? Then she figured she'd help him claim his son back. She was the one who called and then handed him the phone. You'd like her."

"Sounds like I would."

Mags imagined a blonde with curves but he took from his wallet a photo of a thickened, grey Jake with a tattooed arm and a slight, curly-haired mixed race girl in a T-shirt that said Glastonbury. They both wore sunglasses but her smile was freer.

"I do!" she told him. Which she'd never actually said to Jake, thank God, even though he'd proposed after Cam was born.

"Will you come to the funeral? She'd be happy if you did."

"Oh Cam, I don't know ... give me time." She'd had thirty-four years but he didn't remind her and that felt kind.

"Yeah, I'll keep in touch. I haven't booked my flight back yet but I can't stay forever."

"Oh, of course, no forevers."

She was trying to recall his job title these days but it featured the kind of words that wouldn't stick and carried no pictures. She reached up to hold him and it was so comforting suddenly that she almost cried, but he'd hate that. She did know that much.

She supposed as he headed upstairs that she should eat something.

The flat was grotty and the grot was visible as well as lurking. Mags had to find somewhere better but on her cashier's wage that would take a while. The main thing was safety and staying hidden.

Cameron had been grizzly at bedtime, which always made him flushed, but there was no sound now from the bedroom. She crept along to look inside where she'd left the door ajar and he seemed peaceful with his hand curled beside his head and his lips apart. If he slept deeply enough she wouldn't wake him when she crept in beside him, but she'd have to buy him a second-hand bed for himself once he'd stopped clinging and things had settled. For now she liked him warm under the same blankets, even if they were old and scrubby. There was restoring to be done and they could help each other with that, no one else to do it.

She heard footsteps outside, clicking, almost like a water pipe at night. Even so, the doorbell caused the physical reaction that shocked her. Not him. It couldn't be, not unless he'd paid some private detective and anyway he wouldn't dare. Not that he'd be expecting a knock on the door from the boys in blue because in his head all that was just normal when a bird pushed a bloke too far. The door was frosted. Anxious to head off a second press of the bell, she drew close enough to see a colour and shape, dimensions. Not Jake but a woman. And not her mother either. With the chain latch on, she opened as far as it allowed.

Under the light was Maureen in a fancy, big-collared coat she'd have bought from her catalogue, and navy courts with heels. Maureen who would have liked her to dress more stylishly and get a nice haircut.

"Tell me Jake doesn't know I'm here," Mags hissed.

Maureen shook her head. "I persuaded your mother to tell me the address."

"I made her promise ..."

"Can I come in? I won't wake the baby."

Mags stepped aside. She wiped her feet on the mangy doormat as if it wasn't fit to touch her shoes.

"I know what Jake can be like. Don won't hear a word of it but I've got eyes and ears. He'll grow out of it, I know he will."

"I'm not going back, Maureen."

82

"That's not why I'm here." Maureen produced a fat envelope from her large coat pocket. "This is my money. I've been saving it for years now, in case. You can put it all behind you, be an independent woman the modern way. You don't need to stay in a crummy dump like this."

The notes were stacked, each with the Queen's head at the same end. Mags didn't actually count, just looked. So much money, like a bank robber's stash in a film.

"Maureen!" She reached out but Maureen wasn't the hugging kind.

"Please don't tell anyone about Jake, Mags. He's not a bad lad."

"Ah, is that right?" The money was to pay for silence as well as better accommodation. "That's the deal, is it?"

"It's a gift. But I hope you'll give him a chance to change. Don would kill him."

"Only if my dad didn't get to him first." Mags flushed. Her father would be cardboard to Jake's fists.

"You'll take the money?"

"No choice really, Maureen." No pride, either. Jake removed it, surgically.

Maureen's smile was tight. She nodded. "Good. I'm all for women's lib. You do it for me. I never had the courage." She was moving back towards the door. "Maybe one day ..."

Mags smiled. It was as if she'd just walked on set with no script at the end of filming.

"Thank you."

"It's being so talented and not making it. He takes that hard. He cares for you and little Cameron. He's broken without you."

"I see. So he was the one who broke when he knocked me to the floor?"

"You're bound to be angry but ..."

"Maureen, thank you, but I don't want to wake Cam."

She closed the door and heard Maureen's heels tap away on the concrete. Then, after checking Cameron was breathing, she counted the cash.

10

There was a time when Mags prayed for the people she loved in a verbal way, along the lines of, "God, if you exist which would be amazing but also make the world harder to explain, please I beg you keep my darling Genevieve safe and whole," or, "God, if you're out there or in anything except people's imaginations, which is a scary idea as well as mysterious, please help Cam to heal, and the twins to survive everything the media throws at them to try to steal their souls." At thirteen she prayed for Grampy and Grandma to go to Heaven after they'd been crushed on an A road in their little Beetle, but it was a formality. The hard bit was the space where they used to be.

When her mother was ill in the hospital, shut down but for the mechanics, she prayed to her closed eyes and pale skin: "Don't die, don't die please, I'm not ready, I need to be good enough first." But when her father died, so suddenly after years of sour and ashen lingering, she said, "God spare me this glowing relief. Help me love him somehow so I don't have to carry this weight."

Long before the deaths she prayed fervently, "Please Jesus, bring Georgie back. Make Daddy sorry. I promise I'll be good for ever and wear dresses and try not to be a rebel or cheeky or messy. Forever and ever amen."

Nowadays she sometimes pictured people who needed love most, and imagined around them a kind of soft, rainbow aura with warmth as well as light. If she focused hard enough she could see it wrap around its wearer like a sari. The process was silent, apart from the name she heard in her head, and she sometimes felt wrapped herself as a result. It seemed the best kind of love, the most giving and least prescribed.

Lying in bed, she tried it with Cameron as he slept in the next bedroom. Now that the physical reality of him was updated and fresh it should be easier, but she felt a kind of blockage. Was it rejection, blame or just distance he'd set between them? Whatever it was, his father was dead and he didn't know whether he loved or hated him, which made it hard enough for anyone to behave in the world. She supposed the twins would be partying, so instead she pictured Genevieve drawing, all those wristbands of hers stroking the thick textured paper she'd bought her, and surrounded her with sensory love.

It was tiring, and even more intense than proofing an essay for Kara. But once begun it was hard to justify stopping. Rudi used to follow, or sometimes lead if she was anxious about a choice he had to make – money or integrity, the divide he hated her to raise. Now she could only picture him pulling on the jumper that morning he left, or sitting at the kitchen table as the air filled with lilies.

Poor Dan must be reeling under all the prayer Mel lavished on him.

And as for Jake … hadn't there been times when righteous justice had seemed the Old Testament kind that involved hell and rotting? She knew she'd tried, "God, don't let him do it again, not to any woman or child," but the resentment felt too thick. And there had been days when she'd stepped outside her own hurt to ask for protection, comfort or escape for women whose men had less control than Jake, more weight and power and no remorse.

Because he had been sorry. She allowed that; it just made things sadder. It might help to go to the funeral. It might even help Sharon. But how could she begin to guess what Cameron wanted her to do or be?

"What do you think, Georgie?" she asked, not out loud but perkily, like little Mags used to. Just as well he hadn't shown up. He'd need a spreadsheet and glossary, timeline and photographic line-up to make sense of the life she'd recount. He might have imagined she'd be celebrating her Ruby Wedding around now and she supposed that was the future she would have counted on, if little girls counted on anything beyond the white wedding and a heart-framed kiss.

Thanks to Facebook she could picture Georgie and his beautifully shaped white-grey hair and green eyes, looking distinguished in a soft, feminine way. How linear could his own life have been? Not easy. Not conventional. Mentally surrounding him, head and shoulders, in a coloured mist of love prayer, was what her child self might have called, *Piece of cake!*, and made her smile.

"Give me a chance, Georgie Stroft," she whispered, and turned over with sleep in mind. What she needed was a blank page. No reruns of kitchen conversations. No bodies in coffins. No small boy left alone for the evening shift. No cut lip, caught throat, head banged against a wall. No ramming against the side of the pool until her head went under. Just peace.

It was a while since Georgie had felt so empty. He'd had something to fill the space and pushed it away like a child with cooling cabbage. He hoped Mags didn't feel the same kind of vacuum now, since she was herself the cabbage and that was horribly unfair. So much for progress, he thought, and the space ached as if strained by weight. He could be laughing at her now, time racing. He hoped he'd be admiring her spirit, if life hadn't gutted it. Which made him think of fish, and candles dying.

How can I explain? Hearts mislead minds and minds trample hearts and I don't know which to blame but I used to do this a lot – look at the door as if opening it and stepping beyond it carried terrors I couldn't name. You are more than a highlight, a symbol in a way. But you're intact as you were, like one of those hardback books with colour plate illustrations that belongs to a different world. How to handle a different you? What if the updated reality of you uprooted the past, and when I tried to open the book the pages were empty?

I want to keep on loving the child who loved me. What if the woman sees only a loser? What if there's too much living between us – and the past we shared became two different stories?

There it is, my best shot. I let you down. It's a modus operandi but of course I let myself down hardest and now the loss I feel is becoming acute. I don't see why you would want to take this risk a second time but I hope you will.

I'm so sorry. Tell me how you feel.

Georgie x

There was sometimes a case for sending a message without even proofing, or it would never be sent at all. He pressed carriage return. Pulling off the new dress he'd hoped she'd like, he thought it dowdy, conservative. Where could he feel safer than in a vegan café in the West End, with the only person who believed in him when life made him shake inside? He began to think that had she been his tormentor or betrayer, and God knew there had been enough of those, he could have followed through. Toughed it out with scent behind the ears and a bracelet around his wrist. Played the part, shoulders firm.

"How do you know?" he'd asked her, when she named Love Lies Bleeding, Love-in-the-mist, Red Hot Poker, Black-eyed Susan. It was a National Trust garden and the father was tense because the children around them were sober versions of their parents who didn't run or call out like she did.

"There was a book," she'd told him. "I learned the good names. The Latin ones are too long and hard."

He looked awestruck.

"They're whole stories," she said, repeating the names.

"Tell them then," he prompted. "But not the horror one, not blood."

So she told him Black-eyed Susan was a baby wrapped in leaves and found in a forest by a woodcutter, and her mouth was red because the birds fed her berries, and the first thing she did when he spoke to her was laugh and reach for his beard. As she grew, her magic made her lonely in school but strong and shiny with the animals and fairies, and she danced in and out of toadstool circles with a daisy chain crown, until her hair grew bright and petal-shaped and she

87

never had to do sums again but only sun herself, drink the raindrops and laugh.

Georgie had told Julia when they were engaged that he wanted Black-eyed Susans on his coffin, if the timing allowed. For a librarian Julia was rather suspicious of stories. She said she wanted to live with more imagination – but not in the end, with a man who walked the streets in a skirt.

Mags didn't know what to expect exactly, although she'd seen footage of the kind of food bank that had subsumed a church hall and was managed by nice women with manners and sensible shoes. She felt the cool stone walls close in on her prejudices, but there was something familiarly urban about the sights, sounds and smells. Welcomed by a petite Somali woman, she was shown around the stacked shelving on wheels, the excess baked beans, pasta and soup and the inadequate stock of nappies, shampoo, washing powder. The plastic was blue, the volunteers' sweatshirts a Robin Hood green, and the system clear, business-like, tested. They'd found this, tried that, had ongoing problems with the other, were still negotiating the best way of ensuring and preventing … She was told the team kept growing like the need but not as fast. And it was impossible to eradicate misconceptions because people who wanted to believe in lazy repeat manipulators didn't listen to the rules.

Mags was finding it hard, through the tour, to keep up. She started to feel complicit. Just another middle-class do-gooder trying to exonerate herself when revolution – non-violent of course – wouldn't be enough, and ministers could pat these teams on the back and say what a jolly good job people like her were doing in the big society.

Not that she'd started yet and she'd delayed long enough. Yet she might, all those years ago, have come close to this kind of need if Maureen hadn't turned up with the cash. Which went to show, she supposed, how safe a bubble could feel, and how small she was inside it.

A portly Irishman with a long, wispy white beard and a hoop in one ear took the next leg of the tour and explained about the sandwich run, at close of business, from cafés to the local homeless. His mood was as jaunty as Ashkiro's was neutral and brisk. No anecdotes, nothing personal. Mags didn't suppose commitment like his – three years now, he said – was possible without humour, and she couldn't see herself holding on to hers while taking an aubergine, basil and pesto wrap to a guy in a sleeping bag.

An unexpected laugh made her turn as it echoed and a female volunteer smiled back at her. Someone offered her tea.

"Thanks, but I don't think I can stay just now. It's been very interesting." They would think her a journalist or voyeur. "I'll be in touch." What was she now, a boss at a job interview? "Thanks so much for your time. I want to help. I need to work out ..."

"Sure. We'll be here when you've decided," said Paddy – although that might not be his real name. No edge. Just no time to waste on spectators.

A kind of panic had undermined her now. Somehow she got lost on her way out but eventually passed a mother with two pre-school children carrying a bag and hurrying, eyes wary as if a bomb might fall from above or the ground might crack in their path. Or someone like her might understand where she'd been.

"There are sharper realities than yours," she told herself, unable to make eye contact and – perhaps just as well – find a face to fit.

People watched the more dysfunctional soaps to believe their own lives were in better shape. And it was time she stopped acting on impulse and started examining what, why and how. This wasn't a supermarket and it would be hard to find the heart for clowning. But she could do it and she would. She'd prove herself wrong again.

Back at the house she found a call from an estate agent on her answerphone, wanting to arrange a valuation at the request of her husband. Calling back, she introduced herself and added, "Come when you like. I don't give a monkey's aunt," before she realised the clichés were inter-breeding and she might as well be eighty-five. "Sorry," she said. "Too many spliffs," and laughed. "It's cramped in a bubble anyway."

Sometimes change was liberating and if she was going to prove it she'd better do it now before her marbles started heading off for the far corners of the unknown.

It had been decades since Mags had made a list of intentions, Gatsby-style. She found a used envelope and turned it so that the numbers could fit down the flap.

1. Make art happen.
2. Forgive Jake now he's dead.
3. Commit to the food bank and stick with it.
4. Make a love breakthrough with Cameron.
5. Offer more consistent support for Genevieve.
6. Avoid assumptions about premature independence with Kara and Simon (and try to make sure he doesn't father a child) i.e. keep playing Mummy (more convincingly).
7. Find a half-decent terrace/flat no one hates.
8. Don't allow 1. to slip in the chart. Keep it up there like Bryan Adams, Whitney and Wet, Wet, Wet.

A better mother would promote 4, 5 and 6 but they were ongoing: steps back as well as forward. A kind of reflex instinct threw up the first three and it was with them that she needed to make most progress, from a zero base. Until the vegan café, Georgie would have been there, with a verb like reclaim or uncover. And recompense would be in the mix, thanks to Daddy. Now she wasn't sure whether Georgie Stroft wanted to be found, and remembering when she was in hiding herself she wondered whether all she could do for him was respect his choice. Turning the envelope landscape-wise she fitted along the edge:

9. Make sure that whatever Georgie wants or needs, he knows I'll always love him, (reprise Whitney).
10. (she adds guiltily) Join the resistance. People and planet before profit.

Now she felt like a beauty queen who'd just remembered the world she should want to save. She found some Blu-tack and attached the list rather crookedly to the kitchen wall where it would offer no embarrassment should any of her children spot it because it was barely legible, even with reading glasses.

For the rest of the day she cleaned, pulling a muscle in the process of leaning an arm under and up to the hinged glass of the bedroom windows. There were interruptions from people wanting Rudi but blocked breezily by her answerphone message, and a text from Kara to say that she was on the verge of a deadlines breakdown or quitting and she'd update her on which way it went. When the sweat started to invade her hair she made some tea and, sidestepping email and Facebook, found a picture on Instagram of a charcoal piece Genevieve called Urban Pieta which seemed to be some kind of fur-based roadkill. Breathing deeply, she filled in the heart and commented: *Powerful and startling. Xx* Which was both accurate and evasive. Art as expression, she told herself, and therapy and an outlet – all of it healthy and probably necessary, so there was no need for alarm.

She'd only just exited Instagram, where she hadn't yet worked out how to post any pictures of her own but would supposedly need to do so in order to accomplish Intention 1, when her mobile rang. Genevieve.

"You like it then? Or is that a way of avoiding the question?"

"Powerful is always good, darling. Is it part of a series?"

"Why would it be? I don't repeat."

"Ah yes. How are things?"

"It's like a gasp of air – you know, forest air – creating something. You should try it, honestly."

"As a matter of fact I do ..."

"Pa said you had a good talk. I think he misses you more now Mel's grown a halo. It makes me want to swear on a loop but with Dad it's the booze. I hear your Georgie stood you up. You know the past is another country, Mum. As Leonardo di Caprio said to Carey Mulligan, you can't repeat it."

91

Mags remembered that Gatsby knew how but Daisy lacked the faith to cooperate – just as Genevieve corrected herself: "I guess in your case you do."

"How are things, beyond creativity?"

"There's nothing beyond that, Mother! Rudi taught me that the way Trump teaches ethics. Nine to five is shit but at least it leaves my brain with plenty of battery for powerful, startling art and I'm celibate which makes for higher voltage too. You do like it really?"

"I do, Gen. You sound … energised."

"I'm still off the meds if that's what you're thinking. Who needs them once you junk the animal fat and – wait for it – run in the rain? You'd be amazed. You should try it."

"I'd drop dead, darling. I'd soon be roadkill myself."

There was a pause. "You never take my work seriously."

"It was a joke." Calm, slow. "Cracker standard."

"You make too many jokes, you know? And I'm not one of them."

Mags promised herself not to apologise, a determination that should probably be incorporated into Goal 5, and asked her instead whether she'd heard from Cameron. Since she hadn't, this led into a narrative that seemed to smooth away the edge in her daughter's voice. She ended by sharing the forgiveness goal and the question of the funeral.

"I think that would be like … a surrender. Of the truth! As if men do what the fuck they like and once they've died the slate is clear. You know you survived by hating him. Sometimes it's necessary. You'll never create anything if you deny what's real inside you."

"That's an interesting thought but you did say the past is another country and maybe I want to cross the border."

"Clever. Anyway, I'm sorry if it's all a bit of a maelstrom."

That was a favourite word of Genevieve's lately. "It is rather. I'm sorry Cam didn't tell you himself."

"Oh, he gave up on me long ago, and the only thing that makes it OK is that I got in first. You'll never crack the shell, Mum. If you do you'll just find another one inside. My stepbrother the Russian doll." Genevieve yawned. "You know I fire off. By the way, Rudi says we need to do dinner once a month which is nice of him. I used to worship him, you know?"

"Yes. He enjoyed it." She remembered the time Genevieve used to take her own pastels or watercolours to the studio, to watch and learn. It was her awe phase but it lasted longer than roller blades or Robbie Williams.

"Hey! He's just commented that my Urban Pieta is *stunning, almost literally. Visceral.* So that's cool. Or worrying. He'll be doing *Strictly* next."

Mags made a small grunt of a laugh but guessed he'd score eights on minimal training. She said how glad she was that Rudi was keeping in touch and that the work was so fulfilling, and expressed a hope that Genevieve might be able to visit soon, seeing as she couldn't commit to Christmas. She might like to come house-hunting with her …

"I might not. Too much time, you know? A distraction. I've got to go, Mum, but you sound like you're dealing with stuff. I guess you've had the practice."

"Hoho!" cried Mags. "And I think a female Santa is long overdue. I might start a petition."

"Shit, yeah! Take care." Genevieve chuckled. "Unintentional rhyme. Love you."

"Love you too."

Ending the call, Mags wasn't sure whether that was a promising start to Intention 4. But Genevieve loved her and that was enough for now and, with a historical perspective, a turnaround the Mels of the world would call miraculous. Remembering the Russian doll analogy, she sent Cam a text saying she hoped he'd had a painless drive and Sharon was doing OK.

After sending similarly innocuous messages to the twins, she emailed the food bank with an offer of Tuesdays or Thursdays and had forgotten all about the valuation when a girl appeared at the door in dangerously high heels and a short purple skirt that would once have been ra-ra.

"Come in!" she cried. "Have a Sloop John B and you can try me with any questions but I can't promise any sensible answers." Oh dear. Even the girl's parents probably wouldn't have bopped to the Beach Boys. "A snoop," she said, "as in a tour. Tea? Coffee? Glass of red?"

Nicolette introduced herself as she offered a neatly manicured hand, asked whether Mags had any diet coke and mumbled, "No worries then," when she didn't.

"One benefit of a messy kind of life with regular set changes," Mags told Nicolette as she began a panoramic sweep around the hall with a tablet, "is that walls come and go until they only have to stand up in a gale without sprouting like old cheese. Do your worst!"

With a cheerful grin she returned to the kitchen and peeled a banana. Less space would be cleansing, a liberation of a kind. She might find a sense of substance and feel less of a lone pea in a colander.

I'm bonkers, Georgie, she thought, *except when I pretend to be dull. Or dull except when I pretend to be bonkers.*

She picked out a thick black marker pen from the oversized mug in the corner of the worktop and took it to the plain wall that framed her when she ironed beneath a minimalist steel clock. Nicolette found her minutes later finishing a large squared eyeball a foot above the skirting board, where it turned towards a splurge of a brutalist nose connected by a tear to parted lips.

"Ooh!" said Nicolette. "Shall I come back when I've done the bedrooms?"

"If you don't mind," said Mags. "There's just a pair of eyebrows to crawl off, one round the corner and the other through a hole in the wall."

"Oh! Awesome! You're an artist too. Mr Shaw didn't say. Can I take a picture when you've finished?"

It wasn't quite as imagined when the caterpillar brow hooped its exit and she stepped back to assemble the whole, but she printed IMPULSE 1 down along the door frame and winked at it. Sometimes intentions couldn't wait.

Nicolette the estate agent returned eagerly to declare a passion for improv and stand-up and flash fiction: "You know, instant stuff. Not overthought." She admired the wall and Mags told her it certainly ticked that box.

"My husband says I have facility, but if you take the adjective out of the word and look it up it's not exactly praise." She could see the girl was floored. "If it's too easy it's too shallow. If it's too fast it's cheap. I lack depth and substance." Mags rippled her fingers, arms outstretched. "Watch me float!"

"Well I think it's cool. You should do that live on *Britain's Got Talent.*"

Mags thought it was time to switch to numbers and was surprised by the inflated value of the house Rudi had bought just a year or so before they met. Nicolette said she'd contact Mr Shaw directly, of course, but, "Honestly Mrs Shaw, you're my kind of artist. It was lovely to meet you. I bet there are meanings in that if you look hard enough anyway."

"You're very kind."

When she'd shown the girl out, Mags realised it was Georgie she wanted to tell she'd defiled a wall with marker pen, even if he hadn't made contact at all, not even a sheepish emoji if there was such a thing. The blue balloon stretched down further than any bubble gum could and it was full to bursting. She read the message twice, and then aloud, wishing she could hear his intonation and be sure where the pauses lay.

Georgie you are a human, a vulnerable one, and I'm not sure that without vulnerability much humanity is possible. You are free to choose and free to be you. I love what you have written and am happy that you have been so honest and true. I'm afraid that it's all made me want to meet you even more than I did before but only when you want to meet me. In the meantime if you'd like to write a letter, tell me anything – about your favourite film or book or of course, me as you remember me (down, ego) or what you see around you as you write. Anything. Just write. Here's my address. I love letters and will buy a proper pen to write back. Messily.

Then she framed the kitchen wall with the camera on her phone and tutted her way through a kind of longhand way of sharing it with him, labelling it *Facile Art: a protest or a start. Praise not required. Xxx*

He must be offline but he would write.

It was 3:12 on Christmas morning – the second and last she shared with Georgie Barkle. Holding her stocking in one hand, she tiptoed into his room, placing her bare feet to avoid the creaks. Eight o'clock was Daddy's limit and warning but she was wide awake, and it would be no fun alone. In any case, the two of them had promised each other. She swallowed a giggle at the sound of Daddy snoring across the landing: a sound that grated the air as if his nose had holes to work cheese. Georgie's door was almost closed but the gap was to let her in and she squeezed through it. At once, even though she'd been as silent as a kitten, he stirred under the blankets and turned towards her. It was dark but she knew he'd be smiling.

Mags crept across the rug, sat on the end of his bed and switched on her torch. The beam was old and faint but enough to illuminate the stocking hanging there. She passed it to him, feeling some of the same bulges that shaped hers.

"Happy Christmas!" she whispered and he echoed it back. He always sounded as if he had a cold and Daddy kept telling him to blow his nose, barking, "Harder!" if it was unproductive.

When he asked the time and she told him, he pulled a fearful face.

"We'll be in trouble if he hears us," he said, looking towards the doorway.

"Not through his own racket he won't," whispered Maggie. "Satsumas first."

They raced to pull them out and pair them with, "Snap." Then there was the red net bag of chocolate money they didn't dare break open, and the ritual of pretending to stab their own fingers with sharp new pencils. This year they both had a fat plastic pen that could be switched to change colour, which was quite exciting, and the miniature notebook was fun because it could be kept in the tree house for small, magic visitors to use. When they found their equally tiny packs of raisins they grinned and risked untucking the lid and eating one, then two, because Daddy wouldn't count as long as they checked their teeth for black traces.

"Now you," said Maggie. This was where the boy bits and the girl stuff began.

"You first," he said, so she pulled out a knitted doll's dress that would fit Jemima because Mummy would have measured but she'd forgotten that Jemima liked dungarees better.

Georgie hesitated. What he produced was a cricket ball wrapped in tissue. "I knew it was there," he told her. "I lost the old one over the hedge when he wasn't looking."

Maggie gave him a what-can-you-do face and promised, "Don't worry, I'll whack it to kingdom come."

The stockings were deflated now but she could see something curved in hers. Soon she was holding an Alice band with fake little daisies sprouting from it, which called for the same expression because she didn't have the right kind of hair for decorating. It wouldn't be flattened. Any hair slides Daddy thought would neaten it up were just swallowed by the wilderness of curls like a ball in a jungle. This daisy band wouldn't stay in place any longer than the paper crown in her cracker, which once landed in gravy.

Georgie was reaching for it. Maggie looked back to the door and listened. The snores had stopped – but not for long. She handed the hairband over and Georgie fitted it. On his full but smoother hair it was snug, reminding her that she'd never found the red velvet one that would suit him so nicely.

"Fantasmadocious."

Maggie searched and all that remained in her stocking was the usual mirror, this time with a polka dot frame. She supposed she could use it to make fire in the summer like a Boy Scout. In the meantime she showed Georgie how he looked, which was fuzzy in the darkness but lovely anyway because of his smile.

"Secretly yours for ever," she whispered. That was what they called a double meaning.

Then his face changed. He tiptoed to his chest of drawers and reached into the back of the bottom one. When he turned, he was holding the hairband she'd lost. He'd pulled his mouth inwards.

"I'm sorry," he said. "He was cross with you."

"You looked after it." She smiled. "You can keep it."

"I don't steal."

"I'd biff anyone who said you did!"

She danced around the room like Cassius Clay, who said he was a butterfly, and imagined stinging Daddy like a bee.

11

The last time Mags went to a funeral it was her father's and she felt as if she had gravel for a heart. Rudi thought the multicolour dress was reckless but she wore a short black jacket and her legs were silky black down to the dark red shoes. She gripped his hand through the service and tried to erase everything false so that only the reality of the body in the coffin remained. But how real was that, how true to the man she knew? Because sometimes when she made herself visit him in the home, she thought he'd turned to charcoal already, inside.

Today she wouldn't be playing the hostess with a whole tray of clichés and a jug of smiles to pour as required. Most of the mourners wouldn't know her from Adam, especially if she could rely on Cam to resist any urge to embrace her.

You'll have to make your own decision, Mum had been followed a second or two later by: *But I'd maybe keep a low profile. X*

Fine, cold rain soon made her dress cling as she walked across the churchyard. A hand to hold would have helped. She supposed she was the pariah here, her presence challenging the lies implied, even heard. And it was natural for Cameron to want to believe them.

Inside the church she saw him a few rows from the front, substantial in a creamy grey suit. Someone gave her a booklet with Jake grinning on the front, aged around sixteen and not so different from the *fella* she'd fallen for a few years

98

later. Sharon might have been a daughter, not a wife, her thick hair piled up high with stray curls trailing her long neck. Small beside her was Maureen, her hair a bright white and her suit immaculate but her reduced body low in the pew. Mags had expected to feel many things but not tenderness. As the two women squeezed hands she knew she shouldn't have come. She was from a different story with a bad ending and they needed a nice, regular fantasy.

The back row seemed the best place now she was here, and in anything but the middle aisle she'd be visible for being alone. Further along the pew a compact, dark-eyed woman around her age glanced in her direction with an anxious-eyed smile, which made it hard to leave the gap between them that Mags had intended. Smiling back, she drew nearer but used her handbag as a divide. The service was due to start soon and she'd have to endure it for Cameron's sake. She reminded herself that when Bertha's brother intervened in Jane Eyre with a truth no one wanted to hear, it made a villain of him.

Mags had a feeling the woman on the other side of her bag was looking at her. As the music turned Hollywood she shifted closer and leaned across it. The woman's perfume was of roses but the spicy kind, a hint of ginger. Her make-up must have taken some applying.

"You're Mags, I think? I've seen your photo."

"Yes! I'm sorry …?"

"I'm Liz. Jake's first wife – except that was really you." She held out a small hand, surprisingly mottled. "I didn't think you'd be here. I wasn't planning to come myself but Maureen kept in touch. I'm here for her. That's what I tell myself anyway. And you're here for your son." Her eyes identified Cameron.

Now the coffin was carried past; the two women rose together. With a sudden disjunction the organ was obliterated by a chord sequence Mags recognised. Instantly the volume of guitar and drums was lowered. She looked at Liz, who knew it too. The voice around them was Jake's, and the song one she told him, just days before she left, was slush. *I love you really, please believe me, it's hard to let it show. I'm not worthy of your loving but I know you can help me grow.*

Liz slung her bag onto her shoulder and with a shocked glance at Mags, began to walk out towards the rain. Slowly, on her toes so that her little heels wouldn't betray her to those at the front, Mags followed. Once outside, Liz lit a cigarette, her hand shaking. Already they were both wet and Mags had no umbrella.

"Nearest pub?" she asked. Liz nodded, and began to walk rather precariously down an uneven path towards the road. Mags remembered Cameron. "I'm sorry," she called after her. "I can't ... my son."

Liz turned and nodded. She exhaled smoke away from Mags but the wind blew it back. She pointed to the lych gate with seats on both sides. The old, worn wood was dark and a little damp but they both sat, facing each other. For a moment Mags just watched her smoke hungrily.

"Jake hit you," she guessed.

Liz inhaled deeply and blew out slowly, her head turned from Mags. "I was pregnant. He knocked me to the floor. I miscarried a week later but as Maureen pointed out, the two don't have to be connected. He said he wrote that song for me but he didn't, did he?"

Mags shook her head. "I'm so sorry." It was too far to reach across and place an arm.

"You get to an age when the past seems bigger than the future ..."

"Oh yes."

"And the difference is, you think the past is kind of ... in the bank. Then the best bit gets trashed." Liz stubbed out her cigarette. "Maureen said it was a one-off and I stayed. Then when I was pregnant again I found out about you. Saw your picture in a drawer. I said he'd better tell me or I'd walk. He had me up against the wall with his hand round my neck."

Her voice was so flat and cold she might have been talking about a check-up at the dentist, but her eyes had a sore kind of wildness as they looked back to Mags.

Mags shook her head and mumbled, "I'm so sorry." She could have drawn the storyboard.

"Then he cried and said he'd never forgive himself because he never meant to hurt you and now he never saw his son and it broke his heart. I told Maureen I wanted a divorce, not him. She was really generous. It must be horrible to have a son like that."

"You had a child together?"

"Another miscarriage. I married again years later, someone a lot older. No children." She took another cigarette from the pack but didn't light it. "Sometimes I heard the song in my head and believed that Jake did love me when he wrote it and it was just a tragic romance, you know? One we could have saved if he gave up the booze. I was mad about him, you see. The time I was with him was the only time in my whole life I ever felt … you know, almost …beautiful."

Mags watched in silence as she lit the cigarette, struggling to protect it against the wind. The song must be over inside; she could hear no rhythm. But who wanted it, allowed it? Maybe Maureen hoped everyone would take it as their own personal apology.

"Love of my life, the bastard," Liz said, with something close to a laugh. "You?"

"First love anyway, and that's always hard to shake off."

"You're married to that artist. He's on Wikipedia."

"Mm, but the Personal Life section will have to be updated before long."

"Yeah? That's a shame. But you have your son. You should go back to him. I'm going home now anyway. It was nice to meet you, Mags. Good luck."

"You too, Liz."

Liz turned a few paces on to add, "Say hi to Maureen for me and tell her I'm doing fine and would love to see her any time. She's frail, isn't she? You don't know the widow?"

"Only that Cam likes her."

Liz nodded. "Take care then."

"And you." Mags had read that when humans hugged a friend there was a rush of oxytocin. She would have like to receive that as well as generate it, but Liz was about to cross the road. Mags turned back towards the church, a mist of rain suppressing her hair but frizzing it too around the Japanese comb Genevieve had bought her.

Banks could crash these days, but wherever people stored it the past was never safe. Rewrites could happen any time. It was possible that the whole of Jake's final marriage was a whole different genre rather than a sequel. But not plausible.

She didn't want to re-enter during the prayers. A sudden thought broke in. Her first love was Georgie long before she heard of French kissing, wore suspenders or sanitary towels. Not Jake at all. Her smile was big before it fractured.

She waited for the sound of the organ lurching into life before she pushed the doors open. The hymn was *Abide with Me*, which would probably have made Jake cry because Arsenal lost to Ipswich in '78, when she was pregnant. Through the verses she watched heads: not just Cameron's, tilted slightly upward as he sang, but Maureen's, wobbling as she leaned a little towards Sharon, who held hers perfectly still. Mags thought this widow would probably be stylish in a dressing gown. Her arms hung down as if ignoring the words on the service sheet. Then suddenly her shoulders lifted shakily and behind her Cameron placed a hand on one of them. She turned a little and nodded a kind of thanks with no smile.

Cameron, who didn't touch! Mags breathed deeply. It made her feel not excluded exactly but clueless, out of it, a kind of fool – just like poor Liz.

The hymn turned out to be the last. The coffin disappeared and from the delicate frame of the grieving mother came a gasping moan that broke into staccato notes. Mags thought she could hear muffled cries from Sharon too as she linked arms to support her. *It's All Over Now Baby Blue* jumped in on the organ and the congregation of not more than thirty-five or forty slowly took their seats. Mags wondered how soon she could leave without seeming disrespectful and cold hearted, but she didn't want the family in front to turn and find her, walk past her like the bride and groom at the end of the wedding, and not know what face to show her. Just as she wouldn't know what face to show them.

As the second verse began she rose and edged out. She could wait, fairly well hidden in the lych gate, until Cameron emerged. This kind of thing was harder alone. *"Come with me, Rudi? One last double act?"* she could have asked and he would have nodded and said, *"Sure. Of course,"* although he might have added, *"I won't be mourning."*

When she'd told him, in bed, just a few days after they met, the narrative had had a profound effect on chilled, slow-talking Rudi, who'd tightened and sworn, then cradled her and kissed the top of her head. Even though she had edited out the pool scene, inside she'd reclaimed an old status, not sexy and funny and free but damaged all over again. "Now forget," she'd said. "Please."

Today Mags tried not to keep looking around to check who was stepping out of the church. Realising the rain had stopped, she felt sudden sun break in.

"Mags," she heard. "I hoped you'd come." Maureen's style hadn't changed anything like as much as her skin, frame and posture. Her coat was almost indigo and made her white hair look blue-edged. She was too frail for a hug.

"I didn't know what to do for the best, Maureen," she said, accepting the cool, light hands offered and clasping them briefly. Her handshake used to seem brisk and formal; she remembered her own mother saying so.

Maureen smiled. "You haven't changed. And look at Cameron. Can you use the word bonny at his age?"

"Let's," said Mags. "It fits."

"He's been a great comfort to Sharon."

"Ah ... good."

"Jake calmed down, you know. I knew he would. He settled with Sharon. He wasn't a well man for a long time but we didn't expect to lose him like this."

Mags waited for more to follow or the right response.

"You didn't see the best of him," Maureen told her.

"No."

"But I hope you don't bear any grudges."

Mags would have welcomed an interruption. She looked towards the church, and there was Cameron – heading their way with Sharon and holding an umbrella over her.

"I'd be glad to shrug those off," she said, quietly, and wasn't sure Maureen had heard.

For a moment she made eye contact with Sharon, who said something to Cameron. He closed the umbrella as she walked across the churchyard towards a group of people her age who might be their dinner party friends. That was hard to imagine but so was a Jake calmed down and settled.

"Mum," said Cameron, holding the umbrella out like a sword so as not to wet her. He leaned over, though, and kissed her cheek. And the other one! She wasn't sure she'd managed the choreography of that; her second was a miss. With his grandma, in spite of the stoop, the score for artistic merit would have been higher.

"Are you all right, love?" she asked him, as if he could answer such a question or ever would.

"I'm fine. I've learned a lot. About Dad, I mean."

From the address by a vicar who had never seen Jake in his life? She'd missed it, which was most likely fortunate for her and essential for Liz.

"Oh," she said. As if even a word like that could be neutral.

"There's always more to people than meets the eye, I find," said Maureen. She looked up at Cameron. "I've been getting to know my grandson much better too. He's such a lovely lad, Mags. You must be very proud."

Mags smiled. Maureen said she'd leave the two of them together and went to join Sharon. Cameron's eyes followed them before returning to her.

"You had the worst of him, Mum. That song he wrote for Sharon – it was about him wanting to be a better man."

"Is that right?"

Cameron pulled the service booklet out from his inside pocket. He grinned at the photo on the front and for the first time she saw a flicker of a match. "I don't know what to say to you, Mum, but I'm sorry. Gran says he was sorry too."

"All right," said Mags, nodding slowly. "Thanks, love. But I don't know what to say either."

He asked whether she was going to the reception at the pub and she said she thought she might head for the station. "You'll stay?"

"At Sharon's. It would be too hard for her to be alone. Did you know Dad built an annexe for Gran?"

"That's nice. You'll have to talk to me, Cam. Please? Will you come home tomorrow? To the house, I mean, Rudi's."

He said he thought he might stay another night or two. Mags asked him to text when he was on the way back and she'd get the right food in – presumably the sort of thing that would make Genevieve rage or cry.

"I will," he said, and hesitated a moment before embracing her, for rather less time than she would have liked it to hold.

12

That evening Mags came upon an item about Rudi on Channel Four News – or rather, about a retrospective exhibition that had been in the offing for months and stalled, but was now scheduled to open at Tate Britain early in the new year.

"Oh, Rudi baby, you're Establishment now!" she cried as his face appeared, relaxed and well-groomed in that edgy and alternative way of his. If she'd never seen him before she'd be finding him attractive right now, and part of her – the detached, reactive part that didn't consider or reflect – still did. But she didn't really want to hear him talk about his "creative energy" and how he would be looking forward, in spite of this retrospective, to "new artistic challenges."

She should find a flat. He was all around her here, and she'd had enough retrospectives of her own for one day. Switching off the TV, she searched Facebook instead. No posts from Cameron. Genevieve had shared films about animal welfare and cries for social justice, most of which Mags 'Liked'. Gen seemed to be a fan of a little Swedish girl called Greta, and showed a sudden concern about the climate. Mags feared she wasn't keeping up. Then she saw for the first time, on Simon's wall, the girl he loved. Their heads were joined in hoodies and the girl had one of those nose rings that made Mags think of bulls, along with a collection of studs in her ears. She was wondering whether it was legitimate to search for her and scroll down her wall when Kara sent a text: *Only got an A for that essay. Don't know how that happened. Must stress less. X*

Fab job. You underestimate yourself – stop!

I will when you will. Hugs. X

She was just going to exit when a new Facebook message appeared, from Georgie.

Mags, I thought I'd warn you that a letter is on its way, on writing paper like people used in the old days! It felt like a kind of therapy to write it but I hope it won't lower your spirits. I like to think life hasn't suppressed those. Handwriting seems to bring out the Jane Austen in me but I promise I can talk in 21st century sentences. What have you done today?

Mags grinned.

Hello Georgie. I'll have to save the answer to your question for a letter but it might be a very long and not exactly spirited one. Jane Austen eh? So ... I shall look forward with eager anticipation to receiving yours in due course, and in the meantime thank you kindly for your trouble which is greatly appreciated... I can't keep this up myself! I'd have liked to fit the word bestow in there just because I like it! What about you? Did you go anywhere?

She waited.

Only back in time!

Wish I could! she replied, but no more followed. He'd written! She switched off her laptop and decided to excavate her collection of albums in ragged covers. Going back in time had its attractions, she thought, fingering through them – but to which era? *Space Ritual* by Hawkwind from '72 was probably safest. At that point she was a stroppy but not very wayward fifteen-year-old whose Janis Joplin style was misleading because she'd never smoked a cigarette or drunk anything stronger than shandy. Next to it was *Tea for the Tillerman* from two years earlier, when she was in the Lower Fourth and in love with Cat Stevens. "Needs a good haircut!" said Daddy. "He looks like a girl." Which had prompted a passionate declaration: "I think he's absolutely beautiful. And you're just jealous." Finding Cyndi Lauper's *She's so Unusual,* she remembered that Jake had bought it for her as an apology because she used to sing the chorus to *Girls just wanna have fun* as she bopped around the house. 1983, the sleeve said: the year she left him.

She'd almost forgotten *Broken Arrow* by Neil Young and Crazy Horse, and shouldn't possess it by rights since it was Dan's. Smiling at Dan's conviction that he had Lakota Sioux blood, she realised she was fond of him now and wasn't sure how or when that had happened.

The number on the phone bill might as well be in bold, underlined or starred. It was like a chorus in a song, *Hey Jude* on repeat. And she hadn't called it, not for weeks. Dan was lazy about phoning. He was the one who let her call his mother because she was 'so much better at chat', and never rang anyone to fix or arrange anything without six reminders.

The number spoke for itself. And the times of the calls corresponded with her shifts at the supermarket. There was one afternoon when he'd called it ten minutes after the previous conversation ended.

"Want to explain this?" she challenged.

"What's that?" he asked, relaxed as ever, unsuspecting.

"The phone bill," she said. "I couldn't think why it's so high."

He'd been high himself the night before; he didn't seem to appreciate her point that Genevieve was impressionable and far from stupid. But he was funny that way, and extra-warm, eager to nestle up against her afterwards and ask her to stroke the back of his neck.

He didn't connect at first. He was lying on the sofa with his notebook, his knees up. "Yeah?" he said, unfazed.

Genevieve was at school and Mags was due to start work in the next hour. She moved into the hall where the phone sat on a unit with the directories stacked on a shelf underneath it. As she dialled the number on the bill her fingers didn't shake. She was strangely calm; it unsettled her.

"Dan darling," said a voice she knew, even though she generally heard it outside, on the street. At book club, or over coffee. Not down the wire. "I was willing you to call. Come round right now if you're home alone."

"Hi Anne-Marie," she said. "You used to be my friend but I see I haven't been keeping up."

There was a pause. Mags felt Dan's presence in the lounge doorway behind her. Maybe she'd heard his big, clumsy slippers in the shape of gorilla heads, or smelt the marijuana in his hair.

"Hubby dear," she called, sing-song, "it's your mistress."

"That's very dated," said Anne-Marie, suddenly sounding as if she studied Classics at Oxford. "I prefer lover."

"Mags," Dan said. "What are you doing?"

"Getting to know Anne-Marie a bit better than I thought I already did," she told him. "But take over, go on. No need to wait until I've left for work."

She pulled the receiver as far as the twisty cable would stretch but Dan didn't move. He looked as if he'd just had a submission rejected.

She heard Anne-Marie: "Mags, please ... Dan said you're just friends these days. Fond friends."

She let the receiver fall; it swung against the wall and off again. Dan moved towards her now. "Not this time," she said.

"Mags, listen, love." But he reached for the phone.

"Love? Too many punctures. It's starting to leak away. You talk to Anne-Marie. She's dangling."

Her voice was even. There was no element of surprise. She'd told herself the others were all diversions, temporary and

108

meaningless; she was his muse and soulmate. Walking away, she took her time to sway, as if she was perfectly loose. Then she closed the lounge door behind her.

The shaking began in her legs and arms and for a moment she gave in and let herself be jolted, her jaw slack and wobbling. Then she clenched, and stopped. She sat on the sofa and turned on the TV, volume raised.

The door, which had been stiff for years, juddered open. He had the there-there look of an adult hoping to reason with a child.

"Mags, you know we connect. We mesh."

"I should go to work." She'd forgotten. "But why don't you move in with Anne-Marie? You can just carry a few bags over the road and save a lot on phone bills."

Dan's chest lifted. She could see he was tired of this already. "Don't make me choose …"

"Because you want both: the poetry and the wages, the family and the cannabis, the wife and the affairs. None of it meshes! And I choose divorce."

Motionless, he stared back at her as if he couldn't comprehend a word she said.

"It's not *Ulysses*, Dan, or *The Waste Land*. Nothing complex or original about this. I'm going to work. Don't forget to collect Genevieve after Drama. And tidy the place. Open the windows."

Turning away to grab her jacket and bag, she heard a sound she didn't recognise. He was crying. Looking back, she saw his hands cover his face and his shoulders shake. She had to remind herself that helplessness was not always appealing.

"What can I do?" he murmured. "Anne-Marie's pregnant and I don't want to let anyone down."

Mags liked to imagine that news bouncing off her as if she was the Michelin man. "No, I know you don't," she told him. Anne-Marie had sworn she'd never do marriage or children. "Stand by her. Go on. But stand by Genevieve too. Don't make me chase you for money. But more than that, don't deny her your time because you've got new demands on it. She loves you fiercely. Unconditionally."

109

He nodded. "But you don't?"

She didn't answer. Sometimes words lacked precision and she needed clarity. No doubts. She opened the door and stepped outside into a turbulent wind that made a blindfold of her hair.

"I'll always love you, Mags," he called as she walked away.

Mags sang along with Curved Air under her breath and remembered when she wished she could look and sound like Sonja Christina. Who looked, in fact, a little like Anne-Marie – who rented a place five miles away and only lived there with Dan until the baby was two. Anne-Marie, who would be earning more as an editor in a big publishing house than Dan could from royalties of the collection they published, under the title *Rose-coloured Rain*. Anne-Marie married a fat crime novelist in the States and would probably be posting Mags another Christmas card any time now. It wouldn't surprise her if Dan got one too, time being such a famous healer.

Had she forgiven Anne-Marie? Up to point, and beyond the limits of Genevieve's forgiveness. But Gen had decided to love her little step-brother, until she saw him posing with a toy gun and miniature combat uniform. She still sent him something educational for Christmas and birthdays, often solar-powered.

Mags suspected that she was the only one of Dan's lovers who still enjoyed his company, but that might be considered a weakness ...

She was thinking how to begin a letter to Georgie – and bring it to a stop – when she found a text from Cameron: *Glad you came to the church. I will stay on here a couple more days. X*

She replied that he must be a comfort to his granny and Sharon. Then she noticed a voicemail from Kara and listened to it, trying to mentally exclude the backing track of some kind of pub or club.

"Mum," Kara projected, "have you got company? I know where you've been. Saw a photo Cameron posted on Face-

110

book and you're in the background looking shit. You really don't have to put yourself through it."

Mags deleted it, frowning at the idea that Cameron was even on Facebook when he kept his whole world private from his own mother, and that Kara was an online Friend of his when she described him as *boring as hell* on the basis of very little actual rather than virtual evidence. Still, it was kind of her. And Mags decided she did have company in a way – not just the messages in various forms but the music and everything it stood for. The scenes that stayed with her.

The doorbell rang, with a battering of knocks to follow. Abida's rhythm. The clock showed after nine and the door opened on Abida, wrapped in her red velour dressing gown and holding a bottle and a warm plastic tub which she handed to Mags. Even through the lid Mags could smell the pakoras. Abida stepped inside and out of her trainers, explaining:

"Kara called me. You went to your ex's funeral, the one who beat you?"

"Well, that's a tabloid headline version, Abida, and I'm unbeaten. Just a bit whisked."

"You shouldn't be alone. We can dance the darkness away and if that doesn't work we can pop the cork."

Abida's dancing began with her fingers and spread. Mags smiled and nodded. "Thank you, sweet thing."

But she didn't dance. What would happen, she wondered, if she chose to be alone with the past from now on? Wondering whether the twenty-first century allowed anyone to escape surveillance, she thought she might as well be an MI5 target. Abida stopped, her arms falling gracefully. She tilted her head, disappointed.

So Mags did her best moves to some rap in her head, which had Abida holding her stomach, her giggle soprano.

"Would be way better with a hoodie on," Mags said, finishing with a fling of her fingers that probably went out of date with Ali G. She unscrewed the top of the bottle and Abida fetched glasses from the minimalist glass cabinet Rudi had chosen. Mags put Crosby, Stills, Nash and Young on the

111

turntable. They sat on the sofa and seeing that Mags would rather not talk about the funeral, Abida offered better memories instead, of Kara and Simon at their most endearing.

"If I asked what they wanted to eat when they came to tea, they'd reply in perfect unison: 'Pakoras please, Abida' or 'Can we help you make dahl?' Like monks at prayer!"

"It was an act, you know. Or at least, they exaggerated it for effect, like a party piece." Mags helped herself to a pakora.

"Tch, don't spoil it, Mags. You can't make a cynic of me! Sweet children they were. One soul divided but connected."

"If you say so," allowed Mags. It seemed pretty clear that a bond like theirs would endure longer than their love affairs and quite possibly their future marriages. Abida reminded her of the time she had measured the twins for outfits to wear at her nephew's wedding. Kara had loved her salwar kameez and insisted on wearing it to sleepovers until she outgrew it.

"I'm glad I raised them in London," said Mags, "not some all-white, gossipy Fifties place."

"Like the one you grew up in?"

Mags nodded. She admitted that Rudi had done a little raising himself, as a kind of hobby. "That was unfair. He was the only decent father I managed to find my children." Then she asked Abida to tell her some of her childhood stories because she didn't want to talk about any of those fathers, living or dead or her own.

"No!" cried Abida, eyes bright. "Tell me about you. The most interesting Englishwoman I know and you keep too much schtum!"

"Come on, Abida, you can always ask my children!"

Mags sat up meerkat-straight. There was someone in the hall. She put her hand to her mouth; Abida heard it too. Their eyes widened as they messaged each other.

"Mags?" It was Rudi's voice. The living room door opened wider. "I rang the doorbell and knocked a few times. Then I used my key."

Mags frowned. "It's hardly Steppenwolf, and we're not that deaf in our old age."

"I did try."

"Maybe not hard enough?" suggested Abida as Mags lifted the needle from the vinyl.

"I came because Kara called me. You went to Jake's funeral. She wanted me – I wanted – to make sure you're all right."

Mags felt a laugh overwhelm her but it had more breath than sound. "Help yourself to some wine, Rudi," she told him. He hesitated before crossing the room. "You know where the glasses are. You can help yourself to that unit anytime you like, too. It's too pretentious for moi."

"Shall I go, Mags?" muttered Abida.

"No need," said Mags, but Rudi's expression sent a different reply.

"You're a good neighbour, Abida."

"You're a friend," Mags corrected him and embracing her, "and a diamond."

Abida kissed her on both cheeks and told Rudi, "Be your best self, please, the one I like a great deal."

Abida didn't resist when he leaned to kiss her too. Mags sat down and held out the tub of pakoras but Rudi shook his head.

"Happy ending please!" Abida called, and shut the front door. Mags shouted, "Bye! Thanks, pal."

Rudi was looking at her, waiting.

"Was it horrible?" he asked, sitting opposite her but with his body almost off the edge of the sofa. "Did it stir everything up?"

She nodded, determined not to cry just because the question came from him.

"Bastard," muttered Rudi. "You didn't owe him any kind of respect."

"I went for Cam, and Maureen and Sharon."

"You've never met Sharon!"

"Well I have now, and if she saved him she's a better woman than me."

"I doubt that." He drank a little. "If you ever need … I could have gone with you. I would have liked to support you. You know I'll always care for you. I really want to be your friend."

Mags chewed the pakora; it was lukewarm now. The fingers on the stem of the glass were greasy. "I expect you do. But there's a fact of life you're missing. It's easier for the person who ended a marriage to reach out the platonic hand of friendship than it is for the person who got severed to take it. Especially, in a hypothetical sense, if she still loves him more than is good for her. So it's kinder, in fact, to keep that hand in a pocket. And skip the mercy missions. I'm fine. I'm adjusting; it's a full-time job the way things are going. So much as I appreciate your concern, I feel stronger without it. Thank you."

"Mags ..." The gentleness was thick as pity. She hoped he wasn't going to repeat that he never meant to hurt her.

He stood. "All right. If that's how you feel. You do know I love you too? Just ..."

"You can leave it there."

"But I don't want to leave."

"I think you already did, Rudi. I'd rather you didn't mess with me if it's all the same to you."

His face showed as-if. He reached out to hug her and somehow she let herself be held. Everything about him was so achingly, deeply known: the contours, textures and smells. The warmth of him – as if it was August out there and not November. The fit that made her think of tessellation. As she gave herself up to the hug like a child who'd been afraid, his hand stroked her hair – always a challenge with the tangles that could trap him – but there was no snagging, just a wild kind of peace that was a wish and a dread.

Lifting her chin he kissed her forehead, her lips.

"Stop," she said.

"I'm sorry, Mags. I miss you. I wish I'd been there for you today."

"I'm a big girl, Rudi," she told him, and tried to separate herself, but still he held her gently by the arms. She could see he was a big boy in his own way now, but that wasn't possible, desirable, sensible.

"Let me be your husband," he murmured, and pulled her closer for a different kind of kiss. As his tongue grew urgent in her mouth, her own quickened to life. He was pressed against her now but his hands were soft and slow as they caressed her. Mags wanted to live right here, in this moment, for the rest of time – and to escape it, reject it, draw a line that couldn't be crossed. She withdrew her mouth.

"Your lover," he said, kissing her cheek once, twice, again.

"I can't."

"You love me." He kissed her again, like they hadn't kissed for months, years.

"That's not the issue here."

"I'm wooing you. You needed more romance, more passion, intimacy. I need it too." His kiss was long, beautiful. She welcomed the wildness back. Her hands explored his chest; he threw his leather jacket onto the sofa. Then he smiled and cupped her breasts as another kiss began, until she led him up the stairs.

13

It was almost three a.m. and Rudi slept beside her, one leg against hers. It was a while since he'd been so eager, but as she watched his passive face, cleared like a screen of age and all other data, she wished it was happiness she recognised. Or the kind of satisfaction that begins with the body and frees something like the soul. Instead she felt a heavy sense of doubt and loss. Another funeral, she thought, resisting the impulse to take his hand.

She could tell him she understood what it meant and that was less than commitment. She could open the door for him and wish him well – adding that any time he felt randy or lonely she could still be his wife for the foreseeable future. She could say that a lover with kind hands was a gift and she was grateful for it, and she could repeat what he took for granted: that she loved him.

"Whatever love is," Prince Charles had said, unforgivably, with Diana luminous and quivery beside him. It had prompted Mags to leap to her feet with "What!" followed by "Run like the wind, girl!" but now ... experience complicated things. That was 1980, when she still lived for Jake. Now she had children to love, unreservedly – even in moments when she wasn't sure she liked them much. But that was such a different feeling. She remembered drawing an amoeba in Biology, detaching a new being from itself – more like a photocopy than an embryo – and supposed that mothers were guilty of self-love as well as greedy possession. Except that her four were such renegades, all as unlike her as they could manage to be.

Mags closed her eyes, continuing to picture Rudi's face. He was meant to end this. "It was supposed to be a reawakening," she murmured, knowing how deeply he slept, "but grown-up at last. A mature passion that could outlast sex if it had to." But the sex had proved for her what he'd known and she'd resisted – that it couldn't. And she wouldn't know how to explain because it was a body and spirit thing, not a rationale.

If she knew, Genevieve would be angry with them both but save the most serious charges for her. Submission was in Gen's book the cardinal sin. It was feistiness she aspired to, and applauded in Mags. But what if sex was the limit, the way men liked it to be? Perhaps that was all he wanted, as well as all she was prepared to give. *Hello, wildness, my old friend. You came to mess with me again.*

Mags touched his shoulder. So boyish and slight, it made her feel thuggish as she shook it just enough ...

"Rudi," she said, and he stretched from the chest up, his eyes opening to a reluctant squint. He made a kind of protest noise and rolled away, his back to her. "Rudi," she repeated, her whisper thicker now. She could have kissed his neck and spooned her body around him, but instead she raised her volume: "Talk to me."

Slowly he turned to face her, looking past her to the alarm clock. "Mags? It's the middle of the night."

"I need to know where the hiatus is."

He breathed deeply. She hoped he wasn't thinking hernias – hers, the diagnosis of which had made her feel much too old.

"Hiatus," he said, his eyes closing. "You've mislaid it?"

"Was it in the marriage you left – on hold, to be started up again? Or in the separation, temporarily, when you walked in?" He frowned. "Do you see the marriage continuing after the hiatus, or the divorce?"

"I never said I wanted a divorce, you know that."

"But you didn't want me."

"I missed you like hell." He reached out a hand to stroke her hair. "My work's been crap."

"That's a doggone shame," she said, best Southern twang. "But I asked you what – as far as you're concerned – the coitus interrupted ..."

"Sweetheart ..." Rudi kissed her forehead. "Let's talk over breakfast."

"If you don't want to tell me," Mags continued, "I can explain how I see it." He opened his mouth but she didn't wait. "I didn't want to lose you but I did and now I'm busy finding something else. So if you were thinking of resuming married life, I don't think I can, because the search tab isn't closed yet."

She was astonished at these words she hadn't known were thoughts, but at the same time pleased to hear them sound so plausible. Rudi seemed wide-awake now. He sighed and she tasted his breath as it blew over her face. She had a theory that end-of-the-night halitosis was uniquely individual.

"I thought you'd be happy," he murmured, deflated. A birthday boy with no presents.

"I did too. I thought I was ..."

"So did the rest of the street!"

"Rudi, I felt loved; everyone wants that. But I didn't know what else I wanted – what I didn't want – until you offered it."

He held out both hands and lifted his shoulders in the look that meant she was impossible to understand.

"So instead of a husband you'd rather have a fuck buddy? Is weekly enough? Oh, I remember now, that's plenty, overkill."

"You're putting words in my mouth, Rudi. Teenage words."

"Because I can't make sense of yours."

She thought he was rolling over again until he was out of bed and reaching for his clothes. In the dark, his skin looked soft as he stood, shuffled and stumbled. Mags wondered if he had any idea how lovingly she watched. If she sat up, leaned and reached she could touch his arm, pull him back into bed.

"I can't give you sense!" she said, like a joke. "It got pulled up like weeds and thrown in the air and when it landed it looked different. And started to wilt."

He shook his head at that and she couldn't blame him. Then she heard his TV interview voice, with a dismissive edge for a fatuous question.

"That's perception, Mags, not reality."

"Says the artist."

Dressed now, he ran a hand through his hair. "Let me know if you see things differently in daylight."

"You don't have to go right now, Rudi. It's cold out there. We can cuddle." She remembered a picture of baby otters sleeping but holding paws.

"Thanks. I'll take my chances."

A swell of guilt and tenderness. Now he was leaving again; he was through the door and onto the landing. In a few moments she would hear the door close hard the way he always banged it.

She could have kept her big mouth shut and waited for thoughts to take a different shape.

When the letter arrived next morning it woke her out of her doze. Seven forty-eight and she'd slept for the last three hours – in spite of an apparent lack of organs, and the regret that had almost worded an apology to hurl at him on the stairs.

Dear Mags,

When we meet we will talk about the distant past we shared but maybe I should fill in the rest – or some of it. I came to you after a couple of other foster homes where I didn't settle, but before that I was an abandoned toddler, not outside a hospital but a school. I remember wandering around huge gates that looked like prison and the police coming for me so I thought I'd be locked up with bread and water.

Research has shown that my mother had an affair with an Italian POW in Wales. You may have seen the extraordinary chapel they built from newspaper and bully beef cans near a village called Penwrhwllan. I can't pronounce it either. Now I know that my mother left me in the care of her Welsh aunt – not because she was a girl but because she was forty-five and married. That's less romantic, don't you think? I'm guessing my father, who was younger but no boy, had a wife and children in Italy too. The aunt – my great-aunt – died when I was barely four. I think I remember the smell of her washing and the face powder she wore on Sundays.

That's probably enough to be going on with. We'll both be obliged to leave gaps. It may help you to understand why the boy who landed with you was so odd. Damaged, I could say. I don't suppose you've forgotten my preference for your dresses. You hated them yourself but I wonder whether that's changed? My habits haven't. It's a big subject but let's say that I was planning to meet you in a long skirt, pretty blouse and cardigan.

I am a man, but not, perhaps exclusively. Or perhaps I'm a man who would have been happier in the time of George Villiers, Duke of Buckingham – have you seen the portrait? I wonder why we have to subscribe to one gender or the other when many of us are a mix of both. Today's young people see that, of course, and I'm glad for those who don't have to struggle to fit the right label. Your father wasn't the only man who feared and loathed what I am.

I was married to Julia for three years in my late twenties until she fell in love 'properly'. We keep in friendly touch. We had no children together, but one of hers, Troy, is a kind of godson. He's gay and a gentle, buoyant soul. Since Julia I've been mostly alone. I have a few friends who are patient and loyal but my moods make me hard work when they reduce me; I disconnect and wish the world away. In between I sometimes come close to peace and manage laughter! I want that to be the Georgie you find.

Thank you for your patience, now and then. I hope you have been doing more home decorating.

Georgie x

Mags turned back to the first page and read the letter again. The matter-of-factness of it, and the honesty, seemed both sad and heartening. She liked the rhythms of it, the word choices, even the rather unruly and uneven handwriting which she could see he'd tried to control. She liked a man, however male or un-male, who wrote the word *soul* and didn't cross it through.

She must shower Rudi away but this changed everything. Or rather, it confirmed it all. She had so many questions she must ask when they met, about the mature love affair – or casual fling – that made Georgie, and how he knew as much as he did. Had he traced his mother, or even his father? She wondered whether either of them would want to be found.

But Georgie did, and so did she.

While showering and having breakfast, Mags composed her reply to Georgie. Nothing had yet been recorded in anything more reliable than her memory, but she had a sense of honing, of editing her way to the truth. After clearing her plate and mug she woke her laptop and phone and was surprised to find messages on both from Cameron, up early and apparently not running or lifting weights. But presumably still with his grandmother? *Mum I need to talk to you. Can I call? Are you up?*

Dismissing a frisson of panic oddly mixed with joy, Mags could supply no obvious explanations. She began to reply that of course he could call when she changed tactic and rang him instead, only to be greeted by the answerphone that made him sound so bored.

There was a message from Kara, who should probably remain unaware of the consequences of her actions even though she asked, *Did Dad come round? I didn't want you to be alone after the funeral.* Mags replied that she was fine, really, and almost told her daughter about the encounter with Liz, who wasn't. But she could keep that story on standby for when she needed a distraction even more badly.

The ringtone on her phone was sudden. Cameron. He really did want to speak to her.

"Darling, are you all right?"

There was a pause. She wondered where he was calling from but there were no clues.

"Well ..." he said. "What about you? Was it tough? It must have been. I hope I didn't ... that you didn't go for me."

"I suppose I was curious too." Mags cut herself off. "What's wrong, Cam?"

"I'm in love." He made a little noise like a laugh that meant it wasn't funny.

"Really? Like in *Four Weddings and A Funeral*? You met someone across the coffin?" That sounded horribly flippant and she began to admit it, but her apology was cut short.

"No. I've been in love with her for ... I can't say. It snuck up on me. She doesn't know and I can't tell her."

Mags had never heard this sound in his voice. If she'd named it, helplessness would have been the closest she came.

"You mean she's married to a friend of yours?" She remembered seeing a photo of him at a wedding – a second marriage for someone he used to work with – and being dismayed by the glitzy excess of the whole thing, including the bride.

Another pause. "No. Look, Mum, you're the only person who might not tell me I'm crazy and it's hopeless. But don't tell anyone – Rudi, Gen, the twins."

"All right." She waited. "I promise," she added, moving to the sink and running water into her stained mug just to keep normality running.

"It's Sharon."

For a few seconds Mags expected a surname or more details. Then in his silence she understood. "As in Sharon the widow? Your ..." She left off the stepmother tag that had presented itself. "Oh Cam."

"I can't even ask her about my father – whether she loved him, you know? Whether he was a shit to the end." His voice had flattened but after a pause it lifted again. "She's a private person. All she does is lay on food and make sure I've got everything I need but I don't want anything but her. I've never felt like this. I don't do what you'd call romance – you know, roses and all that. I'm out of my depth and she's just nice, you know? Concerned for me – you too! If she'd just let go and weep I'd get some idea ..." He sighed. "Talk to me, Mum. You've been through this stuff ..."

"And back again." She sat down at the kitchen table and hoped he wouldn't hear her breathe in deeply for some kind of help. "Most people would say wait, give her time and space. I'm not really one for patient self-control myself." But he always had been. It was unnerving to find herself shocked by her own son. "I'd need to know how she feels, so I'd ask her and I'd listen. Tell her you want to know your father better, but her too."

"Yes." Another pause, presumably while he told himself he could. "I will."

"I love you," she said. "I'm glad you called."

"So am I," he said. "I'd better go," he added, lowering his voice.

Was he in Sharon's house, her spare room? Would she have any idea? Surely women always knew, even new widows who were apparently saints?

He had ended the call. Mags put down the phone and walked to the window. Rain struck and beaded the glass. Running down the slope of the road by the kerb, it made the morning grey and black as any old photograph. The fairy lights on the house opposite thought it was still night.

"Oh Cam," she said.

14

Dear Georgie,
Your letter moved me. Why is sadness so beautiful? I'm not
sure happiness can match it. Not that yours is a self-pitying
letter; I think it's brave. I'm tempted to say I'll come to Wales
with you and see the chapel but that's why my kids call me
pushy. We haven't even spoken yet, not in voices we'd recognise.
My life has lurched off kilter rather dramatically in the last
few weeks so I wouldn't know where to begin but the people I
thought I knew as well as loved keep peeling off layers I didn't
know existed, like in the John Donne onion poem. Feel free to
do the same by the way. I'm getting used to it.
Maybe I should go back to the beginning too but I don't
remember much until you arrived. You were the biggest deal
of my childhood – apart from the ongoing battle with my
father. I'm not sure whether I was trying to change him or
myself or just protest and resist. Either way it sometimes felt
like a full-time project. When Mum died I recovered a great
box of my childhood drawings, some pastels and a few watercolours. She'd dated them all on the back, bless her. But the
thing is, I know I drew pictures of you, and they're not there.
I think it broke her heart too when Daddy decided you had to
go. We should have joined forces and defied him. He'd probably have shrunk like spinach in a pan. I wish ...
I pushed him pretty hard as a teenager but if his gasket
hadn't already blown, it must have done an Apollo-Some-
thing impression when I shacked up with Jake. I don't think
I want to give you a character study of Cam's father right now
because he's just died and things that had been overlaid have
pinged their way back through the cracks to the light. To put
it in a thimbleful, he knocked me about as well as up. You
don't say why your marriage ended but I'm hoping it wasn't

acutely painful if you're still friends. That's what Rudi wants us to stay, and the truth is that when he says it, I despise myself for listening – not in spite of loving him but because.

But I've jumped around on the timeline now. To go back one husband, you can look up Dan Turner, the poet. I wasn't out of my mind with love like I was with Jake but I thought that was progress. He was kind and I think the plan was to nurture and grow him and his talent. That's pretty much my M.O. By the umpteenth affair he called meaningless, I'd stopped believing anything much. Genevieve adored him and hated me for ending it. She's high voltage but her breakdown as a young adult was so terribly silent. Rudi coped much better than I did, bless him. Now she's passionate again, about art as well as animal rights, and she might turn out to be more talented than the stepdad she's decided to cut loose.

You didn't mention work. I see you as a gardener. You had lovely hands; I remember the way your fingers taper. Most people do boring jobs that sound soulless and I'm no exception. My career has been in supermarkets. Over that time I've been on the receiving end of more quiet words from management – about my hair but supposedly outlandish earrings and scuffs on shoes – than your average Punk. But in recent years I've been Rudi's PA so now I've got days to fill and I want to get that right.

I lost faith in any potential I ever showed as an artist myself, but I'm starting to imagine again – that I could create something worth the time and effort, something Miss Tralee would approve. Did you ever have a great teacher who saw the best in you? I hope so.

You see what you're in for in person: me rambling on. Perhaps we should stick to favourite music and movies next time. I love Mary Cassatt with a strange fervour, by the way– do you know her paintings? And I'm still mourning Bowie because I didn't love him enough when he was alive which is inexcusable.

I want to meet very much but I am in emergency mode with Cam and to be honest also with myself, just for now. I hope you're not?

M x

When she reread the letter, Mags hoped she hadn't misjudged anything but especially the idea of a crisis for Georgie, whose life had been harder than hers and who apparently suffered from depression. She sealed it anyway, copying the address in her most decorative capitals, and found a stamp, First Class. She wasn't in the mood for editing herself. As she collected everything else she needed in order to brave the rain, and had to make do with the umbrella with the loose and deformed spoke because the good one was in hiding, she realised there were times she rarely remembered. "Ill," was the word she used, out loud at the time and in her head when something took her back there. "Genevieve is ill." But it didn't explain what happened to her wildest child.

Such a beautiful building, she thought, as the taxi from the tube station approached it with the driver tapping the steering wheel to a Westlife ballad Gen claimed made her vomit. The grass outside was perfectly tamed and the borders were like artworks. Yet the creamy white walls, and the surprisingly dramatic turrets, could have been transformed by a coat of black into Hammer Horror. It was a blend, she supposed, of peace and turmoil. Rudi was on his phone, but she was sure he saw everything. His aunt had been here once, he'd said, for mental health issues of some kind. And what kind were Genevieve's, exactly? Maybe they'd be told.

She would like Rudi's hand to hold but he was still talking so she paid the driver – clumsily, coins tumbling. No mother expected her child to stay here. He ended the call and caught her up, taking her hand. His always felt cooler than hers, and never seemed to redden or swell. They checked in. The security was quiet but tight.

"Could be a ballroom," he said, looking up to the ceiling minutes later. Mags wasn't sure the red panels were a good idea. Wouldn't leafy green be calming?

It was a long walk, and oddly quiet, but when they found Genevieve's room it seemed, from the corridor, almost virginal, the window opening onto a lawn and a cherry tree. It was

125

so neat and clean, with its softly billowing curtains tasteful enough for a church elder, that Mags almost cried. Then she smelt the tobacco and saw the butts outside.

"I wish Genevieve wouldn't smoke," Kara had said, perplexed and anxious because they'd been taught about the dangers at school. "It's cool though," Simon had said, casually, because of Radiohead, his big step-sister's new favourite. All she'd told the twins was that the illness was in Genevieve's mind rather than her body, nothing to be ashamed of and quite common. And she'd soon be well because she was in a place where she'd get the best care. They were old enough to see through her lies but too scared to say so.

Now here was Genevieve, long and thin on the bed in dungarees, her hair a dark wine-red, her eyelids closed and edged with Amy Winehouse eyeliner. And the word that burst out in Mags was *why*, when she knew there was no short answer. "It's not your fault," Rudi had told her. "Oh it is," she'd said. "Everything's always the mother's fault, except when it's the father's."

Genevieve was still but Mags felt sure she was awake. Her arms were stacked with woven and beaded wristbands but she knew she mustn't be seen to look, to check, to doubt. The doctors here were expert. They would save her.

"Hey, Gen," said Rudi, as if they were in a park and she'd been snoozing carelessly in the sun.

She opened her eyes and smiled. "Step-pa," she said. "Looking good."

Mags crossed to the bed and embraced her. She felt slack and slight.

"Mum," she said, "I'm bored as hell."

Mags produced some books, painstakingly chosen. Together they showed her the art materials.

"Thanks," she said, without managing to conceal the listlessness. "For when I'm ready."

"Has your dad been?" asked Mags, although she knew he had, because he'd sent a text, a brief one to say there was more colour in her cheeks, more life in her.

She nodded. "Sure. He's paying, Mum. I'm sure he can't afford it."

"Don't worry," said Rudi. "We'll sort it."

"Yeah, you're famous now!" She smiled briefly. Mags noticed an anarchist symbol drawn on the sole of her bare foot and remembered how ticklish she was as a child. It was always extreme, like everything else with Genevieve – as if she might giggle until she died.

Rudi was talking cheerfully; Genevieve seemed to be listening. Maybe Dan would have written a poem by now about the breathless girl who called because she'd cut deep this time, while the pills found their way through.

Genevieve asked about San Francisco, where they'd learned the news. Mags hadn't even wanted to go. It was all flim-flam and wasted carbon. All precious and excessive, especially the smiles. As Rudi answered, Genevieve reached for her tobacco pack and began to roll. Mags filled a pause with her own anecdote about discovering that quinoa didn't "rhyme with feather boa but boudoir" as Genevieve lit up and moved to the window before exhaling.

"Let's go in the garden," suggested Mags.

Genevieve shook her head.

"It's lovely out there," added Mags.

"No, all right?"

Mags heard the click of footsteps and a doctor knocked on the door before stepping onto the beige carpet. She was elegant in a Sixties way, her hair flicked and sprayed and her suit fitted around Monroe curves. Her shoes were slingbacks, pointed and narrow with kitten heels. Genevieve looked round and blew smoke towards her like a bad girl to a prefect in the toilets at lunchtime.

Doctor Willis asked her gently to be respectful. Genevieve threw her cigarette out of the window, and when she turned back, a tear began to blur her make-up and streak her cheek.

Now another one of her children was in love, equally misguidedly. Perhaps it was in the genes, but she hoped that Cam was as robust as he used to seem. She decided it was time to resume her habit, interrupted recently, of sending them all a morning message on waking, sometimes the same one. Simon rarely replied except with the occasional thumbs-up or *hehe* and any replies from Kara were delayed until lunchtime. In Genevieve's case, history suggested that no response meant she was busy, which was good, a relief – except when it meant she was low, or worse. And Cam tended to wait until the texts stacked up the way unpaid bills used to when Mags was his single mum, before attempting a form of clearance.

When Mags discovered group chats through Kara she suggested someone should set up a family one but Kara said, "We're not that kind of family, Mum." "Just because we're a bit of a patchwork of step people," Mags had answered, "doesn't mean we're not connected." But Kara had pointed out that they weren't. Especially Cam.

Mags sent him a non-standard message, wording it carefully in case someone else saw it – specifically Sharon, who might presumably be serving his breakfast. Or even Maureen, with her specs on.

Mum you're awake. I'm going to take your advice today. X

Oh jeepers, Cam. It has to be what you think is best. Breathe and decide. Xxx

Breathing I can manage but I'm not sleeping so I'm in no shape to reason anything and besides this is love which seems to be insanity. X

Ah yes. I'm here. Love you. Xxxxx

Mags had a memory of him being less than sympathetic when Genevieve was infatuated with Dr Willis – or anyone, male or female, before that. Maybe Michael Ball had a point about love changing everything.

She had a letter to post. How annoying that it wouldn't go until five o'clock. It was tempting to catch a bus or tube to deliver it herself but that would be a breach of the rules and might alarm him. A glance at the calendar reminded her of a commitment that would change her perspective.

At the food bank she was put on sorting duty because the van had just collected from the nearest supermarkets, including her old workplace. Mags felt ashamed of the customers when the big, deep box was almost empty, and often meant to add something nice on her way out – but usually forgot. She'd been told on her training day which items were *high need* and which were currently or always surplus. Now it was just a question of shelving everything in the right large plastic drawer on rollers. An experienced volunteer called Chamian smiled and shook her hand very lightly.

"It's an easy job," she said. "But ask me if you come across something silly we didn't ask for and probably can't use."

"You mean asparagus in honeyed brandy?" suggested Mags. "Caviar en croute?"

Chamian chuckled. "You'd be surprised."

As they began, Chamian found time to point Mags in the right direction while placing her own items at speed. Mags asked the obvious question and learned that Chamian had been volunteering for a few years now.

"I've had it on my intentions list since the 2015 Election," said Mags, but steered herself away from political polemic because she wasn't great at multi-tasking, especially when she became aeriated. "I was desperate once myself, for a bit."

"Yeah?" It seemed Chamian hadn't been expecting that. "It can happen to anyone."

"I'd better concentrate," said Mags. "You do the talking. There'll be less risk of tampons in with the dough sticks."

After another chuckle, Chamian didn't say much, except to advise. She was a wide-hipped woman around the same age as Mags but there was nothing slow about her. She wore her glasses low on her nose and there were fat red beads around her neck. Mags imagined her with eight grandchildren, laughing freely, but here she was focused. The thought prompted an attempt by Mags to increase her work rate.

"Doesn't it make you angry," she asked a minute or two later, "that so many people are hungry and can't afford to stay warm in winter?"

"Sure," said Chamian. "That's why I'm here. No good steaming away on Twitter."

"Oh I like a good Twitter steam," said Mags. "Especially about ever-so-generous people who donate champagne truffles." She held up the fancy gift box and squinted at the small print. "From last Christmas."

Chamian showed her where to put items that seemed random or inappropriate. "Not sure they can use those as a prize at the shelter, though. There's an alcohol ban."

Mags thought better of admitting a fancy for a truffle or two. She had no idea the night shelter existed and although she tried to conceal it, Chamian was probably equally astonished by her surprise.

"You're remembering to check the use-by dates?" she asked Mags, who realised that she might have missed a few.

"Sure," she said. She was afraid her shelf-stacking experience wasn't helping her impress. "What field were you in, job-wise, Chamian?"

Chamian slotted a tray back in place and paused a moment as if she might suggest Mags focused on the task in hand. "I was a midwife," she declared with a smile. "And I fostered too."

"Oh, that's why I imagined you surrounded by children!"

"Really?" Chamian seemed pleased. "I hate to see little ones here." She nodded towards the room where the bags were distributed; Mags winced at the thought. "We'll chat over a coffee later."

Mags was reaching in for a split pack of custard creams and hoping she wasn't to blame when her phone rang.

"Aagh! My son." She looked at the screen and cut him off, wincing. "I should have turned it off. He's having a crisis."

"Then speak to him!" cried Chamian. "Call him back."

"But not this kind of crisis …"

"Please, call."

Mags felt guilty as she hurried out of the building. The sun had broken out and the wet pavement shone like wet paint, but she needed a coat. Seeing a young mother enter with twins kicking their legs in a battered buggy, she smiled at the children. They were chunky in zip-up bodysuits and festive in Santa hats, while their mother looked drawn and pale in a denim jacket, leggings and pumps. "Morning," she said, smiling at the girl, but the response was a quick pull of the mouth, as if she was out of the habit. Regretting the cheeriness in her voice, Mags didn't suppose solidarity counted for much when only one of them had nothing in her kitchen cupboards.

She stood and called Cameron but hesitated when invited to leave a message after the tone. "Sorry, Cam. I'm volunteering. Hope you're OK. Call me at lunchtime?" She'd seen something online that morning about being a *good enough* mother and children learning from parental mistakes, but hadn't dared read it in case she fell short of the criteria. But this wasn't Genevieve. If Gen's skin was papery, Cam's was rhino-tough.

Ah yes, she told herself, but that was then and this is now. Shivering, she went back inside to apologise again and do better.

15

The sea was the colour of steel and the waves looked strong enough to knock Georgie down. Daddy always chose Frinton because it was *nice and quiet*, even though Mags had heard about a funfair at Clacton, which sounded a lot more fun. She didn't like the groynes because they were as slimy as a witch's hair, but they marked off a beach that was more or less their own for the day – unless the sun came out of hiding. Wild gusts kept beating the sides of the striped windbreaker into a fierce flap. Mummy had an anorak on, with the hood up, but Daddy wore a jumper she'd knitted even though he called it his *mini dress* because it was so long and baggy. That was rude when Mummy wasn't silly, just kind.

Maggie had never seen anyone's teeth chattering like they did in stories, but that was what Georgie's were doing. His body only trembled, right through the layers Mummy had made him wear. His thin legs were blue-white from the end of his shorts to the bare feet that clung to the damp sand.

"Let's jump the waves!" she cried. "Come on, they're titchy!"

"The water will be icy," grimaced Mummy. "You won't warm Georgie up that way."

Daddy was digging stumps into the sand. The bails blew straight off and rolled in the wind but Mags raced after them. When she brought them back they were gritty and damp. Daddy tutted and brushed them off, but either the wind snatched them again or he scraped too hard, or his fingers were too cold to hold on, and one of them escaped. Laughing, Mags charged off after it again, and Georgie ran after her, grinning. Mags liked making games out of things when he was worried.

To make it funnier, she waited when she was crouching right over the bail – to give the wind a chance to drive it on. Then she laughed and had to chase it again, with Georgie forgetting to shiver.

"Oh for goodness' sake!" yelled Daddy. "Bring it here."

She let Georgie pick it up and take the credit because she was the one *mucking about* the way Daddy said she was always doing. But Georgie decided to prove himself with an overarm throw and instead of falling for Daddy to catch, the bail just flew away towards the water and the next thing they knew it was bobbing up and down like driftwood.

"Oh NOOOOO!" yelled Maggie, overacting and throwing her hands to her head before laughing to make sure Georgie didn't feel bad or silly. "Bad wind! Be-blooming-have your-self!"

"Language, Margaret!" cried Daddy as he hurried down to the water. "Leave it to me."

"It's not language," said Maggie. "I bet the Queen says blooming. Her roses do it!"

"Don't answer back," said Daddy. "Go and bowl to Georgie."

"Not with one bail, Daddy! That wouldn't be cricket!" That made Maggie splutter a laugh she tried to hold back because things not being cricket was one of Daddy's sayings. He turned from the waves to give her a narrow-eyed glare.

"All right!" she said, and took Georgie's hand. "Hope the blooming bail drowns," she muttered to their bare feet. He made a little gasp of a laugh.

Behind the windbreaker Mummy was drinking tea from the striped flask. Maggie looked at Daddy's back, reaching for the bail and trying not to fall in. She knew Mummy wouldn't tell. Sneaking over to the wicket like the Pink Panther, she found the other bail had blown off so she scuffed some sand over it like a dog that had just done what Daddy called its *business* because the other words were *disgusting*. Then she pulled out the stumps one after another and rolled the first two as far as she could. The third one she coated like a sausage with wet sand for the pastry. She'd just finished making it into a ridge when Daddy marched back, his shorts dark with seawater but the bail high in one hand.

"What the dickens?" he cried. "Where's my wicket gone?"

He looked at Mummy who made a puzzled frown.

"The wind must have blown it to Timbuktu," said Maggie, trying not to smirk. Georgie's expression had changed from amusement to panic.

"Margaret," Daddy said, her name lifting at the end into a threat.

"Let's start the picnic," said Mummy. "Hot sweet tea will warm us up."

"Cricket will warm us up," insisted Daddy. "Margaret and George will find the three stumps while I start the sandwiches."

"They'll be food for sharks by now!"

But the two of them started searching with their feet. "You'll have to try harder than that!" called Daddy. Maggie could hear Mummy saying something but Daddy wasn't listening. "Mm, cheese and tomato," he yelled. "It's all right, George, I'll leave some egg sandwiches for you."

Georgie looked at Mags and gagged even though she couldn't smell any egg on the wind. Egg made him sick but Daddy said it was all in his mind and he had to get over it or be a limp lettuce all his life.

Mags nodded towards the groyne and they ran to find the stump she'd thrown, lying on the surface of the water with the seaweed but trapped with one end against the wood.

"I'm going to chuck it to kingdom come," she whispered.

Georgie's eyes widened in terror. "No," he murmured. "He'll shout. He'll spank you."

"I don't care. At least we'll have no blooming cricket."

She picked up the stump. Still his eyes begged her. "All right," she said. "Don't worry, I'll eat the egg sandwiches and you can have my cake."

"Why are you so brave?" he whispered as they began the walk back.

"Because he makes me."

"Well done! I'll find the others," said Mummy as they approached her. "What a nuisance that dog was, running off with them like that."

She said it so nicely, just like an actress in a black and white film. She offered the sandwiches and Maggie snatched the egg with a cry: "Yum, my favourite!"

Daddy wasn't happy. He just drank his tea with his shoulders turned on them all, watching the sea. Mags looked at the back of his neck and wondered how it could be so red when there was no sun to burn anything.

That was before rain stopped play.

The walk to the surgery was stiff and slow. Georgie felt like an old man and didn't like the grimace he caught, thanks to a shop window, on his own face. It was getting worse but he wasn't sure the appointment would yield anything concrete. "You're a puzzle," Dr Da Costa had said last time he presented much the same symptoms.

In the waiting room he checked Facebook on his phone. Mags must be busy with her crisis and she'd had more of those than she deserved. Called in, he was glad to escape the

134

gaze of the square-jawed, red-chinned man opposite, chewing gum so it was just visible like his contempt.

Dr Da Costa was handsome enough for TV, even with no sign of a smile in his repertoire. His hair was very black, with kinks.

"Nice skirt," he said. "Have I seen that one before?"

"Maybe not," said Georgie, and began to recount his symptoms with care not to overstate or make light of any one of them. "I thought it was the depression," he said, "but ..."

"Are you depressed? Taking the pills?"

"Depressed? Mostly not, no and yes to the pills. I could say I've had a new lease of life, or the offer of one."

The doctor waited, his focus intent as he squeezed his knitted fingers together on the desk.

"I reconnected with the one person who loved me just as I am – or was ..." He wasn't sure why he had shared something so private, so new-born and delicate – except that he had nowhere else to word it outside his head.

"An old girlfriend? Boyfriend?"

"No ..." Why had he begun this when he'd stood her up?

"Ah, I'm sorry. You're straight, you said. Forgive me."

"Nothing to forgive," he said, probably sounding weary. "Not a girlfriend. We were children."

"Ah, nostalgia," said Doctor Da Costa dismissively, as if he would tolerate no such thing. "You're telling me you have something to get out of bed for, yes? Or into bed for." Georgie failed to interrupt. "I wish you joy. But we need to do some blood tests." He ticked some boxes on a form and passed it to Georgie. "The nurse will make you an appointment but in the meantime, don't neglect your body just because you respect the power of your mind."

Surely his mind had betrayed him all his life? "No," he obliged.

Walking home, he replayed what he'd said about Mags and wondered why he hadn't told Julia or Troy. He was aware that this conviction of his – that no one read him the way she used to – could be a romantic illusion like endless golden summers long gone. But if he waited much longer to meet

135

her, the weight of all this anticipation would pin him to the floor and he'd be unable to step outside.

In fact, winter felt rather golden too, in unexpected sunlight, but his ears burned in the wind. If he were to buy a festive tree for the flat he'd like it to be hand-made, crafted and ideally a little odd. Maybe Mags would make him one!

Mags started Christmas shopping with a list. Kara was easy; she liked the accessories everyone else was wearing but Genevieve would scorn. Simon didn't care as long as he had chocolate, and Cam was a question mark in human form.

Daddy always did his Christmas shopping on Christmas Eve; Mummy found that stressful and preferred hers wrapped and labelled by the end of October Half Term. Mags manoeuvred her way around a few shops full of novelties no one needed. The world was dancing on a tilting Titanic — except that soon there'd be no more icebergs and the sea would be more plastic than salt. Didn't these people believe in global warming, or did believing make more determined hedonists of them all?

Now that Rudi was out of the picture, she must consume less, check air miles on fruit and veg ... sign up for an allotment, even.

A text from Kara felt like more like a complaint with an instruction on board than a question: *Why can't you give Dad a chance?* No kiss. It was followed at once by another, requiring Mags to reach into her bag once again: *Simon agrees BTW.* Mags breathed deeply.

In the end it wasn't the self-stirring mug or the slim-fit Santa to keep a red wine bottle cosy that drove her off the streets before dark, but the festive old pop songs that staged a coup in some part of her brain. On the bus home she found a missed call from Cameron, but with minimal battery planned to call back from the house. She had only had time to *visit the bathroom,* as Mummy used to say, when he called again.

At least, it was his phone.

"Mags dear, Cameron is driving. It's Maureen. Our ETA is approximately ...?" Mags heard Cameron's voice. "Oh I can never understand what nineteen something means unless it's a year. Not an hour."

"Nineteen forty-five, Mo. Quarter to eight." That was a female voice – with a less than familiar owner.

"You're sure you don't mind us descending on you, dear?"

Mags stalled a moment. The three of them? The last time any of her children did this to her, the twins were sixteen and eight of their friends came back drunk and didn't shut up until morning.

"OK, fine. See you at nineteen forty-five then," she said, when she meant, *"Put Cameron on. I'd like a word with him."* She'd have to throw everything – but mostly potatoes – into a curry and hope Maureen didn't object.

After shaking her head in a way that she supposed made her look like a cartoon, Mags used Judas Priest to obliterate the Christmas hits while she tidied up the kitchen. Cameron could have the double bed in the official spare room – which would accommodate the grieving widow too, if necessary. And why not, really? Who made rules these days about such things?

Soon her phone vibrated on his bookcase, above the stack of childhood DVDs and a couple of Terry Pratchetts. She'd laid it beside the old bear she had denied the charity shop because it was Cameron's first. The text – delayed apparently – said: *Is it ok to bring Gran and Sharon back to yours for a few days for a change of scene?* He'd added three kisses – two or three more than he usually spared her.

But what was his motive really? Was she meant to occupy Maureen, allowing him Sharon to himself? That was at least more achievable than a peace-making plan to reconcile her with his father now he was dead.

"Oh Georgie," she muttered. "So much for taking control of this little life of mine. Just when I intended it to shine." The church chorus played in her head but she wasn't sure how it got there. Presumably during her brief evangelical phase between Jake and Dan. Time to make some space for Georgie before her children and Christmas filled it all.

Sitting on the single bed, she called him on her mobile and found herself tightening as she listened to the ringing sound that wasn't really the one in his home, even though she pictured him, curious.

"Hello?" she heard, a little diffident perhaps. Not an embrace of an answer anyway. Surely her name had appeared on his screen.

"How are you, Georgie?" It was more upbeat than she felt.

"I'm not so bad, Mags. This is a nice surprise."

"Impulse time," she announced. "Let's meet – at the Tate Modern. Tomorrow evening if you can."

For a moment she could hear nothing. No music, not his rain or hers. She'd jumped him, just the way Daddy always objected to being jumped.

"Er ... tomorrow is ...?"

She supplied the day but wasn't sure about the date.

"Yes, let's," he said, and she thought he was smiling now. His voice was deep but light. She identified the warmth that had broken in.

She told him she'd see him in the café on the ground floor at six if he could make it. She didn't even know if he had a job. He agreed and she wanted to ask – along with what he was doing and how his day had been – but only told him she had to run around for some last-minute guests and she'd explain tomorrow.

"See you soon, then," he said. "But they don't have Mary Cassatt?"

"They don't need to," she told him, pleased he remembered – and knew. "Those are all in my mind's eye. Well, that's not true. The paintings are a fuzz; it's the feelings that are sharp focus. Anyway, yes, see you soon. I'm glad I rang."

"I'm glad you rang too."

"Bye now."

"Bye."

Smiling, Mags rose and jiggled her hips, elbows swinging up and down in turn. A childish dance of triumph – and relief. He'd liked her impulse in the end. And those seemed to run in the family; Cameron and his entourage would be here soon and she'd better peel some potatoes. They could amuse themselves tomorrow night. She had some theatre vouchers ...

16

Hurrying to the door, Mags couldn't help feeling that for the women on her doorstep, time hadn't been even-handed. Maureen never used to let anyone see her without make-up. Now her skin seemed thinner and greyer than at the funeral, and in the absence of a hat, her hair looked flat and tired. Beside her, Sharon was vibrant in reds and russets, with large feathered earrings and decorative boots. She carried a rounded woven bag; Cameron put down his gran's neat suitcase with silvery trims and his own bumpy backpack.

Mags reached to hug him. She knew it might be imagination but he felt more elastic, almost unfamiliar. But Maureen's hands were cold as they closed around hers in a gesture of thanks for what she called, "such kind hospitality." Mags thought her close to tears so she aimed to be gentle and not too jolly as she ushered them through and turned the dial on the thermostat. So far Sharon had only made a few appreciative background noises. Mags wondered whether this was awkward for her. Perhaps she'd rather be alone at home.

Cameron took their luggage upstairs. Maureen needed "the smallest room" even though she used to call that the toilet in the days when Daddy thought the word offensive. Mags led into the kitchen, and felt a sense behind her of a kind of fluid grace as Sharon followed silently in socks. If roles were reversed, Mags would have questions. And she did, much the same ones. She arranged herbal teas on the worktop and waited for Sharon's decision.

"Black coffee would be good, thanks."

Mags didn't like to ask people how they were and never seemed to find an answer that was worth airing but also true. But this was a woman whose husband had died less than a fortnight ago. In many cultures her clothes would be as black as her coffee and she'd be howling, or housebound, or locked almost literally in prayer. And Mags believed in authenticity.

"We have such a huge vocabulary for love and sex, but death ..." she began, and filled the cafetière. "It's all euphemisms and tactful avoidance. Doesn't it make you want to spit?"

"I swear a lot," said Sharon flatly. "Not as much as Jake. And only when I'm on my own which isn't often."

Mags smiled. "Good strategy." She saw Sharon look to the door as if watching out for ... Maureen, or Cam? "Did you love him? I mean, were you happy?"

Sharon's face remained impassive. Then her eyes filled and her lips parted. Mags could imagine Cameron's reaction, protective and accusing.

"I blunder in because I can't pussyfoot. You can ask me the same," she added.

"About Jake?"

She'd meant Rudi, but he wasn't dead and that made a difference. "Ah," she said, opening the fridge door. "Ferociously, consumingly happy – and unhappy too."

"I'm sorry," said Sharon.

"Let's go in the lounge," suggested Mags. She looked down at her feet. "Clodhoppers. They don't mean to hurt."

Sharon went first, her flow unbroken. She turned her head and stopped in the corridor. "You can't hurt me, Mags." It wasn't tough, just a statement.

"Good!" cried Mags, and found Cameron behind her, his expression unsure. She told him she'd nudge the coffee and greeted Maureen as she negotiated the stairs with stiff care. Commending herself sardonically on her tactics so far, she wondered what the three of them were talking about on her sofas, but all she could hear was the high notes as Maureen offered something like commentary. That would be on the furnishings Rudi had chosen, all of them more suited to an exhibition than a home but worn now, the stylistic corners softened.

When she returned with the drinks the room was quiet, but Sharon was looking closely at a photograph: the one of Mags and Rudi, Genevieve and the twins, taken by his brother as a wedding anniversary present. In it only Rudi looked comfortable. Mags had period cramps and boasted a cold sore that wouldn't be calmed by teabags or ice. The twins had reached an age when smiles could only be faked with disturbing Cheshire Cat exaggeration, and Genevieve was in Goth mode, narrowing her eyes in contempt for the whole idea.

"Where were you, Cam?" Sharon asked him.

"Out of the picture. And the country," he said.

"But not out of our thoughts," said Mags, because she used to long more than anything to gather them all in the front room, feed them and hear the laughter from the kitchen – even if it was at her expense.

"Don't kid yourself I crossed the twins' minds. And Genevieve once called me too effing straight to be true."

"Oh, teenagers, Cam!" trilled Maureen. "Take no notice. Jake was the same, all mouth and trousers Don used to say."

No one seemed sure how to respond to that although Mags had some ideas she kept to herself. Sharon had moved on to another photograph, this time of Mags crouching down to put her arm around Cameron. They were in Clacton, and Jake was holding the camera more steadily than usual. Mags rather liked the way her hair was caught up in a ragged cloud by the wind off the sea. Cam's curls had been snipped off against her will by his first barber; she remembered the soft V-shape the remainder made at the back of his neck. He wasn't a funfair sort of child, though. It was Jake who yelled and roared, but at least he wasn't angry that day. Not then anyway.

"You look so sweet," Sharon said. "But serious."

"Oh yes," he said, as if that was someone's fault, thought Mags – hers as well as Jake's.

"Do you remember that day?" she asked. "It was a scorcher."

"Uh-uh." He didn't examine it.

"I can't have children," said Sharon flatly. Mags saw Cameron's tender glance but she wasn't sure it was registered. "I wanted to adopt but Jake said he was too old."

"Jake would have liked more children," said Maureen, her volume double Sharon's. Mags supposed she must miss a good deal of what her daughter-in-law said. But had she forgotten Liz existed?

"He was a child himself, really," murmured Sharon, and it was hard to tell whether the tone was fond.

"Coffee will be ready," said Mags. Back in the kitchen she kicked a cupboard door. She was willing to cook, change sheets and make sure they were all warm enough, but Jake-centred conversation wasn't part of the deal.

"Mum? What do you think?" Cameron almost whispered behind her.

"I wish I had a dog I could walk so I could leave you to grieve together. Still, tomorrow evening I …"

"About Sharon? Do you think there's any hope?"

Mags sighed. "I don't know, Cam. But I don't think I can trash Jake just to oil the wheels for you." He looked appalled. "I know – you're not asking me to do any such thing. It's hard to guess her feelings but they're bound to be a muddle." He stared past her and she realised he'd noticed her artwork on the wall. He raised one eyebrow in that way of his that reminded her of Roger Moore in *The Saint*.

"Yes, I know!" she said. "A moment of madness. Perhaps house buyers will see past it to the magnolia that passes for sanity."

"It's kind of … cool," he said, studying it. His mouth curled in a half-smile.

"I'm glad you think so, because the kitchen table is next." She told him she'd better see to supper and put her best pinny on, the one he gave her years back but probably wouldn't remember. As she chopped and stirred she considered what Cupid would do – other than flap his wings and move on to a more achievable task.

At around ten fifteen Mags messaged Georgie on Facebook. *I'm the only one still standing. I think my sag aloo sank them all.*

No reply. Perhaps he was in bed too. That made her wonder how long he'd been celibate, if that was what he was, and whether it was a choice. The possibility of a bedroom encounter between Cam and Sharon raised itself but she dismissed it. He'd never brought girls home. But then once he left for uni he had gone, passed on without a turn of the head, into a space her imagination couldn't fill.

Genevieve used to stay out all night and refuse to say where, which Rudi called normal. "Another sleepover?" the twins would ask, wide-eyed with jealousy, and Mags wanted to freeze their innocence in a cryogenic lab.

On impulse Mags took a photo on her phone of the framed photograph Sharon had liked. Maybe Georgie would find her in it; she was still a girl then after all. She attached it with a place and year, no comments, and hoped he'd find it and reciprocate, but there was no response.

After all this time it was hard to separate the outings; candyfloss might have stuck them together as one. But looking at it again stirred movement in her head. Something surfaced out of the blue sky and heat.

For a long time it seemed Cameron was busy exploring what a bucket could make of sand. Then he ran to the sea for water, and poured it without warning or any apparent feeling on the Roman-style wall Jake had just finished building around the keep.

"Oh thanks a lot!"

"It's melting!" cried Cameron.

"It can't be melting without heat," said Jake, and lit a cigarette.

"It's melting!" insisted Cameron, and ran to fetch more seawater to prove it.

Mags stood on the prom, watching them as she queued within earshot at the Mr Whippy stall. She could smell Jake's smoke mingling with the sea and the sweetness. Suddenly she remembered Georgie and the cricket, the egg sandwiches and Daddy's steel shoulders.

She paid, and took the ice creams, but must have been more in the past than the present because the arms around her waist made her squeal. Jake kissed her lips; one hand moved to her bottom as the other took a cone.

"Where's Cam?" she cried. It was the panic reflex he never understood or welcomed.

And for whole seconds she couldn't see the blue shorts, striped T-shirt, red spade, new boy's haircut. Jake tried to hold tight but she fought her way out. She ran, ignoring her name as he shouted it after her.

It was too hot for running and her hair felt heavy. In a sudden gust it blinded her. There was a dog barking and the smell of chips and vinegar. Unoccupied deckchair seats flapped and stilled as she pulled her hair from her mouth and eyes. And there he was, right where he'd been all the time. Someone's portable radio burst through the soundtrack with *Itsie Bitsie Teeny Weeny Yellow Polka Dot Bikini*. Mags bit her lip because the smallest, most vulnerable thing on the beach was Cameron, crouched down on his haunches – ready for the incoming wave once it had subsided into a low rush towards his bucket. His head down towards the water, his identity was all but lost – until she called his name and he turned, stood and smiled.

Mags realised the two cones in her hands had dropped some of their swirls.

"We lost you!" she cried, her voice surging with relief. Cam took the depleted cone and bit into it as if he didn't notice the difference. She bit into hers too, and said, "Yum. Baby Whippies are the best."

Cameron swallowed the rest of his and wiped his chin with a damp, salty hand. "Come on, Mummy!" He hurried back to his building site with the water, some of it sloshing his legs and bare feet as he tilted with the weight of it.

Aware that she was still cross with Jake, Mags ate the papery cone, looking only at her son and the water that seeped into and destroyed the rest of the sand wall.

"It's disappearing!" he cried. "Puff of smoke!"

But the only smoke was Jake's. She knew before she checked that he was close now. Glancing back, she saw him squinting into the sun without his shades and knew from the line of his slight, faintly tanned body that he wasn't happy.

"You haven't even told him, have you?"

"Told him what?" Unlike him, she kept her voice low. She stepped away from Cameron and walked back up the beach, turning every second to watch him. He was digging now, careless of where he flipped the sand aside.

"Told him not to run off like that," she heard behind her.

"That was you, Jake. You left him."

Silence was a warning with Jake. It was always clenched but sometimes he couldn't hold on to it. She glimpsed him licking the creamy peak, slowly. Then he grabbed her by the arm.

"Let go," she muttered, as clearly and calmly as she could. "He's safe. That's all that matters." She lifted her voice. "Wow, Cam, you're going deep! Watch out for rabbits!" Jake's grip loosened enough for her to break away. Catching Cameron, she tried to switch from neurotic mother to clownish best friend.

Moments later Jake joined them, making a show of savouring his ice cream.

"Want a lick then?" he offered Cameron, but when Cam leaned forward to the lowered cone, he jerked it out of his reach and ate most of what remained.

Mags knew some kids would bawl but Cam's frown didn't break.

"Baby Whippies are best," he told Jake, and turned back to his hole with a determined shovel. Mags felt a rush of pride and sneaked a quick, discreet V-sign at Jake as he stubbed his cigarette in the sand.

145

She could ask Cameron, "Do you remember the Baby Whippy?" or whether he saw Jake grab her by the arm. But it wasn't fair to push one set of memories juddering against another when everyone's were specially theirs. Mags no longer felt ready for bed. Careful to minimise the clatter, she took some paint from her Rainy Day cupboard, wiped the kitchen table and looked for a few minutes at its proportions and bleached pine. With the tips of her fingers she pressed its surface, not entirely smooth. "Let's go natural," she'd said to Rudi and there had been a joke about nakedness because she always claimed to be a nudist at heart but never quite in public.

At Charleston Farmhouse everything must have been improvised. The Bloomsbury set didn't even bother to flatten the bumps and drips into evenness; they let the paint do what it did and be what it was. Rudi was sceptical, calling much of it rough and amateurish, but she liked the exuberance. Art by impulse! Well this would be hers and the National Trust might never take the slightest interest but the time to begin was now.

With the colours to hand she could mix quite a palette and that would be Rudi's way: methodical, like a pianist playing scales. He used to ask her for names of shades he mixed because she'd come out with *Sapped by Joy* or *Monkfish at Night*. Once or twice, having laughed, he used them as titles, and smiled when the works were hung, because theirs was a secret joke no one else could share.

Now she let the Cerulean dictate and began with a slash, not diagonal but not straight either, its depth dissipating at its end. She must let it be. Next, a random encounter with the Gamboge. No interference, she told herself. Let them bleed. Uneven was real. She could experiment with a palette knife, a hairbrush, the flick of a mop as long as it was dry and reasonably clean. And then, when the colour invasion was over, she could let the morning inspire her. Flowers, birds, faces, trees – life and death, hope and yearning. Or she could let patterns develop, repeat and vary like a Fugue. Then she could call it *Discipline.*

Around midnight, Mags walked around the table one more time and nodded. There might not be a tune as such but she heard no false notes either. The surface was textured now. When she turned off the kitchen light, a shine remained in the blackness, like a lake with no moon but a star or two. Would Vincent approve? Mary Cassatt would want humanity to warm its way through but sometimes the story was creation.

Mags realised the heating had turned itself off an hour ago. Cold, she rubbed her arms, her torso, her thighs. Was Rudi alone in bed? Would Georgie sleep?

In the bathroom she grinned at herself in the mirror as she asked herself, *What have I done?*

17

When Mags set off for the food bank the next morning, leaving behind a note explaining that she hadn't mentioned it because she'd forgotten what day it was, no one else was up. She made no reference to the transformation of the table but put notes on cupboards, with arrows pointing to basic breakfast items, and felt a frisson of anticipation as well as escape. It was fun to imagine their various reactions on opening the door. She hoped Cameron would be less embarrassed than proud. So much to tell Georgie, but so much more to find out if he was ready to share.

There was a satisfaction in knowing what to do at the food bank – bar a couple of questions – and she'd never minded a mechanical rhythm to eat up time. It was a surprise when she realised her shift was over and turned on her phone. Not a word from Cameron. She stopped off for French bread, cheeses and fat tomatoes but arrived home to a message in capitals underneath hers: MAUREEN MAY BE HAVING A NAP. WE'RE GOING TO THE GYM.

We now, she noted. Hearing sounds upstairs, she made a pot of tea. Soon Maureen stole in softly in her cerise satin slippers. Her posture was still upright but her steps were small and less than firm.

"Good kip, Maureen?" Mags greeted her, volume up. "I've brewed up."

"Good what, love? Trip did you say? I've been having a nap."

"Yes, a kip! Is the bed comfy? Consider yourself at home," she sang. Mags attempted the Fagin side skip from *Oliver*, which had been a movie favourite of Maureen's when she met Jake. Maureen looked a little alarmed and Mags was glad Cam wasn't there to tell her off as she explained herself.

"You were part of the family then, love."

The lyric caught her by surprise; Mags felt it head-on.

"Indeed I was. But there have been a few changes since then. Where have bell bottoms gone – same way as all the flowers?" She provided another song snippet when Maureen seemed perplexed.

"Jake found the right girl in the end. Don wouldn't have liked it, with her not being white, but she's very patient." Maureen looked at her tea as if it might be the wrong shade too.

Suggesting they make a start on lunch, Mags was told Cameron had already made a nice omelette. Conversation never quite joined up enough to flow as they sat on the same sofa and Mags ate a banana in an attempt to stave off hunger. Maureen began explaining how they'd first known Jake was ill, what the doctor had said, the trouble they'd had to get him to take the medication at first and how scared he'd been, in the end.

"He told me he knew he could have been a better son."

Mags nodded. No disagreement with that.

"He was sorry for all the upset he'd caused me." Maureen's voice was brittle now. "You'd have been shocked to see him, Mags."

"I'm sorry you had to see it," muttered Mags.

"You're a mother. You know about forgiving children."

Mags would have liked to borrow some Jane Austen from Georgie and say, coolly, that she bore Jake no malice. As if it was of no consequence at all. Or to retort that with her kids there'd never been much to forgive. But she also imagined telling Maureen that monsters had to be called out; otherwise the monstrous became acceptable.

"I'm meeting a childhood friend for supper," she announced brightly. "There's a nice Italian in walking distance; Cam will be happy to treat you."

"You don't understand, love," Maureen continued. "Jake asked me to say sorry."

Mags hadn't been expecting that. But though it felt like fantasy, she had enough imagination. The scene had sound as well as colour. It had touch, and tears – but whose?

"Only to me? What about the others – like Liz?"

Maureen stood stiffly. "If you're determined to see the worst in him and forget the rest, even now he's gone ..."

"I'm determined not to break again," Mags told her, steadying her voice as it wavered. "Not to let anyone break me."

"Mags, love, you broke Jake! You'll never see it! He never knew where he was with you or how to please you. Don knew. *She's leading him a merry dance*," he said. He was only flesh and blood."

"I don't think," said Mags carefully, "that flesh and blood are the best subjects in the circumstances."

Had Maureen heard, never mind understood? Mags stared at the glass cabinet and imagined everything in it shattering. This was an old woman, a bereaved mother. She should let it all pass. She could have ...

There were voices in the hallway.

"Ah," she said. "The gym addicts will be hungry."

Cam and Sharon were scented and glowing. They could have passed for a couple, but not the kind to finish each other's sentences. Their answers were brief. Giving up, Maureen began a story about Netball at the Convent School, but Mags lost her grip on it and remembered as her mouth gummed with cheese that she really did intend to go vegan one day soon.

Georgie hadn't been to Tate Modern for a couple of years or more and as far as he could recall had always been alone. Not meeting a woman. There was something intimidating about the place – not just the scale but the coolness of it all, and the style of those wandering, especially the young. It had a vocabulary that wasn't only words and not everyone spoke it. He was far from fluent himself. The skirt and sparkly scarf had never felt less conspicuous but inside them he felt exposed anyway.

Georgie the boy would be lost here; it might as well have been Mars. He probably wouldn't even understand the menu. He walked in and did his best to gaze around before anyone came to take him to a table. Then a chic boy approached with streamlined black clothes and light blue hair.

"A table for two, please," Georgie said, and was escorted to one on the far side, looking towards the river. If she walked that way, she'd spot him lit up behind glass. He could make jazz hands and try not to wonder what exactly she saw, and how sad it might make her.

Mags could have used the word jangling for what was happening inside her, but at the same time a smile lay in readiness, and the warm pressure of it was like a birthday feeling. Or that moment of seeing her own child in a school production, the only one in focus among all the rest, and unbearably special but vulnerable, distant, other ...

The Thames Embankment was alive with Christmas but the cold wind managed to target her skin through all the hair, wool and layers. She walked fast towards the glass corner of café wall, wondering whether he would be the only cross-dresser and whether, without that sizeable clue, she'd know him. She walked inside, telling herself that to expect disappointment was self-protection and common sense.

The relative warmth of the café made her cheeks flush as she pulled off her scarf. Her ears had a habit, as a child, of flaming; now it felt as if they were reverting to it in Georgie's honour. She'd met a fair few men in pubs, clubs and restaurants, but never for a blind date. Never half a century after they last saw each other.

Scanning the space, she saw a figure straightening by the window. He was fuller than the wispy boy, with a full head of grey hair trailing in curls down his neck and meeting the collar of his floral blouse. He looked intently in her direction. Mags hurried past a waiter about to intercept her and as Georgie stood, she pressed herself against him, arms around his neck. For a moment she clung, and he clung back. He felt compact, no excess; his skin was cooler than hers. Did he smell of vanilla?

She pulled away. "If you're not Georgie you won't see me for dust."

"I'm Georgie, Mags." He was smiling broadly. His face wasn't thin or angular, but lined – although she was sure she could compete, crease for crease. She sat opposite him and grinned.

"That's handy. I ran a lot faster at eight than I could manage now."

"You were Speedy Gonzales if I recall." He poured her some iced water and the lemon slice slopped in with a small splash. "I don't know why I said that. I recall everything about you. Or at least, that's the belief."

"I trust emotional memory better than any other kind," she declared. "How can we verify the when and where? Hopeless. But we hold on to the feeling. That defines the event and everything else falls away. However unreasonable the feeling was, and maybe most of it is when you're a child and can't control anything much around you ..." She paused. "I wasn't going to talk."

"If you don't, you won't see me for dust."

The waiter with blue hair appeared and Mags nearly ordered champagne, but blocked the impulse. That could be tactless. She had no idea what he earned or owned, and she'd often cringed inwardly when Rudi swanked like that with the art world and without it. They agreed on the house red. It turned out that Georgie had already decided what to eat so she said, "I'll have the same. Thanks."

As the waiter walked away she checked, "No jellied eels involved, or dead calves, or live lobster?"

"I'm a new vegan. Didn't I say? I'm sorry ..."

"I'm vegan too! As of this moment – I pledge. Genevieve will be ecstatic but Cam will call the men in white coats, being virtually Australian." Apparently she couldn't say that word without the accent these days, even when Cam was around. Maybe she'd been the same fifty-two years ago. How many other reflexes had got stuck on repeat?

He asked her how the visit was going but she must listen now. His turn.

"I don't even know what you do. For a job, I mean."

"I'm a counsellor." His smile was wry. "But I've been on sick leave. The stereotypical crazy shrink."

"Isn't that a qualification? You have to be able to empathise with the rest of us fruit cakes." The wine arrived. She noticed how polite he was in his quietly spoken way, for a boy Daddy said hadn't learned manners. After thanking the waiter, he filled her glass.

"I was thinking of applying for a job as a classroom assistant in the primary school nearby but I don't think I fit that spec." He looked down at his clothes. "Men are suspect enough, but old men – in skirts?"

"Shit like that needs challenging. That's what my Genevieve says. I agree with her more and more these days. She had a breakdown too." Was that the wrong word? He looked easy to break. "She'd approve of you. In any case, don't you think there's a spectrum when it comes to breakdowns, and we're all on it at one time or another? I sometimes look around me on a tube when everyone's captive and isolated and I think some of those anonymous people are cracked right through in the silence. Only nobody knows because they get used to living with a yawning gap inside." She took a sip of wine.

"I never do," he said.

"Get used to it?"

"No." He looked out of the window a moment, but turned straight back. "That's why you should keep talking. I have this habit, when I haven't come up yet, of bringing other people down to where I am. Or would do, given the chance. I don't want to do that to you."

"I want you to be yourself, Georgie. That's what you'll get from me, I warn you!"

"Hit me with it." He smiled. "With being Mags."

Mags fell back in her chair and opened her arms. "I got typecast in a role nobody would choose. Which is probably the human condition, I know. So being me used to be about longing – before I got angry, but kept on longing. And now I'm in a kind of limbo with goals ... which is another way of saying I can't stop longing." She looked around the café. "If they could hear me they'd say join the club, right? We're all such individualists that we forget how standard we are."

He shook his head. "In your case I know better."

"Aw ..." Rudi had said she always joked or shrugged off appreciation.

"I need to say thank you. I never really said it, not enough. Thank you for everything you did and were. I think as time has gone by I've felt more grateful, not less. Thank you, Mags."

"Oh, Georgie," she murmured, and sighed. "Being your surrogate sister was probably the only thing I ever did well. Everything I've been since isn't much to be proud of – mother, partner, an artist with no art to show. I can't hold on to friends, even if they don't sleep with one of my husbands. So being Mags doesn't add up to a whole hill of beans."

Their food arrived and she laughed because arranged and steaming on their matching plates was something not unlike such a hill, only artistically sculpted and beautifully moated.

"A sign," said Georgie.

"That I'm talking baldergook."

He laughed. It was surprisingly full and rounded, a warm laugh. "You said it. I took a lot of your phrases away with me."

"Sorry about that."

"They were a gift! I stored them but I didn't have a lot to say."

"Because of my father, the bastard." She poked her food. "Sorry, wrong word. That's you. Cam too. Thanks a lot, Shakespeare."

"I was used to being blamed for that and the rest. He wasn't the first or last to find me defective. What hurt was losing you."

He was emotional. She recognised it still, even though he contained it just like he did then. No fissures in the vocals, no tears shining, just a steadiness as if pain was fact.

"I lost you too."

Georgie placed a hand on hers as she reached for her wine. "Temporarily," he said.

"Yeah, what's fifty-two years when it's at home!" she cried, and laughed. "Georgie Stroft, where have you been all my life?"

He was smiling again. She was enjoying it. "You don't have to answer – tell me everything, I mean. Just what you want to. I'd like to catch up on who you've been, so I haven't missed out on you."

"Maybe we can just resume, like we have."

"Like pulling the scrollydoodah along on YouTube?"

"Yes! And taking it back to the beginning is an option but not compulsory."

"OK. I should warn you that I slip back all the time – finding a conker or a sycamore whirlijig …"

"Samara," he said. "That's what they call helicopter seeds. I like it."

"You're an urban botanist?"

"More of a spaceman."

Mags began to hum the chorus until she remembered the final line of the lyric. "Ah but you do exist. You always did, and not just in my memory. Yay!"

"And I watch quiz shows. Dramas are a bit too dramatic."

"Yippedoo!" she cried. He looked puzzled. "A little detail. I like those. Yours anyway."

"What are yours?"

"Oh," she said, and ate a mouthful before adding, "I don't think I have them. I'm a thick brushstrokes woman, nothing hidden. And don't change the subject. It's about you. If you don't want to pull back, keep it in the present …"

"In the present I'm happy."

"And earlier?"

"Excited. Fearful. Wishing time along that bar faster than it would go. Drinking too much coffee. Trying to read – without following the words. Exercising realistic rationality, you know? Useless."

"Always is. Even though it was seriously irrational, I was afraid we might not get on. But it seems we do." He nodded. He did look happy, in that muted way she remembered, as if he didn't want to risk anyone knowing. "Even though you're harder to prise open than a conker. Or a samara?"

He poured them both more water. In spite of doing too much talking, Mags saw that her plate was emptying faster than his. She suspected that her volume had risen too.

"Mags, can I ask you … You've loved a lot of people …" he began.

"Are you calling me a slut, Georgie Barkle!"

He laughed as he swallowed. A little water made a getaway. "I don't only mean men. Children, your mother. What's it like? How does it work?"

"There's a lot of malfunctioning!" She spun the stem of her glass. "Relationships are like those wires you see spilling out of those electric boxes men try to fix on the street. It's a mess." She knew what he wasn't saying. He wasn't tangled but isolated. It made her want to hold him again.

He nodded but no longer smiled. "I'm sorry. I've always hoped you'd be happy. Nothing but happy."

"Dream on!!" Mags didn't want to laugh when it was so touching. "I wished the same for you. Maybe we should get real about happiness, and count it in moments. Two or three a day, bonanza! As kids we learn that on the plate there'll be cabbage as well as chips. Facebook serves us up with climate change and refugees as well as poignant acts of kindness – and cats. Do you still hate the smell of egg?"

"Oh yes. You're looking at a case of arrested development."

"Oh, kiddo, so are you! But don't worry about me. My plate
has plenty of chips and I'll get used to curly kale in the end.
Kids make you happy but they can burn you to ashes, sometimes without even trying. Lovers: different process, same
outcome." She grinned and drank her wine. "I'm officially
shutting the hell up now. So talk about anything you want.
Please."

"I prefer listening to you."

"Please. Let me in."

"I haven't really let anyone in since you, Mags. Not even
Julia, not really."

He told her that when he was twenty-six he'd met Julia at
the library, where she worked and was kind enough to find
him books. "Mostly about wildflowers or Donatello, or coun-
tries I haven't been to, which is anywhere. One day I left my
trousers and jacket behind and went to the counter in a skirt,
not even sure she'd recognise me, but she did, and said hello.
I was grateful."

"So you asked her out?"

"Eventually she asked me. Heady delight! She started ordering in books about cross-dressers from the past like
George Sand. I did wonder whether I was a fascinating
novelty. A kind of research."

Mags supposed that asking whether he was a virgin at
twenty-six would be rude as well as presumptuous. "Did you
ever think you could be gay or bi?"

"I knew I wasn't attracted to men. I just wanted to look like
a woman. Be like a woman in a way – or more like a woman
than a man."

"Because guys ...?" she prompted.

"Can be bullies who hate soft boys like me."

"Along with women who stand up to them, or give in to
them, or are just women." She didn't want to turn it back to
her. "There are good guys too. I hope my Cam is one, and
Simon will be, bless him." Looking at Georgie she could
imagine, suddenly, the Italian PoW. who fathered him.
"Your dad might have been one. Not so much a cheat as a

sweet, gentle, lonely man taking comfort in whatever it was they found."

"Yes. He might."

"How else did you get to be you?! Case closed." She decided not to mention his mother unless he did. She scooped up her last bean and wiped her mouth with the paper napkin. "I'm glad to see you."

"Probably not as glad as I am to see you."

She thought he seemed embarrassed suddenly by his own declaration as he focused on the food. "Let's go to the chapel!" she cried. "The one your dad helped to build or paint ..."

"He may have been too busy with other things to play his part," he pointed out wryly.

"It doesn't matter. It's all you've got, isn't it? It's a way in to his world." She watched him glance out of the window at the illuminated river. "That's an offer. You can keep it for a rainy day if you like – I have wellies."

"Thank you."

Mags laughed. "In fact I think you used to say that more than anything else."

"Mostly to you. I'll say it again," he said, and took her hand. "Thank you."

Mags would have sworn she'd turned off her phone but it proved her wrong. She apologised as she muttered, "Estate agent" and answered with, "Hello. Is it urgent? It's not a good moment."

"It could be, Mrs Shaw, yes. We have a flat that's come on the market today and a cancelled viewing. The owners have asked us whether anyone else might be interested and you were first on the list. I think you'll find it ticks all your boxes and there's no chain. You won't want to miss out on this one."

"This evening?" she echoed, as the agent gave her an address just across the river.

"Let's go," said Georgie. "If you like?"

"All right," she told the caller, looking questioningly at Georgie. "It would have been quicker in Tudor times by boatman."

Georgie named a bridge that probably proved her wrong. She arranged to be at the flat in twenty minutes to half an hour. Having ended the call she checked, "Are you sure? These guys make it up as they go along. It could be a dead loss."

"Or your new home in time for Christmas." He scrunched his napkin and took a sip of water.

It wasn't much fun going to Grandma's, with no tree house and everything too neat or breakable to touch. Daddy said it was all arranged and Georgie couldn't go this time but she was worried. What would he do without her? Mummy looked pale. It must be one of her bad headaches.

"I want to stay here with Georgie. He won't like it without me."

He didn't like school except at playtime when they found each other. But it was still the summer holidays. She hoped he wasn't having bad dreams about that yet. Maggie appealed to Mummy but Mummy wasn't looking at her. She was biting her lip as if she was worried too, or sad.

Maggie could see Georgie out of the window. He was in the garden but he wasn't playing. He just stood stiff and straight, gazing back at the house. Had Daddy shut him out like a dog that needed a bath?

"Let her say goodbye," murmured Mummy.

Daddy said briskly, "Wave goodbye then, Margaret. We must be off now. Grandma's waiting."

"Why can't he come?"

Daddy took her arm and lifted it as if she'd forgotten how to wave. "All RIGHT!" she cried, wresting it away because he was Mr Mean and everything was his fault. "Bye Georgie." He looked afraid. Was Daddy going to teach him how to bat again? "See you later alligator." She made herself smile but his face didn't change so she pulled the kind that stretched and made him laugh. For a moment his face brightened.

"Come on now. In the car."

"Don't make him play cricket, Daddy. It scares him," she muttered as she was ushered out into the hall and onto the drive.

"I've told you before – we all need to overcome these things. Even George."

Sitting in the back of the Rover, Maggie narrowed her eyes at Daddy's head and her mouth curled into a twisty snarl she didn't allow out. She'd been in too much of a mood to bring a book to read or notebook to draw in, so she kept her eyes on the road – or rather, the trees and the Old Man's Beard, the leftover roses and the pale blue sky.

"Don't sulk, please, Margaret," said Daddy. "It's very ugly."

Would he see if she stuck her tongue out at him? She didn't dare risk it, and ignored him when he turned on Test Match Special and started chuckling at the men on the radio as if he liked them more than anyone he could see.

Twenty minutes later she was in Grandma's porch with Daddy, waiting. Pink and white petals lay bedraggled on the border. Georgie didn't like the word *deadheading* or the Queen of Hearts either and she didn't see why he should have to. Daddy asked whether she'd combed her hair and she shook her head as hard as she could to make it wilder. Then Grandma opened the door, looking like the Queen Mother in a dress with a soft jacket that matched. Her grey hair was squashed in a fine net as usual so you could never tell whether it behaved inside.

"Hello, Margaret dear. Goodness, is there a storm out there?"

"Not outside," said Daddy. "Grandma will lend you a hairbrush, Margaret, so you don't frighten the neighbours."

Maggie stepped inside and unbuckled her shoes on the carpet, just a step over the doormat, which made both the grown-ups cry out in complaint. As she padded into the lounge to look for the china figures that were too delicate to play with, she heard Grandma ask, "Does she know?" in a voice that was nearly a whisper.

She didn't hear Daddy answer.

"Know what?" called Maggie.

"I'm sure it's for the best," said Grandma crisply. "He'd never fit in."

"What is?" cried Maggie, back in the hallway now. "Who? Do you mean Georgie?"

"I'll see you after tea, Margaret. Control yourself and remember your manners." Daddy didn't kiss her and if he had she would have turned into an eel to slither away. He hurried down the paving stone path towards the gate and the car, and then turned to raise one hand in a still, flat wave.

Maggie didn't know, not exactly, what it all meant. But she pushed past Grandma, her breath hot and high.

"Sometimes we're too young to know what's best for us," said Grandma crisply, reaching to hold her back. "I'm sure George's new foster parents will suit him better."

"No!" yelled Maggie. Breaking away, she ran towards the road as Daddy started up the engine.

"Daddy, stop!" she yelled, tears burning. She could see the back of his head and it didn't turn. "Don't!"

Grandma called her name but before Maggie could reach the car, step in front of it like Bobbie in The Railway Children or at least grab the door handle, the car drove off.

She buckled, holding her tummy. Her body shook like the sound that came out of it.

18

At nine twenty next morning, Mags heard that her offer had been accepted. Cameron and Sharon were out for a run but she called Georgie first, and then Rudi, leaving rather different voicemail messages. She sent brief texts to Genevieve and the twins, using exclamation marks while aware that her pleasure felt oddly sober. Hearing Maureen upstairs, she knocked and left a mug of tea outside her door.

It was later, after the return for showers, that she showed the three of them the details and photos and said she knew straight away, the moment she stepped through the door.

"Really?" Sharon asked. "I'd love to make quick decisions. I waste so much time trying to be sure."

"Mum doesn't," said Cameron.

"It's just a flat," Mags pointed out. "Nothing's ever perfect but Georgie asked all the right questions. So Rudi can have his house back soon."

"Another new start, Mags," said Maureen, and it was hard to identify the tone.

"Yes, and I'm properly vegan now, no messing, for the animals and the planet, but it doesn't seem right to throw the eggs at the TV News so if you want them cooked, ask Cam."

"Soft-boiled, please, dear," said Maureen.

"Not for me," said Sharon, "thanks. So ... who's Georgie?"

"Oh, my oldest friend. We just found each other again."

Cameron clattered around in search of the egg pan. He didn't seem happy and he wasn't looking at Sharon. Mags was sure something must have happened on their run. The thought of it was disturbing. Was Sharon's suggestion to Maureen that they went through to the lounge an avoidance tactic? Now that Mags looked at her she seemed preoccupied, tense.

But then so did Cam.

"I had a Thomas the Tank Engine jumper when I was six, Mum, but I don't want to wear it now," he said.

It sounded rehearsed and pointed. Maureen's egg rattled a little in the pan as the bubbles reached a frenzy.

"Is that about me and Georgie?"

"It just seems ... irresponsible."

"What does? We're friends, Cam. I know you think I'm soft-boiled myself but there's no need to worry about me. Last night was the first time for ages that I've gone to bed without a great bumpy knot inside." He stood by the hot ring but he wasn't watching the egg. It had cracked and a little white tail trailed out of it, not liquid but firm. "That's done, Cam."

161

He didn't react so she emptied the water and found Rudi's favourite egg cup.

"Sharon doesn't want me. I've booked a flight. I don't think I'll be back for Christmas."

"Oh, sweetheart."

"I should have buttoned it and given her more time."

Ignored her advice, he meant. Well maybe she wasn't agony aunt material. She tried to hug him but his limbs hung loose, his shoulders low. "I hope the flat works out," he mumbled. "And Georgie doesn't get dependent."

"Why on earth would he?"

"Wasn't he dependent before?"

"As a little boy!"

Maureen appeared in the doorway, and sat down saying she expected her egg was ready. Sharon followed and made for the toaster. Cameron told her to sit down; he'd see to it. There was silence for a moment while Maureen chipped at the eggshell and Cameron occupied the corner where the toaster soon began to smoke.

"Ignore it. It's the seeds from Rudi's fancy bread. They get stuck at the bottom. And if the smoke alarm goes off, ignore that too."

But Cameron turned off, removed the bread and upturned the toaster, shaking it at various angles and banging it against the worktop. Mags wondered for a moment whether he might throw it at the window.

"Let me, love," she said gently.

Cameron let go of the toaster. "I need to call work," he said, and went upstairs.

Maureen put down her teaspoon. "I'm afraid I can't eat this," she said.

"I'll do you another," Mags told her, and Sharon left the kitchen.

"Poor dear Sharon. She's heartbroken, you know, and Cameron's such a comfort."

"Hmm," said Mags, exaggerating her busyness with clattering around the kitchen. "So who's going to win *Strictly* this year?"

As Maureen began her answer she heard the front door close. Her phone pinged: *Gone Christmas shopping. X*

Now Sharon was back. "I was thinking, Maureen. Do you mind if we go home this afternoon?"

Maureen didn't seem to mind at all. As they talked logistics Mags sent a text to warn Cameron. This was partly her fault. She should have stayed home to play the hostess, or taken them out and about. And she should have known that since Cameron was as unlike her as a child of hers could be, doing what she'd do in his place was bound to prove a bad idea.

Now all she could do was make cake and produce more photographs of little Cameron, preferably smiling.

Cameron came back an hour or so later, asked for scissors and sticky tape and disappeared up to his room. Apparently he wasn't going to talk to her. Then, while she was turning the cake out to cool, he carried six wrapped packages down the stairs, dropping two and swearing.

"Nothing broken?" she asked as he came in and set them on the table.

"Nothing I've bought," he said. "Did you make that without eggs then?"

Mags grimaced. She'd gone onto autopilot and cracked and beaten without the slightest attention. Now she strained to hear the comments from the lounge. "I'll get the hang of it." She watched him as he filled the kettle. "Things do change, Cam. Feelings, circumstances."

"I can't do on/off," he said. As if she could? Or was she just being sensitive to keep him company?

"I meant, what Sharon wants might change ... given time."

"Yeah well ... I don't want to talk about it now, Mum. I shouldn't have brought her here, especially with you being up in the air."

"I've landed."

His look was disbelieving. "So no new stepdad to look forward to next time I'm back?" He washed out the cafetière, rinsing repeatedly. "Don't answer that. I want you to be happy and stay that way. Course I do."

"Me too, Cam. Both of us."

"I'm sorry, Mum. I know things have been tough enough for you lately."

"Not as tough as me." She grinned, and lifted invisible weights. He almost smiled. "Sometimes you have to simulate the things you can't really be."

"Cameron!" called Maureen, perhaps from the landing. "I'm getting packed. Are you all right, love?" There was something in her voice that made Mags wonder whether she guessed things she didn't want to know.

"Fine, Gran!" he yelled up the stairs.

"Are you all right, love?" Maureen asked.

Mags sat by the pool shivering, clutching her raised knees like a child. Her damp costume had cooled on her skin but she'd only thought about a shower. She rocked a little as Maureen handed her a towel. She didn't think she could speak, move ...

"The sun's behind the clouds." Maureen looked away to the sky. "Did Jake come home for his lunch?"

Mags shook her head. It was easier. She rubbed herself dry, her movements soon faster and fiercer. Would his sperm have leaked away into the water? The skin on her forearms felt sore as she dried it. Maybe there'd be bruises, or maybe they'd be hidden inside. "Bitch," she heard him grunt, before he pressed his mouth hard to her neck.

"He's a hard worker," Maureen said – as if she blamed her, just like him, for the half-term teachers earned.

Yes, he was hard. And that was her fault too.

Mags denied nothing.

There was so much she might never tell Georgie. She could admit to failing as a probationer because the school was tough and her bottom sets neolithic. That was easier than confessing to the art she hadn't created. There were other things that could only be looked at side-on, and never actually named. But didn't Maureen wonder that day? Crying didn't have to be loud to be visible; any mother knew that.

Mags reminded herself of the present. She had one last evening with Cam before he flew off in the early hours and she had no idea what to do with it but if they were a Venn diagram there must be the smallest sector where they could both belong. Maureen and Sharon's departure was so low-key that if she'd popped to the loo at the wrong time she'd have missed it. As it was, she fronted as hostess to give Cam a chance to hang behind. She wasn't sure anyone would have known how he felt as he smiled and produced formulae. It was only once she'd closed the door that she saw his toned body droop from the inside.

"He doesn't do museums or art galleries," she explained to Georgie on the phone the next day, "the way I don't do anything that makes me sweat. And I would happily have talked, or better still, listened, but he just wanted to watch TV. Which was cosy but still … And now I feel a bit overwhelmed and leaky, as if I got my son back and lost him again."

She told Georgie she would have loved and hated to wave her boy off at the airport but even with a fractured heart he remained utterly and dismissively independent. Georgie said he was sorry and sounded so sad that she said, "Hey, not too much empathy. No overdose please."

Then she wondered whether he had ever tried that: pills, a knife to the wrist like Genevieve. Not Cameron's style, surely.

"I'm glad about the flat," he said, his voice lifting as if to put an end to her suspicions. "But we should go back and look at paintings sometime soon. You could teach me a lot."

"Oh I doubt that, but yes, let's. Before I give in and spend whole days Christmas shopping." She supposed Sharon would wait until Christmas morning to open Cameron's gift but maybe she couldn't. What would happen then? What exactly had his step-mum said to him, other than, *Cameron that's sweet of you but I'm mourning your father right now*?

Not for the first time, Mags decided she didn't like the phone: the person it made her, faceless and unable to touch.

The doubts that person raised. She heard them in Georgie too, the *boy of few words* as Daddy called him.

"Well I wanted to thank you. Let's do some art tomorrow, same time but feeding the soul first."

He seemed glad to agree but still she felt a sadness in him, even when she exaggerated the brightness of her goodbye. Mags wondered how his depression worked, exactly. How much he could override it or pretend, now that he was *much better.*

There was cake to eat and Abida could help her with that over a pot of chai if she rang the doorbell. But there were beds to strip too and a degree of chaos in the kitchen to clear first.

She hadn't had a chance, when Genevieve rang on the way home from work, to frame the story – or the only corner of it that Cam would want on show. She felt evasive and much too casual as she said he'd flown off and wouldn't be back for Christmas. Genevieve seemed incredulous that Sharon and Maureen had visited at all.

"That's freaky! Really bizarre. Doesn't Maureen hate you?"

"Well, I wouldn't say that. She was mostly quite nice, just a bit beaten."

Genevieve asked about the flat but Mags had the feeling she wasn't really listening. Then the way she said, "Mum ..." made her sit down.

"It's about Rudi."

Mags could have said, *"The stepdad you used to worship once"* but she just waited.

"A guy at work told me he's dating a hot young artist. I pulled him up on the word but he claimed he meant hot as in buzz, current, you know? I didn't want you reading it in the *Evening Standard* or something."

"I will never read the *Evening Standard*, Gen."

"All right. And I'll never speak to Rudi."

"Please do, darling. I hope we can be friends."

Mags found her body able to digest the news better than she might have expected. She asked for a name. Apparently it was Eastern European but Genevieve's source didn't remember it. They arranged to meet at the new flat so Genevieve could have what she called a nose around. Mags asked about work.

"A bit manic at the moment but you know me, I get off on that."

"And other things? Boys? Girls?"

"We're all just humans these days, Mum. I'm still celibate. It's much less messy. Speaking of which, are you actually seeing Georgie?"

"I have done. I shall see him again soon. But he's not the kind of buddy my Spam keeps offering me if that's what you're asking. He's just a gift. That's how it feels."

Genevieve was silent a moment. "Sounds messy to me."

Mags supposed it might do, to a daughter, but there was no hostility and no obvious disturbance. Genevieve was stable still and that was a gift too. She hoped she would like the flat, stay now and then, paint her something for the walls.

Ending the call, Mags mixed some reds for hearts – whole, misshapen, halved and cracked – trailing across the kitchen table like a vine laden with berries.

Georgie lay on the bed with his eyes open. The street lights split the darkness through the gap in the curtains. It made a difference that Mags Shaw was out there, in the same city.

If Julia walked in now, she'd be alarmed. He remembered the Sundays when he lay, dressed but unfed, unmoving, his face to the wall – unable to speak when she came in and offered tea, coffee, water, a sandwich, apple, piece of cake. Afterwards he'd say how sorry he was, how he wanted to take the hand she reached out, how he would have shaped the words she'd like to hear if his mouth would only move and the ache would ease. That he couldn't explain why, only how, and that it overwhelmed him and everything around him. "It must be chemical," she'd say. As if life gave him no reason. And now the world gave him too many.

Was it fair on Mags, to begin like this, just because her idea of him was an ideal coloured with pity? It was hardly reasonable to expect from her the openness of a girl when adults had to learn to close in.

The fear could unseat the gladness if he let it, but picturing her – in the café, in the flat where he could be functional and focused, at the station where they had kissed goodbye like children – was warming. It let in more light than the curtains. It was a smile inside.

He rose from the bed and opened the curtains. So much movement! So much life. He would see her again tomorrow.

"Come on, George," said the woman with the cigarette and red lips. Her skin was smoother than Auntie's and her hair was pretty but she didn't look at him, only to one side. "Don't dawdle."

She'd pulled his coat round him and buttoned him up even though the sun was shining. Auntie wasn't rough like this woman but Auntie was cold now and she couldn't hear him. This woman was called Annette and she made the food and the beds when Auntie was too tired. Was Auntie still asleep? He hoped they were going to the park to feed the ducks but he didn't know whether Annette had any bread. Maybe she didn't know about ducks, only ironing and medicine.

"Say goodbye to Auntie," Georgie said, turning back.

"Auntie's gone," said Annette, and he frowned at her because it wasn't true. She was in her bedroom.

Annette was in a hurry. "Time to go," she said, and she didn't sound kind like Auntie. It was nearly the first time she'd spoken to him except to say, "Mind out the way" over the hoover. She'd never taken him anywhere before.

She stubbed out her cigarette on the doorstep and closed the door behind her so hard that Auntie might wake up. Even though she was tired of him, she'd wonder where he was.

"Where are we going?" asked Georgie, his voice small.

"Never you mind," Annette said, and looked at her watch. Her hand around his didn't feel safe.

To begin with, he knew where they were because this was the grocer's Auntie used, and the baker's next-door, and then the conker tree where Auntie helped him choose the fattest, shiniest ones on the ground one day when she was being kind. Now the old ones were mushy and when he tried to crouch and touch, Annette dragged him on. But then they turned a corner he didn't know and passed something that must be a church because it was old and grey and the windows were big.

"Nearly there," said Annette.

The building near the church was tall too, with a yard all around and two doors leading off it that didn't quite match. He looked at it through railings that were tall and black. There were circles and a kind of ladder marked on the ground in the yard but no one was playing there like they did in the park. Annette looked both ways down the street but nobody was close enough to have a face they could see.

"Sit down then," Annette told him. "The children will be out soon."

There was no bench like the one Auntie rested on when he was swinging. He sat on the ground by the railings and Annette looked all around her. Then she took a belt out of her bag. Georgie tried to jump up but she held him down by the shoulder.

"I'm not going to beat you. Just keep you safe so they'll find you and make friends, all right?"

She tied the belt round him and a railing so he couldn't move. Then she glanced back at the red brick walls and all around again. She leaned to kiss his cheek. Her mouth was soft and smoky.

"You'll be all right now, Georgie," she said. "Auntie's dead, see. So she can't look after you and it wasn't fair to ask someone like me. So I'm leaving you where you'll be cared for. The authorities will see to that, all right?"

She didn't want an answer and he didn't have one, but he knew he might cry. Dead was more than gone and sometimes with birds it was red and broken. And he didn't like being left like a man in a fast film strapped to a railway line. All he heard when she walked away was her heels.

19

When Genevieve met Mags outside the new flat after work next day, she told her the area was diverse, with lots of community projects. Shown the interior photographs from the brochure over coffee nearby, she spoke of potential. For Mags, it was just space really, with enough light thrown in, so Genevieve's approval was rather unexpected in its steadiness. Some of her daughter's usual staccato was missing but so, along with the physical restlessness and animation, was her wry smile.

"Has something happened?" Mags asked her as she began to roll tobacco ready to step outside. It didn't feel like the right time to remind her she was going to give up.

"Yeah. Something. I don't know whether it's beautiful if I could only look at it right – or a bit sad and stupid." She licked the paper and placed the roll-up against the sugar bowl on the table. "Dad's having a baby, an unintentional one. For him anyway."

Mags took a few seconds to process it, and how sad it might be. "He thinks he's a rock star. She's trying to trap him or redeem him, or both."

"I suppose he might want a chance to do better." It was said without bitterness. "And I'd love that chance, to be a really cool big sister this time round. Plus I could be ... like ... the voice of reason when Mel tries to indoctrinate her with Creationist fairy tales."

Mags smiled. "You could."

She was afraid Genevieve would repeat something she'd said more than once in relation to her own womb: *"But the world's not fit for children, Mum."* She didn't have much of a counter-argument but she would like a chance too, to be a fun grandma.

Mags tried to make sure the eye she kept on the time was a discreet one but Genevieve finished her coffee and said she must go. Although they walked together towards the tube, conversation was difficult to sustain as bodies divided them and Christmas hits flooded from doorways. Mags held her a long time at the station entrance and felt her girlish thinness in spite of the loose layers of shapeless clothes that would label her a Leftie protester in the tabloids. Her long hand-knitted scarf almost trailed to the ground.

"I'm proud of you, sweetheart," she said as they separated.

"Back at ya!" Genevieve told her, and scuttled down the steps.

This was where Georgie had been heading for a few years now and he hoped that his father would have liked to join the Veterans for Peace who'd gathered earlier around the bend under the bridge. As he sat on the road with the Quakers in their circle of stillness, he looked around at the banners stirring quietly. But his mind's eye was dominated by the Chinook that only minutes earlier had appeared above the Thames, lifting the water into a gathering wall that rolled and spat and thickened the air. Again he felt the menace of it, the brutality of its ugliness and power. Maybe it had formed an unwitting decoy – because as it landed by the dock he'd taken his eyes from it to hear the news of another 'lock-on'. Some younger protesters were blocking the road and holding back the next lorry-load of weapons – which towered stationary to his left with clowns staging some theatre at the wheels. It was the first full week of September 2017 and Georgie was a peace activist at last.

Between the circle – prayerful, meditative, Georgie couldn't say but he wanted to support it – and the lorry, some activists sang. Some picnicked. If there were hundreds of them there must be almost as many police and six of them were mounted. *Don't you dare,* a woman had chalked that morning on the pavement, under an outlined equine head, *use those animals against us.* Georgie didn't know what they intended and wasn't sure the officers did either. In yellow-jacketed lines they said little, their faces impassive. The cutting crew must be on their way to slice through metal and remove those who lay across the tarmac, cheerful but barely able to move with their arms in tubes through padded suitcases. But for now everything felt soft, and the sun, capricious all day, shone on his face as he crossed his arms around his legs and tried to focus on peace. To obliterate the Chinook, but at the same time, never forget it. To believe love could defeat the war machine.

For a few minutes he sat, now squinting, now feeling the cold ground underneath. Wondering how he could return after this to a home, work, a life. How he could watch *Countryfile* or *Mastermind* as if there were no wars in the world and no fat cat governments arming them while the poor scattered in terror or died. Then he became aware, even with his eyes closed, of movement. He looked to the left to see police officers threading through the circle to break it. He heard them asking people to move.

"This is an act of worship," a young man said.

Like defenders marking strikers, the police attached themselves to individuals and pressed. The protesters were obstructing the road, they said, which was an offence. Then Georgie saw an officer young enough to be his son but tall, bearded and fit, standing over him.

"I'm going to have to ask you to move," he heard, somewhere outside where he was trying to be.

Georgie couldn't claim to be worshipping because he hadn't accessed any kind of space that wasn't filled by the Chinook. He didn't know what Quakers believed in apart from peace but for now that was enough. He didn't want to move because the road must stay blocked and the truckloads undelivered. He couldn't just spring to his feet with a polite apology. So he fixed his eyes on the blue in the sky and shut the rest out as best he could.

"Again, I'm asking you to stop obstructing the road."

As he tried to hold a space the police couldn't enter, Georgie heard someone outside the circle pointing out that the road was already blocked by the lock-on. The police made no response. Georgie could tell some of the Quakers were standing and crossing to the kerb or grass but others remained seated. The smell of horse dung on the road grew stronger.

Someone was reading something powerful about war and the seeds of war. A woman asked the police why they were facilitating war crimes. The black-shoed feet beside Georgie had edged closer to his own pumps, his crossed legs and his hands. Now their owner's presence felt more urgent, like his voice when he said, just above Georgie's head, "I've asked you to move. If you don't leave the road you will be arrested."

Georgie felt the tightening inside but at the same time he knew he could do it. He could stay there, untouched however they grabbed or pulled. It was a choice and he had seconds to make it. His legs were stiff; he didn't know how quickly he could stand. Still he looked ahead as if he didn't hear or see anything outside his own conviction – and felt a fraud because he didn't have this kind of faith, only a growing sense of despair.

"All right, this is your final warning. If you don't move you will be arrested."

Georgie stood, rather slowly, and tilted a little before walking to the side of the road. A long-haired girl smiled at him reassuringly but he felt feeble. *Weak,* he heard in his head. It was what the men had always said. It was what he had always been. A few of the Quakers were being cheered and applauded into the police van, one of them older than him by a decade or more, his beard long and white.

Someone patted his back. "Here alone?" the young man asked. He was short-haired and thin, in a T-shirt and jeans. He had the open face of a boy.

Georgie nodded. Trouble always made it hard to speak.

"Peace," said the man-boy, and smiled before he walked away.

The mounted police turned and trotted back around the roundabout that led to the docks and the miles of vast showrooms. He heard talk of a critical mass of cyclists at the other gate and wished he had the stamina to go and see. Georgie stood wondering whether to fetch a coffee or queue for the portaloo, or say hello to the Quaker girl who looked angelic in Pre-Raphaelite style.

Then the cutting crew in black lumbered out of a van, their gait a purposeful kind of wading. Their size and bulk as intimidating as their tools, they could have been cast for a movie as the heavies from a biker gang. Or assassins.

Glancing through the crowd towards the protesters across the road, Georgie felt envy and respect.

Next time, maybe.

Mags arrived first and sat outside the café entrance, soon feeling peckish. He might reasonably expect her to impart some kind of knowledge, rather than fancy and titbits with obsessive slants. She wasn't sure why she'd even suggested this place again when she was more at home with the gracious old National and its pillars and altar pieces, its Rembrandts and Vermeers. *To be cool, Mum! To be edgy!* Kara might say, with that mocking gotcha grin.

She checked the time on her phone; he wasn't late yet. As she looked up she heard her name and Georgie was smiling down on her in that understated way of his that showed no teeth and made few creases. She stood and held out her hands in admiration of his long embroidered denim coat, bright blue legs and red ankle boots. They embraced. His skin, as their cheeks brushed, felt cold.

"You look magnifico!" she cried.

"I bought the tights today," he said. "I have this sad habit when I'm in men's clothes of carrying a list and pretending I'm shopping for a wife. It's got to stop."

Mags could picture that and guessed he was pretty transparent. "You can imagine I'm there with you, telling you how fab you'll look in whatever it is – if it helps."

She patted the seat next to her; he sat.

"Thank you. I'll try that. This is London after all. It was different when I started stepping out this way in the Eighties. I got roughed up one night outside a bar – just a couple of bruises and a surface cut but I was pretty scared, even before they knocked me to the ground and gave me a kick or two. I still have the dreams."

Mags winced, but Daddy had kicked him too, in a way. "That's horrible."

"I kept my weird habits to myself for a long time after that."

"So it must feel good to be out and part of a community."

"Except that I'm not. Not a belonger really."

Mags said she often felt like that and individuality was more important than a tribe. "I splurge when I feel close enough to trust. Otherwise I just lark about and keep the real stuff under lock and key."

"I'd love to lark about," he said, and smiled. "I'd sign up for classes in that."

"Oh, stick around and watch. Mine are free!" She straightened. "Shall we start mooching now?"

He stood. Mags slipped her arm in his and warned him, "I can't do murky anymore. There's brutalism and then there's what-brute-beasts-we-all-are-especially-me. Let's be inspired."

He smiled as if he might be inspired already. She told him how much she'd enjoyed the Georgia O'Keefe retrospective and that Frida Kahlo was a bit of a goddess, adding that she found herself drawn these days towards the domestic. "Rudi was appalled by my sentimental leanings but I think it's healthy to prefer a child with a dove to a Spanish war zone."

Georgie agreed and asked whether they'd find any Rudi Shaws on the walls.

"He wishes!" She decided not to mention the impending exhibition at Tate Britain. "I think he'd choose to die now if he thought that would speed things up." Mags grimaced. "I say stupid things."

"We should probably joke more about death," said Georgie. "It'd take the sting out."

Mags suggested that was mission impossible. They talked, in between paintings, about people who'd died too soon, and discovered a shared love of Bowie.

"He made it OK to be weird," Georgie said.

"But no one makes weird as cool as he did." Mags realised that might be misinterpreted and told him, "Present company excepted," her arms including both of them. "My Genevieve said a few years ago that she wanted to be dead by sixty-five. It wasn't a dig at me. She meant it."

"I get that. But what if some of us only start living in our sixties?"

"Presactomundo. That's my plan. Must make a start!"

Mags was aware of what lay in store off the next gallery, but if Georgie wasn't, she should warn him.

"We're heading for the Rothko Room," she said, "and it can blow your head off if you're not prepared. But maybe even more so when you are."

"Explain?"

"I probably shouldn't. Words, you know? Mine wouldn't be right for you. And I love that about it."

She could see he was excited now and pictured the dead artist shaking his head at her, saying, *You've been and gone and done it now.* Georgie followed her into the room and she wondered whether he felt the same intensity – spiritual and visceral. A knock-out assault that was really an awakening.

Huge canvases surrounded them with their layered darkness, some of it bleeding through vivid colour. Mags remembered Rudi bringing her and talking technique when all she felt was grief and a desperate kind of love that was bigger than theirs. Glancing at Georgie, she told herself not to butt in. The silence felt cooler and thicker here.

He stood with his back to her. Suddenly she realised he might be over-sensitized, too vulnerable for this, that no clinical psychologist would recommend it as treatment. She couldn't protect him now; it was too late, even if she tried to usher him on.

"Is it too much?" she ventured, as she drew closer at his shoulder.

His eyes widened and he shrugged his shoulders, then exhaled deeply, but kept staring at the walls. "It's like being at Stonehenge."

She nodded. Not that she'd ever been, even though Rudi said soon after they met that she looked like she danced at twilight beneath the stones.

"I think tomb, and womb," she murmured. "But not doom?"

"Yes … there's a life force too. But what is it? Hope, or just creativity?"

"Same thing!"

He smiled and she was glad he could. They moved around together, saying no more, and she resisted the anxious impulse to check his face. But by the time she looked, to suggest without words that they left, she saw it was streaming. He wiped his cheeks and eyes with his knuckles. Mags reached for a hankie but it wasn't very clean. She pulled a face.

"It's OK," he said, and grinned. "I do this." It was a boyish kind of self-mockery but she hoped without embarrassment. "Thank you."

Outside the Rothko Room everything seemed bright, the air clearer. They talked for a few minutes about other works but Mags could see he hadn't fully emerged yet.

"Rudi kissed me in there," she said, "on the forehead. And do you know what he said? *It's only art.* At the time I thought it was a joke but in a way he meant it. He's got the talent but that's nothing, not in itself."

She saw Rudi's expression shift as he emerged from a place she knew.

"Julia said something similar to me, about a film that had the same sort of effect. *It's just a movie* – which means, grown-ups are supposed to know the difference between reality and make-believe."

"Perish the thought! If I couldn't suspend disbelief I wouldn't bother. Shakespeare didn't write Lear just for us to sit there admiring the language and noting staging decisions. He meant to rip us open. And quite right too."

"Ripped by Rothko," he said, smiling.

"Yeah, better than Seduced by Shaw."

As they walked on, the talk focused on the artworks – although once or twice Mags only twisted up her nose as if they smelt bad. With art there were always so many reminders – of the last time she saw it, of another work or artist, of someone who resembled the subject of the portrait, of something else that had once provoked the same sort of response. But she offered him a few technical terms, delivered with the appropriate – if overcooked – accent, just for the fun of showing off and presenting herself as a caricature. He seemed to enjoy the show.

Mags wondered whether she should be inviting him to take the microphone more often but she knew how much Genevieve hated being prompted to do that when she was quiet. Although hungry, she suggested another room where there was a new exhibition that sounded intriguing, reassuring Georgie that as a member she could get them in free. Although the artist had a Russian name and looked like a pro dancer on *Strictly*, she told him she wouldn't hold that against her. Although she supposed there was a chance …? She reasoned that there must be dozens, all equally *hot*.

"Just so you're aware," said the young attendant at the entrance, "they're filming just now."

The space was emptier than most, and seemed at first glance to be a muddle of textiles, sculpture and painting, the colours ranging from bleached to mottled. Mags had a feeling Genevieve would feel more at home than she could, but it was intriguing all the same.

Around a corner, cameras and sound equipment were focused on a coppery blonde with angular cheekbones and immaculately-decorated eyes who managed to make a skin-tight black dress classy. In heels she was tall enough for the catwalk.

Opposite, in presenter position, Rudi was dwarfed, just a little crumpled the way he liked to be. He'd lost weight. Shagging could do that, she remembered.

She could feel the concern in Georgie's eyes as she looked from a few metres' distance at the two of them, separate but intimate, chatting while the crew prepared. They weren't interested in who, among the punters, might have walked in.

"Let's go," she heard, and felt Georgie's hand in hers. Its size and warmth were a surprise. Nothing tentative about the way he held her. A moment later they were on the steps downward.

"I wish they still had that slide," she said.

"I did it," he told her. "07. In those days I mostly wore trousers in public."

"I went down it too! Rudi was moderately aghast but the twins were mortified." Mags resolved not to say that name again, not to think it. She would have dismissed the idea that seeing him like that could change her composition.

"We could have bumped into each other any time."

"Yes, a lot of bumping goes on in the art world, apparently."

He squeezed her hand. She didn't want the evening to be rerouted but she knew her next sentence might be the one that broke away and fell. She put her right hand to her mouth.

"Maybe you should let it go," he suggested gently.

So she cried and he hugged her.

In the Indian restaurant the red wine and spices soon left her rosy. Crowded and noisy, it felt safe. Mags appreciated the anonymity and colour as well as the food.

"It's funny," she said. "It's meant to be *real men* who make women feel safe, with their muscles and control-taking."

He bulked himself up at the table, face as well as body. "I don't know what you're insinuating."

She chuckled. "I thought you needed lessons in larking about?"

"I must be a fast learner."

He asked about Cam, Genevieve and the twins, and she admitted to trying to shed anxieties. "They wear away at my innards and leave me flimsy. A tissue woman. And I want to be oak. I've got the grooves for it and I'm sprouting bark in all kinds of places."

Mags thought that must sound selfish, or at least like the kind of detachment he wasn't capable of sustaining, but he nodded eagerly.

"People taking on other people's pain, that's a kind of overkill. We have enough of our own," he told her. "That's why I don't want you to carry mine."

"I may have reached my limit. Like a Roman soldier with his kit on his back, in case of uprisings to be suppressed."

"Or bridge building."

"That's you, counsellor. My bridges tend to nosedive."

Remembering her strategy, she told him she'd written down some questions at home and he must give knee-jerk responses, no edits or framing. He looked a little alarmed but she couldn't find the paper in her bag. Coming across her phone, she turned it off. A precautionary measure.

"All right, let's wing it. The dead person you'd most like to invite to dinner?"

He turned a ring on his finger. She wondered who gave it to him and why. "My mother. And father. And yours ..."

Mags scrunched up her napkin. "Veto. If Daddy comes I go. And at your party I'll be there." She sang, *"To love and comfort you."*

"You meant famous people. Eric Morecambe."

"Good choice. He'll bring sunshine in his smile." But did Georgie want to talk about the parents he didn't know?

"I'm bracing myself," he said. "Next?"

"First thing you grabbed whenever you had to move on as a child?"

"The rabbit you gave me, with furry grey ears that were silky pink inside."

Mags opened her mouth wide. Somehow she'd forgotten, but now she could feel those ears between her fingers as she swung Twitch beside her. "Have you still got her?"

He shook his head. "I wish. Twitch disappeared when I was about twelve. Someone probably thought I was a cissy and needed an air gun instead."

"I gave her to you because I loved her best."

"I know."

She forked in another mouthful of daal but it might have to be the last. She wasn't sure whether she owed him some fun

180

or whether probing was better, to help her understand. "All right," she said. "First love, apart from Twitch?"

"And you."

"And me." She smiled and waited, sipping wine. "Was it Julia?"

He shook his head. "Olivia Newton-John. Until *Grease* broke my heart. I wanted her pure."

"That's cheating."

He shook his head. "It felt like love to me. I kissed her poster and stroked her hair, and she always kept on beaming that beautiful smile back at me."

Mags pictured him, teenage and lonely. She supposed he was aware that almost every answer he gave carried sadness with it. Did she dare ask for a recurrent dream? Suppose, like hers, it was of a car driving away? Although lately she'd been more adult than that, dreaming not of sex but what at school they called snogging. If ever a word deserved to be outmoded ...

"All right, I am compiling my dossier – and collecting Christmas present ideas, very useful." She grinned. "Thank you for being so kind. When I rattled and croaked, I mean. I don't usually, not like that. I haven't ..." She offered the remainder of the bottle but he gestured that it was hers. "I suppose you can keep elbowing down the waste in the wheelie bin but in the end if it keeps piling up it'll spill everywhere."

Another smile. Once Kara had said, "Can't you talk like a regular person now and then?" but in the absence of a body of artwork, Mags chose language with colour. She could see Georgie liked it as much now as he used to, long ago.

"Just because you're funny and individual," he said, "doesn't mean you can't be sad. And as a counsellor I have to tell you that elbowing down is not a healthy tactic. Better to root around and investigate – especially the manky stuff. Look at it, touch it, name it."

"Sounds unsavoury to me."

He shook his head. "Just real."

"The by-product of life. Which in my case really does contain a lot of waste. Wasted time, wasted love ..."

"You don't believe that."

Georgie looked so full of faith that she said she couldn't, not with his eyes on her like that.

"Good," he said. "It's what I tell myself. Nothing was ever for nothing. Pain's an effective teacher."

"I'll have to be a better pupil then."

The waiter came to see if they'd finished. As he'd cleared the plates away, Mags checked the time and grimaced in alarm.

"You need to go?" he guessed.

"I'm ace at sleeping but I need a lot of it, or I end up ..." She smiled. "Like this. Hyper."

"I hadn't noticed," he said, and she wasn't sure whether she was being teased or flattered or he was just straighter than he looked.

They split the bill and walked back to the tube in niggling rain but with no umbrella in either handbag. Mags felt separate now, the weather and the people coming between them as they dodged both. Since they would be using different lines heading in diverging directions, she knew when they arrived down the steps into the station that this was goodbye.

"I thought it couldn't be as nice as last time," she said, "but it was nicer. Apart from my outburst. And even that was ..."

"Necessary?"

"Probably. You're lovely, Georgie Stroft. Thank you for a fabulous evening."

"I could do my Jane Austen and assure you, my dear, that the debt of gratitude is all mine."

She grinned. "See you soon?"

"I hope so. I need to find some questions for you next time."

"Revenge eh?"

They stood a moment, smiling, before she leaned in for a hug. It was quicker, but firm, and she realised she already knew how it felt to hold him, as opposed to Cam or Simon. She almost missed his cheek when she tried to kiss it, but he was on target and his lips were surprisingly soft.

"See ya then!" she cried, chirpily, just in case …

"Oh no!" he cried, hand to his forehead. "We forgot that selfie for Facebook!"

She thought for a second that he meant it, before he smiled. They waved a pace or two later and she slowed to watch him from behind as he disappeared down an escalator. A sweet boy still.

She hoped he didn't think it was a different kind of love. Or knew it needn't be.

Georgie rarely allowed himself a glimpse at his reflection on the tube because the face it offered back was provocative as well as diffident, and in the glare of night-time electricity had something pre-death about it. Tonight he was drawn to the glass in the hope – the assumption – that all this had remodelled it. That like an artist she had made of him a better portrait. And yes, there was colour, a kind of gleam. His eyes were full of living.

Smile if you had it last night. The T-shirts and badges used to shame him. But maybe this was what it meant – which only showed that people talked a lot of what Mags would probably call cobblerdash about sex. When people opened into each other, like two tributaries into a river, the power could carry anything along.

He should have told her, and asked her too, but he would write.

20

He'd composed the first few lines on the journey home. Georgie turned on the heating, wrapped his dusky blue robe around him and found his cartridge pen.

Dear Mags,

Such a lovely evening full of things I hope not to forget. Thank you. A generous child grew into a kind woman and I felt treated, respected and cared for. It's a good feeling and I'm holding on to it now I'm home. I didn't want to spoil things so I didn't warn you that I'm going away the day after tomorrow, just for a few days. You may remember that I told you about my godson, Troy. He's getting married between Christmas and New Year. We didn't get away together this summer so he suggested a short break in the Cotswolds. As usual his father is probably as jealous as his mother is grateful but once Troy is a husband I don't suppose it will happen again. His partner, Shakespeare Davis (rather gloriously, that's apparently on the birth certificate) is shy but sings jazz and makes him happy. This brings me to a kind of proposal.

On my e-invitation to the Town Hall on 29th December it says, Uncle George and friend, although Troy knows that my only really meaningful enduring relationships are with him and his mother. I'd be delighted if you'd accompany me. I wanted to ask but was worried it would seem presumptuous, pushy, insensitive or just too soon.

I wish I could write like you. Your letters talk to me. I think that growing up I used to read more than is healthy. It was a substitute for living but not feeling. These days it will be video games, which won't teach anyone about clauses or semi-colons, or much about compassion. Oh dear, Mags. I sound like an old man. I must ask Troy what can be done.

I would love you to meet him. But please be your honest self. I'm not sure I'm Oak Man but contrary to appearances I'm not really tissue. In the meantime I will send you a postcard. Thank you again for being such wonderful company. I smiled all the way home.

Georgie xxx

He closed the curtains and wondered whether he would sleep better than usual or not at all. Her openness thrilled and challenged him but he wasn't sure he'd match it, however much room she gave him. There were things he'd rather guard: flames of a sort. They'd singe things and leave the taste of ash in the air, just when she needed to breathe in deeply.

Georgie addressed the envelope and found a First Class stamp. The blood test results were a relief, of course, but left him with a mystery. Perhaps his body was only the outward expression of what happened inside, in which case he would soon be jogging.

The message from Kara came through so late that Mags wondered at once whether she was drunk and/or desperate, so it was no surprise to read the first bubble: *I've had it with Simon. Not sure I can forgive him this time.*

It was followed by: *He's not coming home with me because he can't manage a night without sex.*

And ended: *So selfish. What am I supposed to do? See you tomorrow Mum. x*

Tomorrow? Mags was sure she'd said 10th, not 8th. Supposing, although she never seemed to remember for sure, that Cameron might be in the middle of his day, she sent him a cheery enquiry about the weather before she realised climate change took the fun out of heatwaves. It was a fortnight since she'd passed a garden that boasted tall white gladioli, and decided that although boasting was what gladioli did, no one could blame them. No wonder young people either slit their wrists or partied as if there would be no tomorrow. *Hugs,* she told Cameron, and added, *As George Harrison said, All Things Must Pass.*

"It'd be nice if Cameron cared that I'm broken," Genevieve had said, in those days after the incident. "*It'd be nice if I had a brother.*"

But these things were never really fair. She supposed he detached because of the life she gave him but he cared now. As if to prove it, he sent: *I guess I should take that from someone who knows. You're up late. Hope it was fun. I am busy at work which helps I guess but pumping iron is better. I won't let go though. Take care, Mum. X*

Thank you. I will. Xxx

She should have said George Harrison didn't necessarily mean love had to die. The rain had eased but everything was clingy and a little heavier than it should be, and under the hood of her jacket her curls dripped. Afraid Rudi would occupy her dream space, she blew out and felt shaken by the memory of what Daddy would call making a scene. She had to outdo Georgie's tears, didn't she? Such a show-off. Maybe Daddy was right about that bit.

Now she felt so tired that even the last few yards gaped ahead and weighted her limbs. Rediscovering Georgie was bound to be emotional; running into Rudi somewhere in the art world was nothing short of inevitable. Combining the two was a kind of excess and she'd gone in without protection.

She hoped Simon knew better.

"Is it me?" Mags asked her mother in the kitchen.

Although the window onto the garden was closed, she kept her voice low, but her mother looked nervously out to the seat where Daddy sat with all the movement of a garden gnome but no smile and no colour. His loose flannel trousers were charcoal, his cardigan grey and his shirt a washed-out camel with no tie, but inside them all her father was rigid.

"No ..." her mother murmured indecisively. "Not entirely. No, dear! He hasn't settled ... adjusted, you know?"

"To retirement? Isn't there a Test Match to watch?"

"Well yes. He's listening on the old radio," her mother said, glancing out of the window. "He's not good with ... it's all the changes, really. We're getting older, Maggie. He hasn't the strength to do the things he'd counted on. By the time he's cut the lawn ..."

"It's like a bowling green."

"You know what a perfectionist he is."

Mags remembered he was never satisfied with the groundsman's idea of grass cutting when he was too busy and important for gardening. Had he lost weight? His face, stiff in profile, had edges that were never so sharp. She could have called his skin sallow, but perhaps that was the light.

186

"But he's sulking because I'm here? Because I'm with a leftie poet who hasn't had a short back and sides since he was nine? Because I don't send him handwritten letters on Basildon Bond, begging forgiveness? I'm here, aren't I? But I can't bring Genevieve, not into this. She wants a granddad but she's scared of the dark as it is."

Mags knew her volume had upped but her father was as stony as the lions he'd wanted for the gateposts at the headmaster's house. Her mother arranged the tea things on an old tray they'd had for decades. No cloth she'd crocheted now, though. Mags remembered giving one of those to Georgie to wear as a hat, and Daddy being so cross anyone would have thought they'd burned it on the fire with an Apache war dance. She used to love doing those down the end of the garden where she couldn't be seen.

"You could take him a cup of tea," her mother suggested. No confidence, just a thin hope.

In her head she could hear him: "I'm not going to stand here and take that from you, Margaret." She never knew whether her mother's memories intersected with hers or floated alone.

Her mother was extracting digestive biscuits from a packet. She put two on a plate and stirred two sugars into a cup. Real china. Did they keep any mugs in the house? She supposed they were a threat to civilisation as he knew it, probably implicated in the fall of the Empire.

Mags sighed but took the tray. Her mother opened the back door for her and she negotiated the step down. It seemed too chilly out there for sitting motionless just to make some kind of point. She saw the thinness of his hair exposing freckles or moles on his scalp. There were more on his hands, which made fists by his side. In the days when she needed him to love her, she would have told herself not to be afraid. Now she felt resentment. After all this time, couldn't he bring himself to turn his head, and nod if he wouldn't smile?

"Daddy," she said. At once she was a child in trouble again. "Tea up!" she tried, trying to be jovial as well as Northern. She heard one of the commentators cry, "And that's another one heading over the boundary!" but she couldn't even tell whether the runs were scored by England or the enemy. Close-up his face looked bonier, his nose dented by his specs, but his expression was simply intent as he leaned away from her and down towards the old radio beside him on the seat.

"Good news or bad?" she tried, but now he had firmed again, showing her more of that straight, narrow back. He was like the cardboard butler she'd seen through someone's window, life-size and well painted but minus organs. "Nice to see you too," she said. Nothing. She placed the tray on the grass. "There you are then. If you're going to talk the hind legs off a doughnut I'll go back indoors for some peace and quiet."

He'd never found her remotely entertaining, even when Gramps and Grandma thought she was funnier than Tommy Cooper. As she turned away, she found her shoulders rising and falling and a loud, tense sigh escaping, but presumed he was too enclosed to hear.

Reaching for the back door she heard, "Did you spit in it?"

Her own shoulders set now. "What?"

He was cardboard again; not so much as a muscle twitching in hostility. Mags muttered that she thought she heard something but it must just have been some rubbish blowing in the wind. She stepped inside. Her mother reached for her hands and held them both a moment.

"Is it dementia?"

Her mother shook her head. "Not the slightest chance!"

"Just hate, then."

"No, Maggie, don't say that. How can I explain? Sometimes people are so … disappointed."

"Tell me about it! That's the ninety percent. Aren't you?"

Her mother frowned. "Why would you think that? Because I didn't have a career of my own? You know I think women's lib was no great shakes. I've always been contented in my own way." She poured two teas. "And I hope you are. You should have brought Genevieve. If she'd skipped out he might have …"

188

"Thawed? Could you guarantee that?" Hadn't Mummy more or less said this was a habit? "Will you write me a letter? Tell me about it. Help me understand – this, him. Will you?"

She could see her mother thinking, but what? "Maybe I will." She lifted the lid from a cake tin like a magician. Mags smelt her favourite ginger cake but it looked a little black at the edges. "Do you remember helping me mix Sneezy Cake?"

Mags nodded. Her *a-choos* used to be very panto when the dried ginger was tipped into the mix. "Not for …?"

"You know he won't eat burnt offerings. But I think it'll be all right if we scrape a bit."

"Too right. Thanks. Make mine a large."

Her mother smiled and took her at her word. She began a few stories about people Mags used to know, mostly told with pity. Then she fetched the atlas so Mags could show her where in the world Cameron might be. On that subject she shared as little as possible, because little was all she'd been told. All the while she was sure her mother was equally mindful of Daddy in the garden with his cricket and his biscuits, and once or twice she caught her looking. But what was she expecting to see?

Her cake eaten, Mags embraced her mother and said good-bye. She didn't bother to wave through the glass, but in the hall she reminded her to write.

"She won't," Dan told her that evening, and Mags slumped with dismay but already she knew he was right.

After her shift at the food bank, Mags filled her trolley with food Kara liked, adding to the pizza, pasta and peanut butter a gorgeously variegated poinsettia for her window sill. She cleaned and made up Kara's bed, listening to Radio Four but thinking too, about the two boys she wouldn't see for Christmas. Feeling what she used to describe as grotty, she sat down for a rest and hoped what she read on the thermometer wasn't a temperature, because she couldn't remember what – in new money – that was. Then a text told her mid-afternoon: *Staying another day for a party. See you tomorrow.*

"Great!" Mags told the poinsettia. "That'll give you enough time to die."

When Georgie's letter arrived the next day she read it twice, sneezing and sniffing for punctuation. She messaged him to wish him a lovely break, realised she would miss him and wondered what his plans for Christmas might be. Not that she could ask without the query being misconstrued. Would he talk about her with Troy, who sounded adorable? She tried to imagine what he might say, picturing them in front of a log fire with mince pies in one hand and a brandy glass in another, while snow fluttered down outside.

Around lunchtime Kara had to bang on the door because she'd lost her key. She was knocking again by the time Mags made it out of bed and down the stairs.

"You look terrible! No hugs – I don't want it thanks."

Mags made way for her bags and was told not to worry, she'd sort herself out. Kara said she might have mentioned being infectious.

"It's just a cold, love." Kara didn't seem reassured. "Hangover? Or still cross with Simon?"

"Yes! What are parties for? And yes. He deserves it."

Kara looked wan, her skin over-scrubbed and sensitive. Her hair, unrestrained by the usual straighteners, reminded Mags of a time when she wanted plaits and Mummy did her best but they ended up bendy as well as wiry. She helped carry the various bags and boxes upstairs, which involved considerable sniffing with no free hand to wipe her nose.

"Mum, gross!"

Mags drew her attention to the poinsettia, wondering whether it had stopped flourishing already. With little response she said she'd go and put the kettle on.

"Actually Mum, don't worry. I might have a nap."

So Mags did the same, waking a couple of hours later to find Kara wide-awake, perfectly made-up and perhaps a little agitated.

"Sorry, love. I just crashed out. You look as if you have a train to catch!"

"A plane! But not just yet. Dad's got some artist friend who owns a villa in Tuscany …"

"Not Russia?"

"Don't be like that. She'll be in Russia. But you're invited. Two whole weeks out of the grey old UK. Simon's going – with *her* tagging along, obviously. Go on, Mum. Gen's probably going to Dan's for Christmas Day. Don't stay here on your own."

"Abida will be here." It was all she could think to say. Kara was flushed with excitement she didn't want to crush.

"So you won't consider it?"

"I can't see how, Kara, really. And flying is killing the planet. Your father should know that; I've told him enough times."

Kara huffed through her nose. "It's not about that. It's about you and Dad. He wants to be friends. Civilised, amicable, you know? It'll be like a crowd, a party."

Mags could tell Kara had given up on her. As she began to explain that she had to be around as a buyer, that she had commitments at the food bank, she was interrupted.

"All right, I can see you're not going to think about it. I'm just off for a drink."

"Now? What time is it? I was going to cook."

"I'll grab something out. Don't wait up."

Mags did ask who she'd be drinking with and where, but the answers were *friends* and *pubs*. She reminded herself that during term time she could switch off anxiety quite successfully but she wasn't sure how. Left alone with a quick kiss on one cheek, she wished she could call Georgie, but he'd be in the Cotswolds by now. All right. Deciding instead to call the architect of the scheme, she had to leave a message on his Answerphone.

"Hello, Rudi. It's kind of you to include me in the Italian adventure but I have plenty to keep me here. You wouldn't want me to lose the flat. I need to be available for Genevieve if she decides to stay here, and Cam should he change his plans, which is very possible. I was planning to have Abida round. And … I have a life I need to live." She hoped that

191

didn't suddenly sound as emotional as it felt. "You know I can't be myself on these machines. Have a lovely time, y'all. But I don't think I'm going to fly any more. Genevieve is afraid for the future of the baby – Dan's. Not sure you heard that news? But I know you don't want to hear negative stuff like that and hey, it's nearly Christmas so let's party on."

Oh dear. She waited a moment, but nothing more composed presented itself so she ended it there.

Time to find the decorations. Maybe she could make a tree, a recycled one from junk. It could be beautiful. But she needed to pop some pills first, and go back to bed.

Georgie freshened up for dinner. The hotel wasn't what most people would imagine for a break in the Cotswolds but it was cheap and clean. Troy had chosen it because the beds were wonderful for a godfather who found it hard to sleep, which was thoughtful, so Georgie tried not to wish for anything cosier or more traditional. There had been times when they'd shared a twin room, equally amused to imagine what the staff made of them, but nowadays Georgie would wake at a turn, a cough, a tiptoed trip to the bathroom. With Troy glistening opposite over a meal, or walking with a waltz-like lift and eager pace to his steps, he felt old, saggy and tired, but glad too – because Troy was in love. Yet Troy chose to be with him for these three days, and he wasn't quite sure what he had ever done to deserve it – apart from understand when the boy's own father didn't want to try.

There was a jaunty knock on the door. Troy smelt of sandalwood. His Brideshead phase over, he wore a short, studded jacket and narrow red trousers that were almost leggings. His hair was shaved up to a sculpted bloom. Without a godfather in a skirt, he could pass for coolly straight, but arty or showbiz. Not that he tried.

Georgie was glad to be told he looked stylish himself. They walked the corridors, chatting about what they might do the next day, depending on the weather. Georgie said he really didn't mind. He would have liked to walk around here in autumn but his legs weren't as strong as his wishes. Instead they soon reached the restaurant.

"Have you called your mum?" he asked as they waited to be seated.

"Yeah, she's fine."

They both knew Julia worried about Troy's driving and Georgie might admit she had reason, but then he was of an age to prefer life slow. The woman striding towards them in uniform looked a little perturbed. Her eyebrows were verbal as she delivered a neutral, "Table for two? Are you both guests?"

Somewhere ahead as she escorted them to a table, someone male was laughing. Georgie recognised the tone of it, but if Troy registered it too no one would know. Once seated, he suggested something sparkling, and Georgie said, "Why not?" just as another outbreak of amusement, louder than the first, obliged the waitress to tilt her head with a, "Sorry, s ..." It wasn't the first time someone had recalled the *sir* and he was ready for the *madam* although the word seemed to him to have sarcasm built in.

"I see the Neanderthals are in," muttered Troy when she'd gone. "Do you want to go somewhere else?"

Georgie shook his head and said he was sure they'd get over it.

"They might need help with that." Troy unfolded his napkin. "Have you phoned Mags?"

"I tried. Her phone was off. I hope she's not ... I'll try again. I want to be sure she's OK." He told Troy briefly about the blonde Russian at the Tate. Troy knew of her work because Shakespeare was a fan.

"But he doesn't rate Rudi Shaw by the way," he added. "If you don't mind me saying, Georgie, this Mags stuff is a bit ... full-on. Like she's shot to the top of your Christmas card list ..."

"That chart's too short for any shooting to be required."

"All right, point taken. You're selective." Troy smiled. "I'm not jealous. I want you to meet someone. Mum's always hoped you would. But Mags Shaw's been married three times, right, or had kids with three men anyway?"

"Oh Troy ..."

"I'm not judging her. As if! I'm just thinking about stability ..."

"I think I also need a spark under all the dead leaves ..."

"That makes a fire!" Troy grinned. "I mean passion is incredible, right, but ..."

"I don't want her like that. It's not ... how can I tell? It's been so long, I hardly know any more. It's not madness, heat, obsession ..."

"You sure about the last bit?"

The Prosecco arrived and Troy opened it and poured.

"Here's to you and Shakespeare," said Georgie.

"Thanks. I can pay for the bubbles ..."

"No need," Georgie told him. He came across as obsessed? Of course he did, but how to explain? "I love her," he tried. "I loved her all those decades ago."

"That's sweet," said Troy, gently. "But do you know who she really is now, as opposed to the person she was then? I mean you can't have caught up half a century over two dates."

"Not dates. There isn't a word for them." He drank, and picked up the menu. "But I know her."

"I'm glad for you, Uncle Georgie. As long as ... well what if ..."

"She knows me too. That's enough."

A waiter came and asked whether they had decided, which Troy did by reflex. Georgie hesitated before ordering risotto minus the cream and butter and agreeing to the chips Troy was sure he really wanted.

"I don't want her to hurt you, that's all."

"She won't. She couldn't."

Troy nodded. "All right." He glanced down the restaurant but the noise from the four not-so-young men wasn't laughter now. One was swearing at the other.

Georgie tensed. He sat upright as a bulky, short-haired man bundled not very soberly in their direction, muttering,

"Fucking perverts," and spitting as he passed. Conversations paused around them.

Troy turned. "Hey! Manners please."

Georgie laid a hand on his arm. "It's all right. His problem." The manager appeared only to watch the man walk out of the double doors onto the car park without a coat. Georgie breathed deeply. It had been a while but things were changing and it wasn't progress. As Troy began to relate an incident Shakespeare had heard about from a friend, he looked at the manager and waiter, pretty much whispering. He wasn't sure where they might be allocating blame. But soon their food appeared, brought by the woman who'd greeted them with her eyebrows.

"Sorry about that," she said, almost casual. "Enjoy your meal. If the others can't behave the manager will call the police. All right?"

They thanked her.

"Most people are good," he told Troy as she left them, hoping that majority included the guys at the back, who were inaudible now.

"My Shakey is," said Troy, and speared a chip. "He's a serious soul, you know? And he's read the climate science and we're heading for total catastrophe. Like, 4 degree temperature rise, cities underwater, food shortages, millions dead. He's a rebel, you know with XR? Got me involved, although I haven't blocked any roads yet. He says there'll be mass civil disobedience all over the world. To make the governments listen and do something fast."

Georgie looked up, astonished. Not because he hadn't assumed the expert consensus was right but because no one talked about it, not the BBC or press, and certainly not Troy, who'd been a party animal for a while.

"Sorry. It's not Christmas kind of conversation," Troy continued. "But you're not going to argue with me?"

Georgie shook his head. In his head a glacier crashed to the sea. But he couldn't allow it, not now. "I'm sure your Shakey knows what he's talking about. I hope he's right about the civil disobedience. I might have to join in."

"He says knowing's not enough. You have to take it deep into your heart. I haven't yet. But I've taken him." Troy placed a hand on the organ in question.

"I know. I'm happy for you."

Georgie didn't know if he could function with a truth like that embedded in his heart, but he was proud of this Shakespeare and Troy too. Whatever happened to humanity, love would still matter. Maybe love would save them. He could ask Mags, except that he didn't want to carve out the same kind of wasteland he felt stretching out inside. It reminded him of a Christian chorus he'd been taught in his teens: *Can it be true?* And he supposed it must be, even though the world didn't want to admit it either.

He was looking forward to the wedding.

21

Mags woke feeling disgruntled, with a damp pillow and a hot body. She was tired of this now. She was tired of this room, with its wooden clock, show-off shelves that tried to float, art deco rug that wouldn't stay still, and absent paintings haunting the space. Hearing Kara retching in the bathroom, she winced, climbed a little unsteadily out of bed and decided coffee was more urgent than a shower.

Her phone rang almost as soon as it woke.

"Georgie! Excuse my incoherence. I'm horribly lurgified but I think one hungover daughter might swap with me just for now. How's it going?"

He said she sounded full of it, which reminded her of Dan's decreasingly fond refrain, with variations: "You are *so* chockfull of shit." But this was Georgie and he was sympathetic, asking whether she'd been to the doctor, recommending Echinacea, honey ... "I'll be right as reindeer any moment," she told him. "How's Troy?"

When Georgie said he was excited about getting married, Mags could hear him smiling. He told her places they'd been, some of them on-the-water and some of them sounding like a setting for Murder in the Vicarage, but she interrupted with sneezes. Asked about her kids, she dodged, "I'll tell you when you're back and I'm more socially acceptable."

"Not good?"

"Not great."

She would have liked to tell him that she'd never felt more unwanted and less desirable. More comprehensive in her failure. But that would be pathetic, with very low entertainment value, and selfish when he was holidaying.

"You sound sad."

"Just a sorry specimen." She thickened her voice into the kind of cartoon cold people used to call in sick. "Say hi to Troy."

If he could see her, he'd know, she thought as she said goodbye. Or was that thought a variation on Troy's romantic fantasy? He'd hold her, and she'd love to be held. Although she must be almost as toxic as the *Daily Mail* just now and shouldn't be allowed into anyone's world.

Kara didn't wake until the afternoon, when she put her head round the bedroom door to say she wouldn't come too close if Mags didn't mind, but she was off to get some animal products and would need to be reimbursed.

"Have fun," Mags said, hoping her voice didn't sound as weak as it felt.

"I was thinking of staying with Gen for a few days, seeing as she's not coming with us. I just don't want to be ill in Italy, you know? And Abida will keep an eye on you."

"She will, and she appears to be germ-proof." Mags sneezed.

"Good plan!" she called after Kara as she hurried downstairs.

Dear Georgie,

I'm hoping this will get to you before Santa. Daddy must have waited until I was asleep and then knocked back the brandy and mince pies Mummy left out for St Nick in the middle of the night. For someone who thought himself a cut above the hoy paloy, he was painfully conventional. I wanted

197

to tell the twins it was all just dressing up fun but Rudi said that would be tantamount to a crime against childhood. Another conformist underneath the hipster bravado. I'd rather be honest but people feel safer with pretending. Why is that, counsellor? You don't, of course, but you're controlled too. That's what they call tact. There was something you weren't telling me about your stay, and yes, there are developments here that make me a bit weedy but let's be open with each other. We can withstand that. It's different as a mum; the kids can't deal with too much deviation from the norm the ads offer – a huge, clean, shiny kitchen and a neat mother with perfect hair. I should know.

I have a suggestion and it's very forward. Outrageous really. Only it depends on Genevieve.

Mags crossed the new paragraph through. That would be tantalising for him, reading it, but by that time she might know.

It's kind of you not to hate Daddy. I wish I didn't. I hate hatred. Genevieve used to hate everything and everyone for a long time before the breakdown but now she's much more tolerant – and patient with me. Maybe it was a phase like pre-loading before clubbing; now she's virtually teetotal. Unlike Kara. Can't young people learn from our mistakes instead of having to make their own? I call it wilful.

You don't blame your parents either and I think that's beautiful, especially since you have more to resent. One or both of them must have been sweethearts. I reckon your dad was a passionate, gentle man who felt very guilty about his infidelity. Your mum is harder to imagine but I bet if we knew her story we'd be able to understand. I don't believe in sin; getting it wrong is in the species D and A, but most of us never mean to. That's my excuse anyway.

You haven't told me about the other foster carers and I suppose that tells a sad story in itself. I just want you to know you can. Don't let me monopolise the blurting and splurging – you can do your share. I've been thinking about my mother and how she bore it, and I reckon she must have loved me! But maybe with Daddy she managed the kind of loving that

*accepts and endures anything in order just to keep doing it. I
don't know which thought makes me weepier! That's what
being ill at (nearly) Christmas can reduce me to.*

*This brings me to love. I may be an expert on this given my
three 'husbands' and a couple of other men in between them.
Yes, I know I haven't mentioned those two. Got to save some
episodes for later in the series! Sex with five men is a total
Kara will probably exceed by the time she's twenty-one but the
point I'm making is that it was always love with me. At least,
according to some emotional definition that might not be
universal. The best way I can explain it is a kind of invasion
of self. I don't want to breathe independently but in sync. It
feels like harmony with the natural world and the known
universe but at the same time it's heavy (man) and to offset
that I goof my way through. It was way over the top with Jake
but I loved that drama until he hurt me and even once he'd
started, I loved the reconciliation, the renewal, the relief, hope
and even faith. So with Dan (ignoring Jeff and Karl for now)
I aimed to rein it in, act the strop as well as the clown and
make it clear I wouldn't take any shit. I tried a lighter kind of
love that messed about and didn't buy into intensity but I
loved the fun we had. It wasn't very sensible in the early
years. Dan's a graduate of the Rolling Stones school of life –
and man oh man, would he take that as a compliment!*

*Rudi was meant to be the love to end all loves. The grown-up
marriage. The proof that I can learn from mistakes. He'd had
too many women to remember but not many relationships of
any length and of course the implication was that he was
wedded to his art. Until he betrayed it and went for a separation, a financially beneficial one. I find it hard to forgive him
for that and I never pretended I didn't mind. I was meant to
be glad he'd committed to me and a family instead but I so
desperately wanted him to achieve greatness. Genius even –
why not? Compromise is giving up. I need better than that for
the people I love. And I love him very much.*

*I didn't know that's still present tense until the leggy Rus-
sian and I don't want to be taken over any more. I want to
leave room for me. So I'm sixty and an ex again, and I can't*

get this loving right. Not even as a mother. Ask my four. No, don't!

If love is an open door, sometimes you get it slammed in your face and sometimes you have to heave hard to close it. Even when it's wide open, there's no knowing quite what's out there, what the weather's going to do, what you'll need to take with you. And sometimes when it's wild and woolly you just want to withdraw, curl up and give up until things settle. Open doors are scary – so many possibilities out there. You invite love in and it can outstay its welcome, empty your cupboards and trash the place. It invites you, and once you've crossed the threshold you may find you're a prisoner. I love you, Georgie, but I don't know that as a so-called mature woman I can make as good a job of it as I did when we were small. That's all.

Maybe it's the jollop talking. I'm dosing myself up with syrupy cures. And I'm feeling a bit surplus to people's require-ments which may be the price of the independence I was aiming for.

I miss your kindness. See you soon.

Mags XXXXXXXXXXXXXXX

Given the closeness of the post-box, and a reluctance to ask Kara to use it on her behalf, Mags put a coat over her pyjamas and slipped bare feet into trainers. She hadn't realised it was raining. Preposterously, it cranked up from drizzle to half-hearted downpour more or less as she scuttled down the path, and at the post-box a passing van splashed the pyjama bottoms drooping over her trainers. Growling privately deep in her throat, she gave up on speed and slouched back with water running down her face. This was exactly the sort of behaviour that sent Jane Austen women into potentially fatal fevers and she was right out of smelling salts.

"I don't want to," she told Dan, when he appeared naked to join her in the bath and didn't really need to say he was *horny*.

Ignoring her, he climbed in, grinning. The water level rose to risky heights.

"You can't possibly mean it," he said, and blew a fragrant bubble from his chest. He pulled her to him.

"I told you what Jake ..."she began, even though she hadn't, not in full.

"Screw Jake!"

"There isn't room in this grotty old tub. You'll flood the place."

"Kevin Costner doesn't let that stop him in that movie you like."

Sending a wash of water slopping behind him, he was reaching his arms around her when she began to heave herself up.

"Mags ..."

"Not like this. You know why."

"I'll make you forget him." His tone was only amorous but it felt like a threat. He tried to kiss her; she turned her head away.

"You'll make me hate you," she warned, and this time he didn't resist as she stood.

She pulled at the towel and made a shawl of it. He submerged his long, thin body with a sudden slide that spilt more water. In the bath it almost reached his mouth.

"Will you ever forget that git?"

"I hope so. I want to. Try to understand." She saw he was no longer aroused but disappointed, hurt. Not his fault. Not entirely fair. "The associations, the memories ... they're right under the surface."

"Don't be a victim, sweet thing, or you'll despise yourself."

Did he mean he'd do the despising? She glanced at herself in the steamed-up mirror, glimpsing only the redness of her skin. She wiped the glass with her hand. She wasn't really young any more.

"I'm not. I'm asserting myself. Not in water. A forest maybe."

"We're in London, Mags." His voice told her he was loose again, warm, ready to be funny. Not like Jake at all. "You might as well say the Antarctic."

"Kitchen table? I like a soft bed myself. Tonight if you're good."

He surfaced with a smile. "Hey, I'm on a promise and I like to think I'm always good!" He reached out an arm to touch hers. "I'm sorry. I get it. No more watery advances."

"OK. Good." She watched her own smile and decided it was quite convincing. "I hear the Antarctic is the new Benidorm for a getaway."

"Yeah. Let's put on a show for the polar bears." As she rubbed herself dry enough to leave the poky bathroom for their slightly less mouldy bedroom he added, "But maybe you need counselling. Get Jake to pay."

Mags didn't answer.

"Or Daddy."

This was a sleek, arthouse bath, and big enough for a small-scale orgy. Mags sneezed and thought about bed and a hot water bottle. Decades when therapy and age made a difference. But if she ever needed a counsellor she knew one now and he'd make her feel whole. Georgie Stroft was the wounded healer. She liked that idea.

22

When she called Genevieve two days later, with a small, scratchy voice, Mags deduced from the laughter that her two daughters seemed to be cohabiting successfully. Passed over to Kara, she told her that Simon had rung and sounded tired, prompting a sardonic, "Go figure!", but had no news to share about Cameron. When asked, she said she was getting better thanks, even though she could understand why Kara responded, "Sounds like it!"

She told Kara that Abida had brought her oranges. "Presumably the house smells more Mediterranean than your Tuscan villa will manage. My nose wouldn't know."

They were all packed, she was told. Simon and his girl-friend would arrive in twenty-four hours' time ready for a flight in the early hours. Suddenly Kara softened and asked whether she'd be all right.

"I'll be there to keep her company," called Genevieve, and took back the phone. "When I'm not at Dad's. That all right, Ma?"

"Fine and dandy," said Mags, and smiled.

Nobody asked whether she'd seen Georgie. Nobody seemed to consider him relevant, which made it easier because she'd have to admit that barring a Facebook message wishing her better, she'd heard nothing since sending her letter. Too much about love, perhaps – because he didn't love her the way she suspected, or because he did?

She didn't want to get this wrong, for his sake – because he needed love, deserved it. People would tell her to cool off and let the intensity level drop. Perhaps that was how Georgie was counselling himself. But she didn't want him to think she'd cooled any more than she wanted him to imagine any heatwave.

Still no Facebook messages and no texts. She decided to shrug off her pyjamas and pull on an old sweater and leggings, but her nose saw this as a cue to run just when she couldn't reach and staunch it with her head inside a polo neck. Dressing was one hurdle she could clear on a short-term basis but the prospect of housework seemed to raise her temperature. Perhaps a good book …

What would Jake say if he saw her now, a sloth in polyester but minus the charm – and leaking and erupting uncontrollably? But alive.

She hadn't bothered with emails for days because they were mostly Spam in another folder, or messages for Rudi from people who didn't keep up. Opening a collection of a hundred and twelve, she saw georgiebarkle@ some provider she didn't know and the message header *In case of delays in Christmas mail …*

Dear Mags,

What can I say? I loved your letter. It opened up so many thoughts and feelings that stayed with me, like some of your words, around the house and on the street. As an emotional soloist most of my life I want to understand more about love – familial as well as romantic. I sometimes think that having no children preserves the child in me, which could be tragic or exciting depending on how you see children. I love the way the world of the imagination is as real for small people as the visible and tangible. I have lived a lot of my life in books, suspending disbelief, while you have lived. I see you as strong and wise as well as honest. I am all theory.

I read an article online, from one of the less trivial and bile-fuelled papers, about the four key questions for humans in relationships of any kind, sexual or otherwise. Here they are, as remembered but possibly not as printed. 1) Do you see me? 2) Do you care that I'm here? 3) Am I enough for you (or do you need me to be different)? 4) Can I see in your face that I'm special to you? The article points out that for a dog in a relationship with an owner the answer is always yes (except that no, dogs don't need their human to change) and that made me emotional. No dogs in my life! How stupid. When we were children, our friendship meant I could have answered YES to every one of those questions and I am more grateful for that than I can say. But you owe me nothing. I don't want you to feel sorry for me. My admission to the sadness in me isn't an appeal to be looked after, I promise.

You don't say what's happening at Christmas and I know it will be painful this year; I shall think of you and send you good vibrations. Then I shall see you for the wedding unless you change your mind, which you must feel quite free to do.

Georgie x

P.S. I hope you are out of bed with a healthy temperature but if not, and you need shopping or hoovering done, please do ask.

Mags read the second paragraph again, slowly, in an attempt to commit the four questions to memory. At the same time she visualised Rudi, and herself with her eyes on him as she asked them. No. Not really. No. And no. Which was not enough, and should never be, not for anyone.

But what would Rudi answer? Perhaps the same. Maybe the door was only ajar, not open. People knew when they'd fallen from someone else's pedestal.

Georgie, what a revelation. I am not grieving or broken. I am free. Thank you. Yes, I am regenerating! Yes, I am coming to the wedding. Let's be BFFs (not to be mistaken for FFS) and make each other happy if we can. That's what love is for. And yes let's see each other soon. We really SEE each other!

Genevieve is coming to stay on Friday night. Once that would have scared me. Now it doesn't and that feels like serious joy.

Happy Christmas.

Mags xxxxxxxxxxxx

Announcing to the kitchen that she felt galvanised, she began a Christmas plan involving lentils, nuts, beans and tofu, lots of good coffee, an acute political play if London could accommodate any, *Dr Who, The Secret Garden, Fawlty Towers* and card games. Genevieve could shuffle like a pro at seven, which was about five years before she started smoking and nine before she frayed her wrists.

The first photographs from Tuscany appeared on Facebook with skies that were surprisingly grey. Simon's girlfriend Gayle looked washed-out and sleep-deprived, her attempt at a smile half-hearted. But Rudi was the wide-mouthed host, central and beneficent in a cricketer's knit and black drainpipe jeans. Most of Kara's other pictures were of the interior of the house, which was so beautiful Mags could almost taste it.

She found herself recalling the scent of basil and ripe tomatoes, realising her sensory imagination was courtesy of the supermarket shelves, when Cam called.

"Mum? How's the cold?"

"I'm calling it flu but I'm vertical again, part-time anyway. You sound ..."

"I'm on cloud nine!" She imagined him in shorts. She hadn't seen his chest for years but it must be impressive. "Sharon called. She's flying over, just after Christmas. I can't believe it. I mean, I asked her, but I didn't think she'd get a flight. I didn't think she'd try."

Mags stifled a hallelujah and asked about Maureen.

"She's staying with old Golf Club friends. Sherry on tap! Mum, I had to tell you. I haven't felt like this ... well, ever. And if she wants the spare room, and, you know, arm in arm and no more, that's still amazing. To be with her, that's enough."

Mags nodded, not trusting herself to speak.

"Mum, you there?"

"I'm happy for you. You know the kind of happy that's not quite dry? Of course you don't, you're virtually an Australian male. Be kind to each other. That's way more important than sex anyway."

To be with her was enough. Oh joy. She told him to hold on to that and wished him a wonderful Christmas.

"Cammy," she said. "OK to come in?"

He didn't answer. She couldn't hear any sniffling. He was face down on the bed with one arm around the heavy articulated lorry she picked up from the charity shop. His hair was growing again and she counted on Dan never to suggest it needed cutting the way Jake used to. In fact Dan's was long enough for pigtails and she might try that one night, at jaunty angles.

"Is it something that happened at school?" She sat on the bed and stroked the back of his neck. Eight years old, nearly nine. Dan said she shouldn't baby him. He rolled over and looked at her, his face puffy.

"No."

"What then? You had a good time with Dan at the park? You two look like best buddies to me these days."

"I don't like his smell."

Beer? Fennel toothpaste? Weed? Mags wasn't sure what to do with that but dismiss it as his imagination, even though other children had a bigger supply.

"When's Daddy coming back?"

He hadn't asked, not since the first week after they left. Pained, Mags didn't know what it meant. Was it fear, or a perverse kind of need?

"He's not, Cam."

She waited. He would adjust eventually, wouldn't he?

"All right," he said. "I want to play tennis."

"Great idea! Tennis was my best sport at school." Truthfully, that was table tennis, but she would have upped her game if she'd spent more time hitting the little white ball and less sitting on the corner of the green table chatting with a friend, keeping one eye on the field the teacher would have to cross to check on them.

"I want to play tennis with Dan," said Cam.

She nodded. Sometimes Cameron was see-through but sometimes she couldn't follow his inside track. It was like a Scalextric to which no car could stay attached. "I think that can be arranged," she told him.

Dan was no sportier than she was but less likely to hit Cammy a softie to whack. No need for hurt, even if that was what Cameron intended.

"I can paint something cool on your new bedroom wall if you like. Dinosaurs maybe, or funkadelic creatures from another galaxy." She'd had a few ideas, sketched them on a ring binder and hoped Dan would smile.

"Why?" Cameron sat up. "I want my room red for Arsenal."

"All right. I'm sure that could be arranged too." Jake's team. Some things he didn't forget.

"Does Daddy know where we are?"

"No, Cam."

He pushed his lorry off the bed and made a gassy explosion of a noise as it rattled onto the carpet.

"I saw Dan kiss Anne-Marie," he said, without looking up.

Mags laughed. "Of course! Like the French do. I kiss her whenever I see her too. She's our friend. You like it when she babysits."

He nodded. "I stay up late."

Anne-Marie had no children. She said she didn't want any, or a man either, but Mags didn't really believe her.

"She's practically an auntie," she added.

"But not a real one," said Cameron, and pushed the lorry so hard it rebounded off the wall.

When the estate agent called to say he hoped contracts could be exchanged in the first week of January, Mags asked to drop by with a tape measure. If this was her last home before a large one with a staff of carers, she would have it just the way she wanted it.

In the meantime there were more presents to buy. She was rather grateful to Genevieve for loathing mince pies because last year her home-made pastry had been so thick that Rudi and the twins had scooped out the filling and left the rest behind, as if eating oysters. Best of all, there would be no turkey to apologise to as she invaded its privacy. She hadn't quite got round to investigating nut roast recipes online but knowing Gen, she'd probably want something Mags couldn't spell.

Every list she'd made before the flu felled her was in hiding, there wasn't a trace of sparkle around the house and she hadn't sent a single card, mainly because this year they would in fact be single cards, minus Rudi's indisputably beautiful signature.

She messaged Genevieve: *I have decided to strip down Christmas. No meat, no drunkenness, no money wasted on stuff nobody needs. X*

And no fucking plastic x was Gen's reply.

She'd never claimed to like a challenge and that seemed a fairly large one but worthy of the attempt. When she called in to measure up for curtains at the new flat, she put a pencil, rubber and fat black pen in her pocket. It wasn't a plan, exactly, just a seed that sprouted as she walked from the tube station.

Three hours later, she stopped drawing and looked – long and slow, like the fans at a Rudi Shaw exhibition. An extended murmur of a look. If she'd blocked it out mathematically the fit could have been no better, and it took her to where she was: the next and last new start. The estate agents wouldn't check and even if they did, there was nothing that couldn't be erased. Not yet. About to leave and lock up, she stole a photo on her phone, just in case, and was about to send it to Georgie with a caption: *Timeline* when she changed her mind.

Instead she told him: *I had a creative splurge at my soon-to-be new abode. Might go back to ink it in tomorrow. Time I took artistic risks! M x*

Wow! x

Hope you'll say the same when you see it. BTW I have an idea about communication. Let's exchange one email per day and you can unleash Jane Austen. I will burble, cry in words and make jokes to offset. How does that sound? M x

Wonderful, my dear! I eagerly anticipate your first epistle. G x

Georgie hadn't anything particular to do on an icy day with visible blasts dragging hair from faces and unsettling Christmas lights. Maybe he'd get in first. Seeing Troy always brought Julia back, and a sense of gaps and disconnections smoothed over with good manners and kindness that made him both grateful and frustrated.

Dear Mags,

I thought I loved Julia because of what she didn't do. Your father wasn't the only one who related to me like a headmaster to a hopeless schoolboy who needed comprehensive rebuilding whatever that took. Without ruling out electrodes to the brain. Julia had manners. She could have been a vicar's wife. There was something old-fashioned about her – no swearing, make-up or tight man-made fabrics. I knew she felt

209

pity but I thought she accepted my fractures and foibles. I'd told her I preferred women's clothes – more colourful than her beiges and taupes, creams and greys – but I was working. In the evenings I'd swap my suits for a bath robe and slippers. It was really only at the weekend that I'd wear a skirt and blouse at home.

Then there was a day off. She was at the library. I wanted to surprise her with flowers when she came home, and the afternoon was warm. I only had to cross the road to the high street and I felt ... I was going to say the call of the wild, which was really the same thing as freedom to be myself. Ten minutes later I was home again with a palette of alstro merias and nothing more bruising to report than a couple of funny looks and a "Lovely, darlin'!" from a biker in black at a crossing. I felt a shaky sense of achievement and I wanted to tell her straight away so it didn't become a sneaky secret.

She looked frayed when she came home. She saw the flowers in the vase but only in the way she'd see an unopened letter from the bank. She didn't embrace me when she said thank you. I said, "I didn't change when I went out" because I could see that if I didn't tell her then, it would grow between us. "I know," she said, and didn't look at me. "You were seen."

She said she didn't want to talk about it because she didn't want to say the wrong thing and hurt me when she knew it had been a hard thing to do. "It's a hard thing to hear at work, from a regular in front of colleagues." I didn't ask who or what. "I never meant to humiliate you," I told her, trying to touch. "I know," she said. She was never angry or accusing; she tolerated people without effort. When she headed for the stairs I asked her to stay and talk about it but she said she couldn't, not yet. We spent the evening in separate rooms and when we did meet in passing she pulled a taut smile that was meant to reassure and only alarmed me.

I think it might have been easier if she'd hated me for it but I didn't realise, not until eighteen months later when she left me, that it was herself she despised – for not being sexy or glamorous in the world's eyes. For being the kind of woman other women pitied or looked down on, with a husband who wasn't a real man. In exposing myself I'd exposed the self-perceived inadequacies she'd lived with. We both cried a little but I understood.

She said she still loved me and felt bad about letting me down. I suppose that's why we've stayed friends, so she could make it up to me. And she has. I couldn't have stayed for ever with a wife I'd mortified and reduced. I think she found what she needed in Troy's father. These days we'd call him an Alpha male. She wears lipstick now, and skirts that fit fuller curves, but she's still a gentle woman. When she made me Troy's godfather I felt moved and profoundly grateful. Hers is not your feisty kind of loyalty but then even as a child you knew yourself and didn't apologise for being Mags. Bravo – a word that sounds like courage, something most of us habitually lack.

Now we have both written about love. We've faced up to its flaws and kickbacks as well as our dependency, one way or another. That's the human condition. Thinking about your Simon, in love for the first time, I wonder whether, if it turns out to be that rare, lifelong kind, it could make him a smaller person, closed in and limited by love. How, with such great fortune, could he understand the crises and heartbreak of the world? But perhaps the truth is that it's harder for someone like me to imagine that kind of happiness.

Julia is the only person I've slept with. There. I said it. The older boy in one of the foster families made me unzip my trousers and called what he saw a worm. For weeks he'd leave worms in my room, shoes, pockets to remind me. Words. I love them but I admit I fear them too. Not yours, though.

I plan to make some mince pies for when Julia calls round on Christmas Eve. She'll miss Troy this year because he'll be with Shakespeare as he should. I hope Genevieve will make you happy and vice versa. Like you I have a good neighbour. Winny is from Namibia and too creaky, as she puts it, to go anywhere, so we'll pull a cracker or two and wear the paper crowns. She left during the South African occupation because she was dating a white boy active in the anti-Apartheid movement. Such stories on our doorsteps! She's seventy-one

now but her childhood remains vivid with elephants and
some days it's just what I need. She'll be delighted to relieve
me of any mince pies Julia leaves behind.
I am in good spirits. Thank you.
Georgie xx

Mags could have replied at once, vilifying the Worm Boy and
marvelling at Georgie's forgiveness, but it was all too delicate for jumping in with both wellies. Sex with one other
human, who failed him ever so kindly! None of her men could
live without it for three months, never mind thirty years.
They'd despise him. Jake would suspect, stare, mutter
abuse; Dan would turn him into a performance poem; Rudi
would find his a life hard to credit and a species he couldn't
identify. As if promiscuity and sexual harassment were
easier to believe in, and a lot more normal.

People should take more care of the people they loved, deep
down where they were most rawly themselves, and that
meant forgetting their own rawness for a moment or two,
just now and then. Like Georgie did.

But maybe they shouldn't have explored love quite so surgically. Perhaps she should reroute to favourite albums.

"Mum!" she heard, picking up her mobile which announced
Genevieve. "Can I come to you after work tomorrow? Mel
doesn't want me around, apparently. Never did. Dad has
about as much spine as a mollusc. So I'm not going where
piercings and tattoos make me some kind of Devil worship-
per unfit to hold a baby."

"Oh, Gen. Don't let her ..."

"She has."

Mags tried to offer pregnancy to excuse Mel but Genevieve
was too wired for listening. "Anyway, love, tomorrow night is
fine, but leave the fags at home – for me? Substitute chocolate; we can binge on it. You can't allow a silly remark to
undermine the balance you've found ..."

"She's unbalanced."

"Well, quite possibly, by hormones ..."

"But it's Dad who kicked me in the guts."

"I'm sure he didn't mean ..."

"Don't stand up for him. And don't push me, Mum."

"All right, love. See you tomorrow."

Dan never wanted to come round to talk crises. He preferred to avoid such a word, as if it was a female exaggeration. Until she found the old-style razors, he'd always said, "She's a teenager, Mags. This is what they do." Spread on her sofa, he said she'd no right to turn cop when she bounded up to search Gen's room. She would only alienate her and drive her underground.

"Have you seen her wrists? Or her legs?" she asked. She'd been looking for drugs – not the joints Gen could get from Dan himself during the weekends she spent with him and any woman who was around, but coke, crack. Now she tried to remember the last time their daughter had worn anything with long sleeves, or a skirt. She mimed cutting her own skin.

"Why would she do that?" Dan murmured.

He looked helpless, as if suddenly emptied of all his blag and wit and theories.

"She probably can't tell us. But a professional can help her find out."

He picked up a cushion and threw it down again. "Can't we just talk to her first, Rudi too? I mean, overreacting won't help. I know what you're like."

"All right, I do, better than you. But let's try wisdom here." She offered him coffee and he followed her into the kitchen. "Don't duck this, Dan. You know she's in turmoil. This ... it's about dying. That's where it leads."

"No. Don't say that. She's experimenting. That's what ..."

"I'm not going to lose her to an experiment that went wrong."

She had to hold him then, because he was crying – from above, where his shoulders softened and sagged. "Our baby," he murmured. "Our little girl."

Mags stroked the hair down his neck. "She'll be all right," she said. "It's O.K."

On the noticeboard behind Dan there was a drawing Genevieve had brought home from school when he was a full-time daddy, mounted because the teacher had displayed it and awarded her five merits "in one go". It was of a whale leaping out of starry water and Genevieve told Miss Green that the whale was dead and trying to find a way to heaven. That was why the water had red roses on the surface, for blood.

"We just keep on loving her, without judging and without understanding either." She felt him nod. "She'll try to shut us out but she'll know we act out of love."

That was three days before Gen rolled up her sleeve at the doctor's surgery and showed the livid grid, the skin around it white but swollen. It was a hashtag of red before hashtags were born, ringed by wristbands of rubber, wool and leather. Her arm extended like a challenge, Genevieve didn't speak but her eyes brightened before they looked down and away.

The following Saturday morning when she left for Dan's, Genevieve was pale but glowering, ignoring the stepdad who'd insisted she let them all see the "Nothing!" she hid. Mags watched her embrace the twins, her goodbyes for them only. Comprehensively ignored, Mags felt Rudi squeeze her hand as if to say, *hold on,* but Mags couldn't think for imagining.

Georgie, I am not ignoring your beautiful email. I have read it twice. I have thoughts and feelings about everything you tell me. But Gen is upset and angry and I can only think, just for now, about how I can be a better mother this time round. Winny sounds wonderful.

Mags xxx

23

It was a while since Genevieve had arrived with a holdall rather than a tasselled or studded handbag. Her thick black eye-liner reminded Mags of days that in Gen's case had been as dark as she looked. Not for the first time, she thought how appalled Daddy would be. Little did he imagine that Cam, the son of "that oikish lout of yours", would turn out to be the grandchild he'd approve. But then Cam had the look of a boy who'd been to his snobby school and earned his colours at Rugger. Genevieve had spent a lot of her youth looking dangerous.

Mags boiled the kettle, concerned by the way Genevieve spun the coaster back and forth.

"So you're off now until …?"

"Day after Boxing Day. I might quit."

"But you liked the job …"

"The novelty's worn off." The tone suggested that line of enquiry was closed. "It's a holiday. Let's drink ourselves stupid."

"I thought …"

"I was clean living? Don't panic, I am. I'm not turning into a pisshead like him. She'll leave him before the baby's a year old and I won't blame her although I won't forgive her either."

Mags told her to sit down, drink her peppermint tea and tell her all about it. Genevieve said Mel had blocked her plans to spend the next couple of days with them and had already appointed godparents for the baby, mentioning *people of faith* and *stability*.

"I mean, what does she know about how far I've come and how hard it's been? You'd think Dad would be proud of me."

"He is, Gen." He used to be, of her attitude, and then of her recovery. But that was when he used *conventional* as a term of abuse.

"She's banking on saving his soul. He jokes about everything but he's a spineless wuss. And I think – this'll shock you – he's cheating on her."

"Oh, shit." Would he have cheated with her if he could? She didn't rule it out.

"The baby would be better off with me. I'd love her properly."

"Of course you would!"

Part of Mags believed that. Could Gen be any less ready than she'd been herself, at nearly ten years younger? This daughter of hers was a teen-woman with the kind of history the tabloids owed celebrities for their headlines, and all that experience must count for something. She offered food but Gen said she'd eaten.

"She doesn't think I'm good enough."

"You are!" More truthfully, no one was, Mags supposed.

"I only ever hurt myself." Genevieve's anger was losing its edge and Mags recognised the timbre.

"I know." Mags laid a hand on hers, feeling the coldness of the fist of rings. "Dad knows. No one will stop you seeing your sister. I'll talk to Mel ..."

"Don't. She's jealous of you."

"Jealous?!" Mags blew out through her nose. She realised that had made her smile.

"She threw a hissy fit about that dinner you had together the other week ..."

"She's no need. I have no designs ..."

Genevieve drew a pack of tobacco from her bag. "When he's been drinking he thinks he can pull anyone."

"This lady ain't for pulling!"

"Not even by Georgie boy?"

"I'll have to ask you not to smoke indoors, Gen."

"All right, all right, I'll put my coat and hat and gloves back on and get hypothermia."

"As long as it's not catching!"

"Ha!"

Banter was heartening in its way, but evasive. Mags hadn't worded any update about Georgie for any child of hers who asked, or even for Abida. The only clarity she could muster came from what he wasn't, it wasn't and they weren't.

She would have used Cam and Sharon as a diversion but she'd been in trouble before for sharing with one child fresh developments in the love life of another without permission. Gen said she'd already seen the photos from Tuscany but expressed no feelings, not of envy or disapproval.

"I might go up." She stood and yawned. "Don't worry, Ma, I'll remember Nina Simone. I'm practically in love with her."

Mags smiled. When Gen first took up the habit, she used to play *Don't Smoke In Bed* in the evenings as a hint, until one day the CD went mysteriously missing and turned up years later under the seat of the sofa with some pound coins and fractions of Bombay Mix. Then there had been nights when she didn't come home, and the possibility of her being swallowed up by an inferno was just one of many horrors to keep a mother awake unless sex with Rudi stole them away. "You're a bit of a rock," she told him. "And roll, I hope," he said.

Genevieve's fingers itched around the roll-up. "'Night, Mum. I'm sorry Rudi turned out to be a jerk."

Mags shook her head. "He wasn't a bad father, or husband, or man. Just ..."

"A crappy artist. These days anyway. I used to think the sun shone out of his paintbrush."

"These days that delusion is mainstream. It's practically a pandemic!" Mags had made Genevieve grin but it felt disloyal, cheap. "Maybe he's doing his best work and we're the only ones not to see it. I hope so. I hope it makes him happy."

Gen shook her head and said Alisa Vasnetsova was interesting. "But of course I hate her on your behalf."

"No need. I'm fine and dandy." And not remotely randy, she thought, which had felt true until she'd come to Rudi's defence, and little shards of evidence for her testimonial broke in with light and warmth to back her up and leave her sad.

Maybe Genevieve felt it. When they hugged, she was slow to let go.

"Love you, Mum," she murmured. "This is better than Mel's or Tuscany."

"You akidding me, bella!" It was an impression of the Italian manager in a coffee shop round the corner but not one he'd recognise any more than Genevieve could. "No contesta!"

Dear Georgie,
It's after midnight anyway so call this Christmas Eve in embryo form. Baby Christmas curled up in the womb in a

217

Santa hat waiting to be born and blowing a party popper.
Does that sound irreligious? I'm not really. I'd love there to be
a God that makes us better people and I could probably do
with one of those myself. I suppose Daddy gave religion a bad
name because he believed in God but had no faith in people.
We haven't touched on this, have we – or politics either? Scary
stuff. I did note your peacenik badges though. Good on you.
It's time I stood up for things I've always believed in, in a
horizontal, sometimes mouthy way.

Genevieve is troubled. It's about self-worth, or the need to be
valued by others which is probably the same thing unless
you're made of granite. She isn't. I hope I can make her feel
loved. I have to be prepared to absorb some of the emotional
heat but I must be working towards immunity by now.

Who would have thought that of my four children, the one
with an obsessive addictive personality – and rings through
various holes in that baby flesh I wrapped against the cold –
would be the one I understand best? Not Cam, my stand-
alone hunk, or the twins who might as well have been born
with phones attached. That may be the latest evolutionary
development: little keyboards on palms and Sim-cards for
brains. My twins are so normal by current middle-class
cosmopolitan standards that they sometimes seem beyond the
reach of my imagination! They're super-smart but they're
mostly hedonists. I guess anything else would tarnish the
future that's so much bigger than the past. Spot the differ-
ence! The past is with us; it clings, it intervenes, it tries to
dictate terms and we have to put it back in the corner of our
consciousness and reclaim the present. Redeem it, maybe.

Whereas Gen... she breaks my heart because she can't seem
to help breaking her own; it's what she means by living. And
even though I bounce a lot, I get it. She feels the world's pain
– prematurely but acutely. She's the soft one and I can't
protect her but for a few days I'm going to try.

Anyway, Georgie, Christmas is beginning and I have a
proposal. Will you come to lunch on Boxing Day? Can you get
here? I hope so. I think you have a bike!
M X

She pressed Send without checking because otherwise she would doubt her instincts. Genevieve would understand, even approve. What was the point of any of this if Georgie Barkle was home alone at Christmas?

Done.

Georgie opened the email early the next day, even before he processed the date. Moved by her thoughts about her children, he found himself detaching from the page before the end. Valued. Self-worth. A past dictating terms. They were echoes that resonated in consultations as soon as clients unlocked what they feared, and she wasn't the only one developing immunity. But there was more here, more than she knew because he hadn't told her. He'd never told anyone at all.

Julia cried out. The sound made him run, sweat. But she'd locked the bathroom door. He tugged at the handle, calling her name – urgently, then softly – asking her to let him in. The noise she made changed from a groan into a wail that shook, rattled.

"What? Darling …" A word they didn't use in their friendly marriage. "Open the door."

A pause. What he heard was more of a whine, staccato but low. No footsteps. The handle turned and he saw her holding the hem of her full skirt, her leafy favourite, up above her knees. Blood smeared her thighs and calves. She let it trickle. He watched as the privacy she guarded was surrendered without words. Behind her the toilet seat was splashed with red, and in the pan …?

Julia's body folded in against his, her skirt falling. "Don't look."

Over her shoulder and head on his, he tried to see. And the world's words, the kind that accompanied a ladder in tights, a missed bus or a spilt drink, passed through his head: *Bloody hell.*

"It's dead," Julia blurted.

"I'm sorry," he said, and stroked the hair that curved tight and sleek down to her ponytail. "I'm sorry."

Twenty weeks. Should she go to hospital? He had never felt such warmth burrow into him from her body. She wanted this baby now, after all.

Pulling herself away she turned to the toilet. "Can you see it?"

"It's just blood. I'll flush it away ..."

"No!" She stood looking down the pan. "The baby's there. It's so tiny it's like an amoeba. Hardly human!" She cried quietly now.

Georgie held her to him, wondering, needing to see and know but afraid. She was the one who checked in baby books: charts, diagrams with measurements. Why didn't he know?

"I'll call an ambulance," he said.

He thought she'd argue, but instead she began to reach for toilet roll, wetting it under the tap and rubbing at the blood on her thighs. She moaned as it broke away into pieces that dropped softly to the floor and lay there, sodden and pink, until he threw them into the toilet bowl and flushed.

"You need an ambulance – don't you?"

Julia turned from the pastel trail on her legs and shook her head. "No!"

"All right," he said. "All right." *Cry baby,* they used to sneer. Did she need him to be a real man? It was hard to tell and he'd learned to do his sobbing inside where no one knew. *My child*: it sounded there, like a priest with a hand of blessing on a head.

He didn't know whether they needed A and E. What could anyone do now? "Bed rest," Dr Cartwright had said, and she'd calmly taken a pile of books and a flask of tea with her. Julia didn't panic. She relied on the sensible thing, and that meant sidestepping drama.

"I'll call a taxi for the hospital," he said, and she didn't contradict.

He offered to run a bath but she didn't answer, so he turned on the taps and shook in some scented bubbles, swishing the water with one hand. Looking round he saw her stooped and holding herself, arms crossed like scaffolding. She never undressed in front of him, not unless she turned her back – which was pretty, girlish and lightly freckled. Now, though, he helped her, lifting her blouse over her head, unfastening the hook on the waistband of the skirt, and she submitted, still crying, wiping her nose with the back of her hand. Arms pressed across her breasts, she might have been shivering with cold but it was June. The baby would have been born in late October; he liked Autumn for a girl or boy, but Julia wanted a name that wouldn't stand out from the rest. *My child.*

She'd asked him, not long before the wedding, "Would you rather be a woman?" and he'd reassured her that there must be a spectrum of maleness and he was some way towards one end – while Rambo, he supposed, never having watched the film or anything like it, was at the other. It was the day they'd made love for the first time, and she'd said, coyly, that in her opinion he was closer to Rambo on that spectrum than he realised. And he smiled at the thought that worms might be underrated.

"Are you still getting cramps?" he asked her as she stepped carefully, almost nervously, into the water.

"I don't know," she said. "It hurts."

"All right. We're not taking any chances. I'll be back when I've called."

"I'm not going to drown," she mumbled. It was so unlike her that as he made for the phone it worried him a little. Then she called after him: "You'll change?"

He stopped. Did she mean that without his child he wouldn't want her? He'd embraced the pregnancy sooner than her. But no, he didn't think so. His shirt and trousers lay on the spare bed where she'd smoothed them, because he always left them crumpled just as he peeled them off. It was weeks since he'd been seen on the street in a skirt; he had allowed no repeats.

He looked in the mirror at his Princess Diana collar and sleeves puffed at the shoulders.

"Yes, I'll change," he said.

221

Mags couldn't be expected to know what he didn't tell.

Dear Mags,

Thank you for your email. I hope you slept soundly after-wards, Genevieve too. If I tell you that your words touched on a kind of grieving long ago, please don't feel bad. I should have told you that Julia lost our baby at twenty weeks. That was in between the sighting of me out and about in a skirt and her leaving. Cause and effect can be a complicated busi-ness. I never really showed her how distressed I was because I thought I needed to be strong to support her. I had great hopes of raising a child to be free as well as loved. I'm sure that I wanted to eradicate my own childhood in some way, like Rembrandt painting over an old canvas. Of course I know now that technology exposes the old lines and colours that remain underneath.

We didn't talk about it, unless you count me asking her if she was all right, which was meant to be kind. She wasn't of course, and neither was I. I cried a few times but only alone; I didn't want to add to her grief. Meaning well can do so much damage, but then honesty is a grave risk without deep trust and fundamental connection.

Had he said too much? He didn't want her to feel guilty or sorry.

Thank you for your wonderfully kind invitation but I'm afraid I can't accept. Genevieve will not want a stranger butting in. He erased that last sentence; it sounded as if he was telling her how to be a mother, or knew Genevieve better than she did. *Can I talk to Winny?* He knew exactly what she would say – go, go with her blessing – but that wasn't all that mattered. *In any case I will see you soon.* Remembering the Rothko room, he wasn't sure he could wish her happiness, and these days pleasure seemed either sexual or superficial. *Enjoy your girl. I think she loves you very much.*

Georgie xx

Around mid-morning Mags was glad to see Genevieve look-ing rosier after a shower, and wrapped in her soft, dark red robe.

"Nice snug dressing gown, Ma. You don't mind?" She sat at the kitchen table and seemed to be savouring the smell of the coffee Mags had begun on hearing her in the bathroom. "Don't panic, I won't smoke in it. I'm quitting again. Don't want Baby to smell me coming."

Mags tried to give her a high five which she said was hopeless as well as dated. She offered toast, porridge, granola or muesli and laughed when Genevieve said she'd have the lot. As she ate, declaring a "rampageous hunger" Mags felt herself wearing a full-time smile until a comment about "Saint Mel" that she ignored in the hope of finding a diversionary tactic. Which could be Georgie Barkle for Boxing Day.

Then it was Genevieve who jack-knifed the conversation with a mouth full of marmalade. "So are we both still celibate?"

"Do daughters ask their mothers that these days?" retorted Mags, thinking of Mummy, and how it almost frightened her to imagine her parents in bed, because surely she wouldn't want his cold hands on her, his mouth around hers ...

"Evasive, Ma."

"I don't need you to answer so I claim the same privilege."

"I'm feeling safer, less exposed. You know I go in for phases and I can't say how long it will last. I'd like to fall in love, soon as possible really. Do you think you'll ever do it again?"

Mags pulled a face that was stretched wide open like her eyes.

"Fall in love, I mean!" laughed Genevieve. "Sex on the brain!"

"Innocent of that charge! But I could say I still love Rudi." She looked above the knife rack at the Surrealist calendar still on November, and remembered Rudi buying it.

"He doesn't deserve it."

"But the answer is yes, I hope so. I hope you will too. That's more important."

"Thanks." The toast eaten, Genevieve stood and watched her stir the porridge. "So what about Georgie?"

"Ah ... would you like to meet him?"

"Why?"

"Because you'd like him and he'd like you, and that would make me happy. He makes me happy – and very sad. It's real. It's a kind of love but not the kind you think. At least ..."

"Not yet you mean?"

"I don't know, Gen. But it's important, I know that much." She tried to explain about age and memory and the past making more sense than the present, but how could Genevieve understand that?

Genevieve took the wooden spoon and stirred her own porridge – the way Cameron used to take over his ironing because she didn't focus.

"Sit down and think," she was told. "If it's love, and real, and important, why isn't it the right kind of love?"

"I don't know. I can't say."

"You can always say! Tell me it's not because he wears skirts."

"Oh dear God, I hope not! Heavens to Murgatroyd, Gen. I don't want to hate myself for Christmas."

"So are you thinking?" Gen harangued her. "About what kind of love it is?"

"It's not about the brain. Naming what we feel isn't always so easy. I don't have the words."

"Then paint him."

Mags looked up from some toast crumbs she'd been shuffling around the table. "I will," she said.

Dear Georgie,

I've only just seen your email. It can't have been easy to share the way you did. I'm sad for you both and I know those hurts heal over but stay under the skin. I'm sorry if I was crass but glad you told me. I hope you're not up too, at this late and unwholesome hour. Gen crashed out soon after ten thirty but I've been busy preparing something adventurous. I'll tell you if and when it ever materialises into something I can own up to!

I think you're being sensitive and trying not to butt in on our heart to hearts, but we've had one about you already and Gen likes the sound of you, I can tell. Of course we can't steal you away from Winny so I shall have to think creatively. I shall finish that feature wall anyway, possibly around four in the morning as the absentee owners now trust me with a key. It seems they're in awe of Rudi Shaw – a common mistake! I'm having an artistic recharge and it's making me quite fizzy. And fast! I need to finish one project to start the next but on that subject my blabbering lips are sealed.

We had tea with Abida today and Gen charmed her. Well, it was mutual. I just sat and enjoyed the show. Abida's niece and family are collecting her on Boxing Day for a short stay in Leeds so she's packing.

Being with Gen makes me feel very old but also young. She was more focused on me today and less on her own pain but one way or another she'll have to speak to Dan tomorrow and if he's drunk – which he will be, unless he phones before nine a.m. – he may be incapable of judgement or censorship. The weather seems to have improved in Tuscany. No sign of any blonde Russian artists in any photos. Must stop enlarging and snooping for long legs sticking out behind curtains!

Mags XX

Mags looked at the time on the screen. 11:13. After so many years, there must be plenty more to reveal, confess, rerun, and she would like to recover memories more sunlit and dappled, gentle or triumphant to offset all the grief. Maybe she would tell him, one day, how Jake raped her in his parents' new pool, with its aquamarine water and enough chlorine to burn her eyes. But maybe the words would hurt too much in the hearing, and not just for her. Now at last the thinking rose above the fear of drowning and let her breathe more easily.

She tiptoed around to check Genevieve was asleep and heard her snoring in a way that seemed endearingly *hamsterly*, although she didn't suppose Gen would agree. Feeling oddly excited and enjoying the prospect of reckless abandon to the creative urge, she packed a rucksack. It was only once out of the door that she considered the question of early closures on certain underground lines, but if necessary she'd catch a bus. Even the possibility of a walk as Christmas Day began didn't deter her as she convinced herself there would be romance in that. She'd revelled in impulses once, and remembered how hard it had been to coax Jake out of bed to experience a bright, frosted dawn in Richmond Park with only the deer for company – but how thrilling, kissing in the cold, dim stillness, and sensing a group of them gathered as if to watch, motionless, like a Christmas card. "Satisfied now, you crazy cow?" he'd asked, once the sun had risen, and she'd nodded, happy because he was nice Jake then. Only on the way home he'd accused her of flirting "like a cheap tart" with a man who passed on a bike, just because the happiness made her free with her smiles.

Once she'd painted in Story So Far, she could start the next chapter with a portrait, abstract but irresistibly interesting, of Georgie Stroft.

24

After four hours' sleep Mags felt too triumphant for grumpiness or regret, and woke at eight on Christmas morning wondering whether Georgie had seen the photo she'd sent him on completing the feature wall – at a speed that was admittedly manic and would appal Rudi. "You're instinctive," Miss Tralee had said. "You don't hang about!"

She hoped Gen wouldn't give her that creased-up teenage look that meant *what the hell* but she wasn't awake yet. There was a time when she'd be up before the twins, demanding "What's wrong with them?" because presents couldn't be opened without them and she was what Rudi called the "big kid" of the family.

Hoping Genevieve would deliver – eventually – on her promise to cook lunch for two, Mags decided as she chewed toast that she might as well sort out some paints from the Rainy Day cupboard where she'd also stored some cheap canvases the kids had never used. Creativity was as elating as sex if a little more one-sided, and it wasn't about sales or prestige. Rudi had no clue. It was in the gut and the soul – a flutter that surged and lifted off and might crash-land mangled but that wasn't the point. It was about taking aim knowing the mark was so high and so tiny that only the gods could come close. Mary Cassatt must have known that too but the knowledge didn't defeat her. And neither did being Degas's lover.

What she intended was as firm in her mind's eye as some of the world's most famous artworks, examined at intervals through decades. What had held her back all that time? Just fear – of translating into physical existence something ridiculously perfect. She didn't need a hundred photographs. She knew enough.

Hearing Genevieve padding upstairs almost three hours later, Mags stopped and covered her mouth in case all kinds of emotions broke out. Her hand shaking a little, she washed her brushes and took the canvas to the study that became Rudi's once no one needed a rumpus room. There it would dry in private until she returned to it, fearful that memory could not be trusted. Realising that she hadn't thought to connect herself to the world through any form of technology, she plugged in, switched on and found a missed call from Cameron followed by a message that read, *Happy Christmas from sunny Oz. x* Nothing yet from the twins but they would call when they made it out of bed. It was up to the wrinklies to make mornings matter and she had – hadn't she?

She threw away the cold coffee turning nasty in her mug and let the day begin again, with eyes that burned heavy and doubt slipping in like a shiver. Traditions like mince pies in bed with a naked husband weren't built to last and artworks thrown together before breakfast couldn't really amount to more than a hill of beans. She must smile anyway. Shaking off the rest to her stretched fingertips, she breathed in. It would be good to believe in a God that loved her but not if that was all. She needed humans too, and most of them weren't there on the day when everyone notoriously needed people most – unless they had plenty of them, and could do with rather fewer. Daddy felt like that with the uncles and aunts and cousins, especially Mummy's, who liked *Tiptoe through the Tulips* and games that made them louder than was strictly necessary. "He has a headache, dear," Mummy would say when he closed the door on departing guests, turned on the television and preferred the black and white people with precise voices because they made no demands. "Volume down!" wasn't for the small beings on screen, or even the relatives who didn't quite obey the rules, but only for her.

"Da-da!" Genevieve was at the kitchen door in jeans and a black jumper, her feet bare and her eyes sleepier than she sounded. "Happy Christmas, Ma!"

They embraced. Gen was deliberating over whether to skip breakfast and start cooking when the landline rang and she narrowed her eyes at it. But it was Kara, who began with, "Mum, Happy Christmas and all that but can I have a quick word with Gen first?"

"Of course!" she said brightly, and passed it over. "Shall I leave the building?" she continued, focusing on coffee. Imagination wasn't always an asset in such situations.

Gen took the phone into the lounge, where she didn't seem to be saying much as she listened. Mags found a sigh had welled too tight for comfort and let it go. Her mobile intervened with: *Happy Christmas, Mags. X* from Georgie, followed by: *Thank you for sharing the photo with me. It's moving. More mysterious and powerful than a photo album. It's raw but joyous too – is that possible? I hope to see it wall-size soon. X*

HCTY2 haha. Thanks Georgie. Feeling the rawness a bit at the mo but hoping joy IS possible! To misunderstand wilfully, as Daddy said was my speciality. Can I call you later? X

Of course, but only if you feel like it. Xx

To her surprise, she found Genevieve returning to the kitchen as her coffee cooled again. Handed the phone, Mags asked, "Kara? Everything OK?" She sounded so thin and distant it was alarming.

"I'm OK. Dad misses you, it's obvious. Alisa's out of the frame if you excuse the pun so don't think he's moved on. Gen says you look like you've been up all night crying."

"Ah. Well I haven't, so don't think my heart is broken. It's battered but robust."

Kara seemed relieved. "Ah, OK. Glad someone's is. Because Simon's so-called girlfriend wants a fucking break! Sorry Mum but relationships really suck. He's putting a brave face on but I know him. He's in pieces. I can't look at her and I'm certainly not speaking to her."

Mags said they'd probably just had a row and it would blow over, but Kara interrupted that *she* hadn't *seen* Simon. Then she changed her tone and offered, with fake lightness, "Want to speak to Dad? He's right here."

"Not just now," she said. Her heart wasn't that robust. "Maybe later."

"Anyway sorry, Mum. Love you. Wish I was home with you and Gen."

"Mm." Mags couldn't always find the necessary platitudes. "I'll pass you back to your sister."

The laughter that reached her from the lounge was another shock but easier to absorb. Gen could be a mistress of dark humour when the darkness wasn't hers and Kara had started to enjoy it at an age when most girls still bathed in soft-edged dreamlight: another word she'd told Rudi ought to exist, since the meaning was obvious enough to justify the need.

She was making some porridge, prepared to eat the lot if necessary, when Gen returned and declared hunger.

"Poor Simon," Mags said, to acknowledge the content of the call in a way Genevieve didn't seem inclined to do. The content as she knew it, anyway. It was distressing to picture him with his zipped-up smile and loose amble of a walk, sealing it all inside.

"He'll be fine. Guys shrug it off. Like Rudi will – don't kid yourself, Mum."

"Isn't that a bit … sexist? And sweeping?"

"I know – Georgie's not like that? But he wears skirts, right?"

"And that's a simplification …"

"I'm just saying, no need to feel sad for other people. Or yourself. We're OK here, just the two of us, and I'm going to cook us something cruelty-free so why don't you put on some clothes …"

"What are these?" Mags protested, looking down on her leggings and jumper.

"They're not you. You do colour swirls and pattern combat. They're sad."

Mags couldn't help pointing to Gen's own choice of festive black but was told, "Ah, but this *is* me. I just need some eyeliner and blood-red lips and I'll be party-perfect."

Mags served the porridge and sat down opposite her, but not for long before she sprang up and said they used to have a CD of choirboy carols. When she returned without it Mags offered to find *Merry Christmas, War is Over* on YouTube.

"Don't bring reality into it," Gen told her. "Or should I say fantasy?"

"Is there some kind of secret Kara's keeping from me?"

Genevieve shook her head. "She asked whether you could handle the news of the big break-up and I said you're tough enough so don't let me down. She wants you to have Rudi back and I don't, so we agreed to disagree. But we both want you to be happy."

Mags smiled. "Thank you."

Remarking on Kara's anger on behalf of Simon, Gen claimed she'd learned to forgive more easily once she passed twenty-five. Mags hoped she'd remember that progress if Dan rang, but couldn't quite find a formulation for saying so. As soon as Genevieve had gone upstairs, she picked up the phone, closed the door and composed herself in detached, schoolmistress mode, and called Dan's landline herself.

Mel answered, and didn't conceal the irritation in her surprise.

"Maggie? Has something happened?"

"Christmas?" offered Mags. "Festive greetings from Gen and me. How are things? Over the sickness yet?"

The answer was detailed and punctuated with numbers and a few giggles. Mel had rather an upper-class laugh; Mags made some interested and sympathetic noises.

"Well, occupy that sofa and make Dan peel some potatoes."

"I think I'll stay in control of dinner. Mum and Dad are coming, and my sister and her brood, so I'd best be making some headway." There was a pause before she called, "Darling! Maggie wants a quick word."

"Thanks," said Mags. "Have fun!" As she waited she pictured Dan stirring reluctantly from the sofa and putting down his glass.

"Hi, Mags," he said, sooner than expected. "What's up?"

"Happy Christmas to you too. And you two."

"Uh, yeah."

"But what's up is Gen. I've only heard her version and I don't need to know yours or Mel's but she's pretty upset. So I wanted to ask you to tread softly – on her dreams, really. You know how Christmas shakes everything up. So speak to her like a poem, not a soap script. I know she's nearly thirty but she needs to know she's your best girl."

He sighed and she knew the face he'd be making. "It's between her and Mel. Some sort of flare-up. You know what she's like."

Mags couldn't resist. "Not really. I barely know Mel ..."

"Gen, I mean! Don't ..."

"But she's not an unsuitable godmother, or sister. She already loves that baby. Talk Mel round – you'll need to for a quiet life – but for today, be nice and kind and affectionate. Be Dad. Deliver it the way your audience likes."

"Yeah, of course. Leave it with me." He yawned. "You having a quiet day then, just the two of you? Or is Georgie there too?"

"Yes, lovely and quiet thanks," she said as the door opened and Gen walked in with Cleopatra eyes. "It's your dad." She passed her the phone, hoping her smile was reassuring and relaxed. "For you."

"Hey, Pa," she heard – guarded if not suspicious – as she left the room.

She wondered how much quieter Georgie's day might be – and why, when he'd be the kind of guest who'd happily chop veg, set the table and wash up, Julia's husband couldn't allow him to join them for dinner. Either the Alpha Male had an octogenarian mother who preferred men in trousers, or he read the wrong papers. Looking at the time, she considered when or whether to call. She hoped it wouldn't carry too much meaning, simply because the date came wrapped with echoes: an emotional resonance.

No raised voices from the kitchen. She breathed deeply, pulled the curtains in the lounge and tried not to feel afraid for anyone. She needed Knockabout Mags, dependable when it came to resilience and humour. Mags who could shrug off the breakages around her because everything she'd known was fractured.

Through the glass her slice of London was almost entirely people-free. A frost was softening under sun, leaving everything on the ground sleek and shiny. The dusky grey cat next-door narrowed its eyes at her as if she'd violated its privacy as it stalked the garden unseen. Perhaps it was missing Abida's tail strokes and secret treats.

She called Simon's mobile but had to leave a recorded message: "Hello, love. Just wanted to say Bueno Chrissmas-sio." A moment's doubt held her back before she continued, "and it's hell and you think you'll be dead for ever but then you just step out, burned but ready for the living to begin again. In any case she might just be experiencing the festive jitters and those don't last any longer than the battery on a dancing Santa. Either way you'll still be you, only you'll have grown inside. And I love you very much." How could any Christmas robin pose outside with that cat slinking around like a supermodel? "Enough I think. See you soon."

It was hard to imagine Simon's face as he heard it, whenever he decided to listen. Only a few years ago he used to text her jokes that made her laugh out loud with pleasure, and she tried to match them but found them even more challenging in the typing than the telling. *Hilarious,* he'd respond, *or Side-splitting or what.* He was softer than Kara, less reactive, with fewer moods as well as words and hard to provoke, but highly skilled in the art of the wind-up. The way he could remodel his voice on a mate's phone to play the part of a talent scout, teacher, police officer or radio DJ who asked to speak to Kara Shaw was masterly enough for Mags to suggest Stage School. But Simon preferred football.

If he didn't ring back, that was another choice she'd have to respect. Outside the sun had faded as she watched.

"Ma!" she heard, no edge. Genevieve had followed her into the lounge. "Shall we swap presents before I start work?"

"If you can't wait, kiddo!"

"It's practically afternoon! Sit yourself down then. I hope you like it. Act even if you don't, all right? Dad's in a good mood by the way and vaguely sober. Well vague anyway. He said he's proud of me. I hope *she* was listening."

Mags offered a hug and remembered not to stroke her spiky hair. "Never mind her. Where's this present I have to pretend I don't hate?"

"Hey!" Gen grinned as she pulled away. "Heading for the Oxfam Shop if you don't behave yourself."

While Genevieve steamed up the kitchen, with the Arctic Monkeys loud enough to overwhelm the fan, Mags tried to picture where in the new flat she would hang her *main* present and wondered whether a visiting Gen would be insulted to find it in the loo. The cyclamen would need careful nurturing in order to survive its ordeal courtesy of London Transport and her best efforts with plants tended to fall woefully short.

Wording everything for Georgie in her head, she acknowledged a wish for him to be happy. And a concern that he needed her to make that possible. Or thought he did. If she'd wanted it enough she could have arranged for him to be there for Christmas. Gen was an unconvincing excuse. So there was no point, with the tubes and buses stationary as lampposts and no car between them, in feeling sorry and cross. At any rate the blessing that was the worldwide web could connect them.

Have you eaten yet? Gen is cooking and when I offered to help she told me to ignore the carnage. She made me a clock from a CD of White Christmas and decorated it with what's meant to look like vomit overlaying the snowflakes. So tasteful. It tells the time, I hasten to add, very efficiently - and I'm the laugh-out-loud eccentric who thinks art should push boundaries. She was gracious about the art deco tights I found for her (yes of course I want to wear them myself really) and the vegan cookery book and we were quite smug about forswearing materialism up to a commendable point until we remembered poverty is back and it's getting Dickensian.

I may have played a bit of a blinder UN-style with Gen and her dad. I don't think I like Mel, though. She seems to be one of those people who use religion as a justification for judging others. Most of us don't need help doing that of course and I'm proving it. You've been on the sharp end of that since Daddy, and maybe he'd have judged just as harshly even if he'd had the originality to break free of the church. When I think about it he was just another conformist, kow-towing to the rules, enforcing them with his big stick and condemning anyone who questioned them. And that's spineless – one of his favourite words of condemnation! But I'm judging again and if I'm wrong he can't enlighten me (I hope! No ghosts of Christmas past, please) so I shall stop. Some people – including Kara and quite possibly Rudi – might be outraged by Cam in bed with his step-mum any day now but that's pure theory. Once you see the two of them smiling, hand in hand – and I can frame that already in my mind's eye – the theory disassembles, like Andy Goldsworthy's stick sculpture on the tide. If there's a God what she wants is for people to love each other. It's the most full-bodied kind of kindness, with or without sex.

I'll update you about Simon and Cam when I see you, by which time the news may be old. How is Winny? Grateful to you, I guess. You're a good human, better than me.
M XXXXXXXXXXXXXXXX

The food smelt good. She wasn't sure forswearing greed was going to hold, but Gen didn't want any help in the kitchen. Mags thought of Rudi, who could have had the self-control to take their kids to Devon rather than Italy. But she wasn't expecting her thoughts to work a Secret Garden kind of magic and prompt an email from the Tuscan villa.

Dear Mags,

I have messed up and sometimes it takes Christmas to throw the full horror of it into startling relief. We could all have been together. I could plead a mid-life crisis but now you're the one reshaping your life. I wish you every happiness. Which was what I had, if I'd only recognised it. I don't want any more of this shit I mistook for freedom. But I made my bed as they say so I'm lying on it and the funny thing is I didn't have to. The words could have remained unsaid that day. Then the last three months would have been as regular and predictable – which with you is pretty irregular and unpredictable anyway – as I didn't want them to be. Words, eh? They're not like paint. Once they're out there between people there's no white spirit to make them disappear. Maybe I'm an artist because I'm not in control of mine. I know I made fun of yours. Now I miss them all.

You're right in thinking I've been drinking but I'm sober underneath. And sorry.

I love you.

Rudi. X

She didn't need to reply, did she – not today, anyway? If she did, she could say, *Please don't write to me like this again.* Or, *I'm sorry too, and I wish you every happiness right back –* which was probably enough, although she'd be tempted by, *The ship's left shore and the wind's in the sail but who needs a compass when this sea's the place I love?*

She almost deleted the email but left it instead. He'd expect her to be busy with parsnips. Then as she began to dance to a track from the kitchen that demanded it, and at closer range, another message arrived.

You will have heard about Simon. She's quiet but opinionated and intense. Best off rid as they say. The world's too crappy to be taken that seriously. As it happens, though, it looks like they may have patched things up this morning. Between you and me I hope that's temporary.

I still love you.

Rudi xxx

Mags sent both emails into Trash, hoping Simon never saw the second and thinking that she'd rather like to meet this unsuitably opinionated girlfriend.

"You can come and load the dishwasher if you like!" somehow overrode the music, reminding her of the brief period when Genevieve sang in a style that was deliberately slurred and monotone, in a band of pierced and sweaty boys. And she was banned from listening to a single bar of their output, but Rudi wasn't.

Mags joined her in the kitchen, eyes widening at the number of pans and utensils occupying the worktops with onion peel and tomato puree smears.

"It's in the oven," said Gen as the CD ended. "It's kind of creative, you know – an experiment. I hope it's all right."

Mags moved to the sink and filled a bowl with bubbles. She never used the dishwasher now she was on her own.

"It'll be great," she said. "Outasite – as we said in the days when this wild stuff would have been tame."

Genevieve grinned but shook her head. "I suppose you want Janis Joplin or Hendrix?"

"That'd do nicely. I'm in the mood for dancing. As neither of them ever dreamed of singing."

The music started in her head even before Genevieve had moved into the lounge and found a tattered old album to play on the deck Rudi had bought her a few Christmases ago.

"Loud enough?" she yelled over it.

Mags nodded, and shook her hair as her rubber-gloved hands began to work the air.

"Typically mad dancing! I like it. Don't stop." Genevieve was right on her shoulder now, her arms briefly round her waist. "When do I get to meet your Georgie then?"

236

Mags turned, smiling, and planted a kiss on her forehead. "Soon?"

A chocolate box had provided the bow insecurely taped to Winny's curls. Now her forehead was equally shiny. She wiped it with the hankie Georgie had included in her stocking and then lifted the cotton to her nose, inhaling the scent of the Norfolk lavender he had wrapped inside it.

"So English," she said, smiling, and briefly closed her eyes.

She'd asked for plenty of roast potatoes but three of them remained alone on her plate. Georgie reached for it, checking, "Too much?"

"Eyes too big for my stomach. Can you help me out?"

Georgie considered with a tilted head and then speared the first with his fork, filling his mouth and counting on the boisterous laugh that followed.

"Oh don't!" she cried, holding her stomach. "You have fish cheeks!"

Her bow fell free. Georgie caught it just before it landed on the ketchup on her plate. He told her it was like a samara floating down from a tree. She liked learning new words and wrote the noun down in the margin of a magazine, checking the spelling.

He took the plates into her little, square kitchen and washed them up with the saucepans and nut roast tin while the kettle boiled for her coffee. How many more Christmases before humans stopped destroying life on earth and spoke the truth that spoiled everyone's fun? Could he make room for it in his heart and keep breathing?

Now that he'd read the IPCC report he couldn't console himself with any doubt. The activists said it was an emergency and the scientists said they were right. But it was a subject he hadn't touched on with Mags, partly because it hardly seemed real. And if she had no idea, how could he break it to her?

So that Winny didn't feel neglected he sang Rudolf the Red-nosed Reindeer over the sink until he ran out of words he knew, and heard her tapping her stick in time next-door.

Wondering whether Mags had eaten and what Gen had served up, he decided he needed to develop a more adventurous repertoire.

Returning to the lounge he found Winny pointing with her stick to the chair opposite hers and recognised her look as purposeful.

"Now, have you called Mags today?"

"No. I thought it might be ... invasive."

"You could make it bright and breezy. I think you should."

"Are you going to write my script?" he asked, smiling.

She sipped the coffee with mischievous elegance as if she was drinking tea with the Queen – an ambition even harder for him to help her realise than a home visit from Andy Murray. "Well that depends," she said with mischievous pleasure.

"Oh yes?"

"On what she is to you."

"Ah, Winny."

"What kind of answer is that!" she cried, in mock outrage. "You love her. I know you do."

"I do. But how?"

"With all your heart! That's my advice."

He'd been told the story more than once and didn't mind repeats. She had loved like that, but only once, as a girl in Namibia – and not seen *that white boy of mine* for forty years – decades that had brought him a wife, children and grandchildren.

"Maybe best friends will be enough," Georgie suggested. "That's a powerful kind of love and there's less risk attached."

"Maybe," she said, her tone making it clear she was unimpressed. "If you want to play it safe in life. Sometimes we look back and think the risks were worth taking if we only had the balls."

He nodded. "I'll bear that in mind." Along, he thought, with his track record in the romance department. Mags was the risk-taker but he wasn't sure whether she carried regrets with her.

"You do that, Georgie. Bring her to tea."

"I might if you behave yourself."

"I want you to be happy before ..."

She talked a lot about passing; he found it hard to listen. He laid a hand on hers.

"I am," he said.